# THE
# SISTERS OF
# GLASS FERRY

## KIM MICHELE RICHARDSON

KENSINGTON BOOKS
www.kensingtonbooks.com

KENSINGTON BOOKS are published by

Kensington Publishing Corp.
119 West 40th Street
New York, NY 10018

Copyright © 2017 by Kim Michele Richardson

To the extent that the image or images on the cover of this book depict a person or persons, such person or persons are merely models, and are not intended to portray any character or characters featured in the book.

All rights reserved. No part of this book may be reproduced in any form or by any means without the prior written consent of the Publisher, excepting brief quotes used in reviews.

This book is a work of fiction. Names, characters, and incidents either are products of the author's imagination or are used fictitiously. Any resemblance to actual persons living or dead, or events, is entirely coincidental.

If you purchased this book without a cover you should be aware that this book is stolen property. It was reported as "unsold and destroyed" to the Publisher and neither the Author nor the Publisher has received any payment for this "stripped book."

All Kensington titles, imprints, and distributed lines are available at special quantity discounts for bulk purchases for sales promotion, premiums, fundraising, educational, or institutional use.

Special book excerpts or customized printings can also be created to fit specific needs. For details, write or phone the office of the Kensington Sales Manager: Attn.: Sales Department. Kensington Publishing Corp., 119 West 40th Street, New York, NY 10018. Phone: 1-800-221-2647.

Kensington and the K logo Reg. U.S. Pat. & TM Off.

ISBN-13: 978-1-4967-0956-1 (ebook)
ISBN-10: 1-4967-0956-X (ebook)

ISBN-13: 978-1-4967-3423-5
ISBN-10: 1-4967-3423-8
First Kensington Trade Paperback Edition: December 2017

10 9 8 7 6 5 4 3

Printed in the United States of America

Books by Kim Michele Richardson

*Liar's Bench*

*GodPretty in the Tobacco Field*

*The Sisters of Glass Ferry*

Published by Kensington Publishing Corporation

*For*
*Jeremiah and Sierra*
*with love always.*

*. . . rock and water, taken in the abstract, fail as completely to convey any idea of their fierce embracings in the throes of a rapid as the fire burning quietly in a drawing-room fireplace fails to convey the idea of a house wrapped and sheeted in flames.*

—Sir William Francis Butler

# CHAPTER 1

Every year Mama has baked her a strawberry birthday cake. And for two decades now that cake has sat on the sunshine-yellow Formica counter for one week in June unsliced, the plump pink roses atop the creamy home-churned icing with powdered sugar-coated berries, beckoning another year for Patsy to return home, mocking her silence, her absence.

"Flannery, I just know this is the year," Mama said in that summer of 1972.

"How come, Mama?" Every person in Glass Ferry, Kentucky—in all of Woolson County even—for every year since 1952, knew sixty-one-year-old Jean Butler had been saying these same things until another cake went stale and got tossed into the garbage.

"I just know it," Mama insisted. "I can feel it somehow, in my bones, in this sweet June air. This is the year we'll slice Patsy's cake, all three of us."

Mama quieted, and Flannery emptied the box of pink birthday candles onto the table and began counting them to put on the cake. More than once, the house awakened and popped, distracting Flannery from her tally.

Breezes pushed through the screen door, slapping at darkened halls and sneaking into dusty corners of the century-old two-story. The bones of the house groaned and creaked like tired homes do from time to time—growled low like it was pushing something away with a warning—like it knew something bad was about to slip inside and soil the sugar-dusted air.

Flannery rubbed at the tightness building in her neck. Mama had always said houses knew things before people did—"knows things only the soul knows"—and that homes like theirs could feel things same as a dog catches the silent clamors lost to the human ear.

"Grab the napkins, Flannery," Mama reminded, scattering the choir of airy protests.

Flannery shrugged off her apprehension and crossed over to the sideboard. Sloping floorboards dipped, rasping under her feet. She hadn't been back to Glass Ferry in a year, and had mostly forgotten how different this rambling old country house sounded compared to her loud city apartment. That's all, she presumed. Flannery never missed making it home when the elementary school dismissed her students just in time for another birthday celebration.

Year after year the quiet of the house, the countryside, all of it, still managed to lull her into its own sleepiness until an unexpected jarring bumped the silence and jerked her back.

She dug through the table linen drawer and handed Mama the embroidered strawberry napkins. "I need to get out of my nightgown and get dressed," Flannery said, dusting flour off her gown.

"Oh, baby girl, wear your prettiest. We're going to have a big celebration," Mama chattered, "bigger than the Independence Parade even." She laughed as she smoothed folds into the cloth napkins and stacked them neatly beside the cake. "Hard to believe my twins are going to be thirty-six this year. Lord, how time flies. Seems like just yesterday when you and Patsy were in your cradles. You up and left for college and married—"

"Mama . . ." Flannery warned that her divorce was not on the table for discussion.

"Speaking of time"—Mama pointed to the old electric daisy clock hanging on the wall—"this morning is getting away from us. We haven't even made the punch. Why don't you start on that before you change into your dress."

Flannery glanced at the kitchen clock and then down at her daddy's old windup Zenith wristwatch on her arm, finding a solace and satisfaction in her cheating. Ever since Flannery was born, she had been stealing—stealing time same as she did Patsy's pearls back then—setting all the wall clocks and wristwatches exactly eight minutes ahead. And when Flannery visited Mama every year for the fake birthday celebration, she'd make sure to do the same to her clocks even though Mama fussed the day into tomorrow trying to break her of it. Mama always said, "It's the devil's doings, and it doesn't make sense to thieve from the Lord's hours when you'll just have to pay 'em back."

But that's not what her daddy had taught her. Nuh-uh. The very thought of that final Reckoning Day was *why* Flannery stayed precisely eight minutes ahead, looking over her shoulder for those lagging minutes when the devil might try to collect.

Flannery followed Mama's most hopeful gaze to the wall. Mama would track those circling black hands most of the day, keeping a vigilant eye on the time and the foyer too, first to move the hands back to their proper time and, second, to welcome Patsy when she burst through the door.

Several times Mama caught Flannery looking to the foyer and gave her an optimistic grin. Instead of smiling back, Flannery turned away. She wanted to believe, but after all these years there was nothing left, just a plait of hope that had been twisted, rubbed too many times, tangled into a useless, knotted wish that would never unravel.

Flannery knew the quiet morning would slip into a quieter afternoon, and soon the lull of evening would gather a cold, silent darkness. Tonight she would find Mama tear-stained, asleep at the kitchen table, plumb wore out from watching and waiting. Flannery would rouse her mama from the chair, take off her glasses, and convince her to go to her room—helping her to drag her aged bones and aching heart to bed until the next year—the next time Patsy's birthday rolled around.

*Time. If only Flannery could snatch some of it back for them.*

"Flannery." Mama pulled her to the task and pointed to Patsy's strawberry cake. "Are you sure I can't make you one, or maybe bake your favorite—cherry pie? It's your birthday too, you know."

"I do love your cherry pie. But this'll do, Mama." She plucked an orange from the fruit bowl and rolled it in her hands. "Doc says no added sugar for us borderline diabetics."

Mama picked up the cake knife and nodded, knowing her youngest had inherited the sugar problem and other troublesome traits from her daddy. "The diabetes took him from us too soon, before the twins' fourteenth birthdays," she told everyone the half-truth.

Mama hummed "Happy Birthday" while shining the blade with the tail of her apron. "*Happy birthday, dear Patsy.*" She plucked the words, sang them soft and warbly. "This is the year, baby girl. Flip on the radio. Let's have some music."

1972 didn't feel any different than last year for Flannery, or the one before that, or any of the others. She clicked on the radio, turning the knob to get a clear station.

Cocking her head, Flannery caught the announcer saying something about a rust bucket being pulled out of the Kentucky River downstream from the Palisades. ". . . this morning when a fisherman found . . . near Johnson's boat dock . . ." She stretched an ear closer to the radio speaker and turned up the volume. ". . . shedding light on the decades-old disappearance . . . Sheriff Hollis Henry of Glass Ferry went on to confirm the mud-caked Mercury . . ."

Mama's knife clattered on the sunlit linoleum, hammering its glint across the walls and pinning the clock's slow-sweeping hand into the final stolen minute.

# CHAPTER 2

*Patsy*
*June, 1952*

The day swept its last hour into the cemetery. There, alongside the forgotten churchyard in the washed light at the end of Ebenezer Road, she'd buried her secret.

Just months before, Patsy Butler hadn't any secrets to keep. Not adult ones anyway, and only the kind an almost sixteen-year-old would primp and parcel: an admirer's note passed in history class, a young boy's wanting touch, maybe a stolen kiss sneaked behind the football bleachers, all locked onto a mostly dreamy-lipped grin and safeguarded to chalk-dusted walls.

But now there was a burdening hush-hush in Patsy's soft green eyes and a quivering in her young hands that belonged to the old.

Patsy crossed the room and opened the bedroom window to let the early June air sift through the curtains. Sinking back down onto her vanity stool, she dipped the eyeliner brush into a teacup of water and swished it back and forth across the black cake powder. For the second time Patsy tried to draw a line onto her eyelids to give herself a perfect cat-eye look.

"Patsy and Danny sittin' in a tree, K-I-S-S-I-N-G. First comes love, then marriage, and then o' then, there's a baby carriage!" Her twin sister's stupid little tease struck like a cold blade.

"Dammit, Flannery . . . just hush," Patsy hissed, peering closer at the mirror and inspecting the sweep on her wing-painted lids. Satisfied, Patsy reached for the lipstick.

"Oh, did I spell it wrong? F-O-R-N-I-C-A-T-I—" Flannery sang slowly as she hung over her sister's shoulder.

Patsy batted her off with a light hand. Ever since their mama said Patsy could go to the junior prom with Danny Henry, Flannery had been pestering Patsy because Flannery didn't have a beau to take her. But this particular tease cut deeper. Patsy and Danny had been arguing about it recently, *it* being *putting out*. Patsy wondered if Flannery had overhead their whispers on the porch. It had to be that, only that.

"What's eating *you?*" Flannery asked.

"*You*. Knock it off, tadpole." Patsy pressed her lips together to seal the paint, dropping the tube onto the wooden vanity. She glanced into the mirror and cast a warning eye to Flannery.

"Don't call me that," Flannery said. "Hey, that's mine." She snatched the lipstick and tossed it into the vanity's drawer, then plopped onto one of the twin beds in their bedroom.

"Someone's acting like a brat," Patsy declared.

"That's because *someone* is working *somebody's* shift down at Chubby Ray's, scooping tons of ice cream and making a million cherry lime rickeys and serving stacks of chili dogs to her whole junior class while *somebody* and *everybody* has a big-to-do prom to go to."

"Flannery, you're a doll to do this." Patsy sighed, leaned back, patted her sister's shoulder.

"Well, you've already missed enough days. I wouldn't want Chubby to fire you."

"A living doll," Patsy said, sort of meaning it this time.

Flannery softened a little. "I guess you'd do it for me."

"I would," Patsy said. "But I wish you would've thought about letting Hollis take you to the prom. Then ol' Chubby Ray wouldn't have made you work my shift."

"Hollis Henry is a senior, a dumb one who failed first grade—nearly nineteen years old now! And you know Mama ain't allowing us to date seniors, same as Honey Bee. 'Sides, I never much cared for him—I don't want to double-date—and I don't want your date offering up his brother as a pity date for me."

Their daddy, Beauregard "Honey Bee" Butler, or *Honey Bee,* as Patsy and all who knew him called him, had a lot of silly rules for his girls, Patsy thought. Rules that were still calling from the grave. It wasn't fair, she felt. Honey Bee never wanted the twins to be around older boys, yet, he'd let them skip second grade and go straight into third when the teacher advised it. Honey Bee'd enjoyed boasting how doubly-sharp his little girls were.

"But that's only because Honey Bee told Mama not to let us," Patsy reminded Flannery. "He's been dead over *two* years." There was a relief in Patsy's words. Honey Bee was one less worry—one less in the mess of her latest troubles.

"That's 'cause Honey Bee was right," Flannery said. "And it doesn't matter if he's gone, or how long; he'll always be right."

Patsy studied her sister a moment. "Honey Bee wasn't *always* right. If he'd listened to Mama, maybe he'd still be here—" she said quietly.

"Patsy Jean Butler, you hush your mouth about our daddy," Flannery scolded.

Patsy hung her head a little, thinking about the day he'd been found dead on his ferryboat. Pushing the horrid thought aside, she said, "Well, it would've been fun tonight with you there." If Flannery went with Hollis, it would serve Patsy in a two-fold way: keep the older brother away from her and Danny, and let them spend time alone. "He's the sheriff's son, so Mama wouldn't mind . . . Danny said it was Hollis who brought it up first, before he asked you—"

"Too late, and I don't care," Flannery snipped. "Sheriff Jack Henry's son or not, Miss Little wouldn't have allowed it. Anyways, I heard he didn't get approval, even when Violet Perry submitted his name."

All girls' dates for school dances had to go through their home economics teacher, Miss Little, for preapproval.

"What? Violet put his name in?" Patsy asked, wondering why she hadn't heard that the pretty Violet Perry had to go back and submit another name to Miss Little, wondering what Hollis was up to now.

"Heard he begged her to do it to test Miss Little, though I bet he secretly wanted to go with her," Flannery said. "And you know if the pastor's daughter can't get Miss Little's permission for Hollis, ain't nobody going to get it."

That was true. Patsy'd thought it would've been okay to put Hollis and Flannery together for just one night, knew Hollis didn't have a sneaky eye trained on Flannery, and then her sister wouldn't gripe about working her shift. But after hearing even the preacher's daughter couldn't earn Hollis Miss Little's good favor, Patsy knew Hollis would never go to any dance, not even his own senior prom. Not as long as Miss Little was alive and kicking, that is. Patsy'd barely squeaked her date's name by the old teacher.

The seventy-four-year-old spinster took not only the name of your date, but also checked his grades and looked at any infractions the boy might've had in the last year. Folks knew she sniffed around better than any hound dog or gumshoe even, going so far as to call on the boy's neighbors, pastor, or an employer if he had one.

If something was amiss, Miss Little would tell you to find another date; the boy wasn't good enough, and the troublemaker wouldn't be allowed to attend. A girl could try to plead the boy's case, but it was rare Miss Little would change her mind and give permission. Parents too. *Especially the parents.* Though Miss Little was indeed small and frail in appearance, in these matters she had a might of influence over all the grown-ups, especially since Alfred Harris.

Long ago, Alfred transferred from another county after his school chased him off for doing bad things to animals. The family sent him to live with an aunt in Glass Ferry, but Miss Little found out his sickness had come with him. After that Alfred incident, no one grumbled about Miss Little's guardian role or her results.

Still, Miss Little tried to be fair, and there was always a chance if the boy's offense was trivial. The teacher sometimes offered to have him atone for his misdeed by attending her Wednesday and Saturday two-hour Bible study at her house. If the boy made a month's worth of meetings and seemed truly repentant, Miss Little would finally nod her consent.

A boy willing to do that punishment knew his date was worth it, knew that come Monday morning after the dance he might be boasting about making it to second, possibly third base even, and, by lunch, he'd fish-tale it bigger and describe an almost homerun on prom night.

The girls' mamas and daddies thought Miss Little's rules were nifty—as close to the Good Lord's blessing as they could get. It saved them big headaches, and they didn't have to worry their sweet magnolias would end up with a hooligan or the likes, and their families disgraced.

The boys' families said Miss Little helped keep their Southern sons honorable and on the straight and narrow, said their boys worked harder in school and at their jobs because of her date-dance scrutiny.

Patsy had been thrilled to pass her first name to Miss Little for the Cupid's Dance. Then again for junior prom.

On that morning, long before the bigger troubles took root, Patsy'd dressed in a modest skirt and a buttoned-to-the-top blouse, and stood in line with the other girls, including the seniors.

Quietly, Patsy had waited her turn to contribute to the pile of papers and place the traditional apple into Miss Little's wooden bowl.

Patsy watched the others in front of her pass their apples to Miss Little and give the chosen name inside their folded papers. Everyone in line stretched their necks, slipped a snooping eye, watching too as the teacher opened paper after paper and peeked, before folding and adding to the pile.

At last Patsy handed Miss Little her polished apple along with the folded slip of paper, the name of the boy she was sweet on taking her to the big prom written in her best handwriting. It meant she was a woman now. And folks would look at her like one. Especially Danny.

Miss Little examined the apple closely before putting it with the others.

Patsy squirmed. She had gone through three pails from old man Samp's orchard until she found one without a blemish.

Miss Little studied Patsy's paper. You could always tell which boys would get a pass right off and those who wouldn't or needed more checking, because the old schoolmarm always hinted with a tiny smile, or a wrinkled worry in her brow, before folding up the paper and placing it to the side. Anxious, Patsy searched the teacher's face.

Danny had been careful not to get into trouble. But lately he'd been hanging with his brother and a few of the other older boys, and getting closer to it. And the more he hung, the more his good grades dipped, and as his lip got a little looser, and his breath smelled a lot boozier—the more Patsy found herself harping. She couldn't dare risk losing the dance. *Her chance.*

At last Miss Little nodded with the slightest smile, dismissing her. For a lingering second Patsy stared at her, agonizing she'd imagined it all.

"Miss Butler, you may take your seat."

Patsy startled and gave a small curtsy, fleeing to her table. But not before seeing the blessing in her teacher's crisp blue eyes.

When Patsy told Mama she'd gotten permission, Mama'd squealed and grabbed her pocketbook. "Let's celebrate." Mama held up her hooked arms in invitation to the girls, then took them to Chubby's for treats, letting Patsy drive the automobile there and Flannery tote them back.

Flannery cheered some at that.

Seated at the slick chrome-polished table inside Chubby's, they'd chatted happily, and in a bit, Mama confided to her daughters that Miss Little had not approved Honey Bee for her own high school dance.

"I can't rightly remember what Honey Bee did to get turned down," Mama began, while she fiddled with her dress collar, plucked it, and looked across the booth at the twins. "Something small, I'm sure."

The girls begged her to remember everything.

"Well now." Mama's cheeks rosied, and she took a sip of Coke, attempting to hide her deepening blush behind the frosty glass. "Miss Little shot him down flat."

"Poor Honey Bee," Flannery said. "What did he do?"

"Lessee, that's been a while."

"Mama!" the girls cried for more.

"Oh, don't you know Honey Bee Butler took me to the dance." She sly-eyed them with a wink.

"Honey Bee agreed to do her Bible study?" the twins asked, and looked at each other, incredulous.

"I sure hated telling Honey Bee she'd turned him down." Mama frowned.

"But what did he say, what did he do?" Patsy needled.

"He never said a word. Not a one. Not a peep."

"What happened, Mama?" Flannery pushed.

Mama chuckled. "Well, he wore himself out walking. I do remember that much."

"Walking?" Patsy and Flannery puzzled.

"Walking." Mama grinned. "Walked himself the three miles to and three miles back—six miles total—all spiffed up in his Sunday suit, twice a week for a month, just to attend Miss Little's Bible studies. Walked himself silly, and wore out those shiny new shoes of his, and nearly knocked the nails off his toes."

The girls laughed.

"He went to *all* of them," Flannery said, admiringly.

"Attended every single one," Mama said. "The next thing I knew, Honey Bee'd hiked the five miles over to my house. He pounded boldly on our door and handed my daddy the permission slip."

"Did Gramps run him off?" A wide-eyed Patsy waited.

"Don't you know Daddy took one look at Honey Bee's busted shoes and right away gave his blessing. I knew right then I'd marry that boy. I'd walk barefoot across Kentucky to have a man as fine as your daddy." Mama dabbed at her watery eyes. "Still got that old paper tucked inside my cedar chest with the quilt Miss Little made us for a wedding present."

Patsy and Flannery smiled, proud of their parents. The one living, and the one not.

"How was the dance, Mama?" Patsy asked.

"I promised Honey Bee the dance would be divine." Mama smiled a little dreamily as if it was happening all over again. Right then and there.

"And?" the girls chorused.

"And we danced, is all." Mama took another drink of her cola, flicked at a tiny crumb on the table. "Danced the jitterbug and the Black Bottom like nobody's business," she said matter-of-factly. "It was all divine. A real gasser as they say."

"*Gasser,*" Patsy and Flannery sang out and giggled.

"Well, it was. The *dance* was," Mama said.

"Did you let him kiss you?" Flannery propped her chin on her fists and leaned in closer to the conversation.

"Oh, hush. Your daddy was a gentleman." Mama shook a finger at Patsy. "A fine gentleman, and I expect nothing less from your Mister Danny Henry. Now drink your colas, girls." She fanned away the discussion with smiling eyes.

Now that the prom was finally here, Patsy wondered whether Danny would have agreed to Bible studies if the old teacher had turned him down. Worried how far he would've walked for her. More, would he still be willing to walk for her after tonight? Patsy was sure she was about to find out if he was a fine one like their Honey Bee.

Flannery leaned over, bumping Patsy's shoulder to grab a ribbon off their vanity.

"I'm sorry Wendell didn't ask you, tadpole," Patsy said. "Miss Little would've said yes. Mama too." Patsy knew Flannery had waited months, hoping for Wendell Black to ask her out.

"Yeah," Flannery said to her twin. "But he has to work too."

"That boy's crazy about you, even if he can't scrape the words off his tongue," Patsy said. "At least you'll get to be with him tonight."

"Humph. A fat lotta good that does me." Flannery grunted softly, taking a chew to the consolation. . . . "You really think he likes me?"

"I do." Patsy pulled out the cubbyhole drawer on her side of their vanity and lifted out a Chicken Dinner candy bar. "Here, tadpole, you can have it," she told Flannery, feeling a little more sorry her sister was stuck working. Lately, Patsy didn't have the taste for the candy anyway.

When Danny went to Lexington with his folks, he'd always save his nickels to buy Patsy the expensive candy. Not made out of chicken, but a scrumptious chocolate-covered nut roll, and Patsy's favorite. She held out the Chicken Dinner bar with the roasted chicken on its blue and gold wrapper.

"Patsy"—the girls' mama poked her head into the bedroom—"don't forget these." She dangled an old string of pearls.

"Gramma's pearls." Flannery jumped off the bed, rushed over to her mama, and reached for them.

Jean Butler pulled back her hand. "You know these belong to your sister, baby girl. Firstborn gets the pearls, and the second child gets the wedding quilt," she gently admonished.

"No fair." Flannery flipped back her braid. "She was born only eight minutes before me, Mama. Only eight little min—"

Mama draped an arm across Flannery's shoulder and squeezed gently. "Come on. Behave."

"A quilt, a stupid coverlet. Can't wear a stupid quilt." Flannery sulked.

"You'll have Daddy's business one day," Patsy pointed out. "Same as his watch."

"Small chance of that happening now that you and Mama sold his stills," Flannery snipped.

"But you got his recipe books," Patsy said, relieved Mama had rid the family of the old whiskey distillery, got rid of almost every trace of Honey Bee's business. That was the first thing

Mama did when he died. "And look what that old female did with just a pile of recipes, tadpole. It made her famous—"

"I'm not Catherine Carpenter. And, he meant for us both to have his secrets," Flannery reminded, dismissing the famous Kentucky pioneer. "But he knew only *one* of us would be doing the work. And 'sides, you told Honey Bee you didn't want anything from the whiskey—still, you got his gun that belonged to that old outlaw." Flannery rubbed the leather band on the timepiece her daddy had passed to her.

Patsy wrinkled her nose.

"Please, girls. No bickering," Mama scolded. "Let's not bring up sadness on such a beautiful day. Whiskey is not a proper business for ladies. You'll be sixteen—young ladies in a few weeks. And I've decided today's the day. Flannery, you can go get your quilt out of the hope chest, and Patsy"—smiling, she handed her eldest-daughter-by-eight-minutes the pearls—"you'll want to wear these to your big dance."

"Thank you, Mama," Patsy said, embracing the pearls, pinning them to her chest. Although old, the pearls were gems. Something precious to add to her beauty. The teen had been waiting for those family jewels ever since she had toddled around in them while wearing her Mama's prized periwinkle-blue church heels that Honey Bee'd brought her back from New Orleans. Now finally the pearls were hers.

"Who needs fancy gems for soda-jerking anyway." Flannery sighed. "I have to get ready for *your* shift if I'm going to make it on time. It's late."

"That's because you wasted *your* time arguing," Patsy said.

Earlier, Patsy had hung her robe beside the tub and bumped her sister aside, calling first dibs on the bath. And their mama had let her over Flannery's loud protests about running late for work. Mama had gasped, "He'll hear! Heavens, what's gotten into you, Flannery Bee Butler? It's nearly six . . . and it would be a sin to make your sister late—no respectable lady has her date sit in the parlor while she's bathing just a hush away. That's just plain wickedness!"

"Scandalous." Patsy's breaths hovered above her mama's. "I can't be naked in this house and have Danny Henry hearing it behind the wall like that, Mama. It's my prom!"

"Indecent." Mama pressed her hands to her ears.

"*Lord*," Flannery sassed. "You'd think I'm committing a crime of moral turpitude the way you two are carrying on like that. Mama, I doubt if God has given that Henry boy, or any boy, special X-ray ears to hear a female taking her bubble bath through the acres of damask-rose skins that thicken our paper-soaked walls. Let me go first—"

"It's my big dance," Patsy cried.

"She's always trying to boss and has to be first in everything, Mama. Everything! If Honey Bee was here, he'd make her be fair," Flannery groused. "He wouldn't let her—"

"Flannery!" Mama and Patsy scolded, running her out of the room.

Minutes later, Flannery poked her head back into the bedroom. "I'm going to be late, Mama. Can you iron my uniform for me?"

"Mama," Patsy said, pulling out one of the bobby pins fastened to her pin curls, "you need to do my hair."

"Heavens," Mama said, "just look at the time." Mama starched Flannery's uniform, making it look out-of-the-box new as only she could, then fussed with Patsy's hair and helped her into the prom dress she had made for her eldest daughter.

"Where did I put my new stockings?" Flannery wiggled into her girdle, held up a garter buckle. "Mama, have you seen—?"

"Look on your dresser under your apron." Mama fluffed Patsy's underskirts, lifting tulle and satin, and then prissed and fussed some more over the dress's sunshine-yellow chiffon and lace puffy veneers, inspecting the pencil-thin velvet shoulder straps and sweetheart neckline. Smiling, she clasped the pearls around Patsy's neck.

"Mama, you go on now," Patsy insisted. "I don't want you to be late." She couldn't have Mama making a fuss in front of her date.

"*I'm* gonna be late," Flannery complained again, foot propped on the bed, carefully walking the hosiery up her leg.

"You could be twenty minutes early and still think you're late," Patsy said.

"I don't like making folks wait like you, *Queen Patsy*."

"Girls, shh." Mama rested her hands on Patsy's waist, looked over her daughter's shoulder into the mirror.

"Flannery can see me off," Patsy told Mama, shooing her away. "Right, tadpole?"

Reluctantly, Flannery nodded and pecked her mama's cheek. "Thanks for ironing my uniform, Mama. Go on and get your stuff. I'll take care of Queenie—so long as they pick her up on time."

"The dress is beautiful, Mama. I'll see you tonight," Patsy said.

"It's one of your best," Flannery agreed.

"We'll make you one just as pretty when it's your time." Mama lightly patted Flannery's cheek. "Okay, girls. I'll just get my dessert and be off. What time is Sam and Carol Jean supposed to pick you up?"

Patsy and Danny were double dating with Sam and his girl. Sam had offered to drive Danny and Patsy to the prom since both were weeks shy of getting their own licenses.

"Soon." Patsy kissed Mama good-bye and turned to the floor mirror on the other side of the room.

Satisfied with Patsy's appearance and her own handiwork, Mama once again lectured her daughters on modesty and manners, then left for her monthly canasta game with some of the townswomen.

Patsy patted the pearls resting on her collar, taking in one more drinking glance of herself in the mirror. The soft glow of the gems warmed her body, dulling the harsh secrets she carried. She loved Danny, she was sure of it, and that would see her through.

Turning sideways, Patsy ran a light hand down her neck and alongside the curves of her breasts, admiring. She looked rather like a princess, she mused. *Yes, a princess.* And her prince would have the prettiest date in Glass Ferry tonight—would walk a thousand miles for her, even farther than Honey Bee had walked for Mama.

The pearls were her crown—they empowered her—and would give her the courage for bigger things. Tonight her life would change—change so she could reclaim the rightful passage that Danny's brother had stolen.

# CHAPTER 3

*Flannery*
*1972*

Flannery had always managed to slip in and out of town, dodging Hollis Henry most of the time. But there was no escaping the sheriff now with that announcement hitting the air waves.

Mama moaned and dropped into the chair, pressed a clenched hand to her mouth. "My baby girl, my Patsy."

"Mama, shh, that Mercury could be anybody's—maybe not even from around here, maybe not even from Kentucky." Flannery picked up the cake knife and set it on the counter. "And if it is the Henrys' car, it doesn't mean Patsy was in there. Lately they've been pulling all sorts of stuff out of the river not even from around here, from places way far away," Flannery said softly, hoping she was right. Still, the "maybes" felt dark, not lanterned near enough to be true.

For many, the river had been a guardian of private matters. A slow, meandering 260-mile tributary of the Ohio River that coursed its way through craggy Kentucky mountains and thick forests, winding past forgotten family cemeteries, small and bigger bluegrass towns. Some of its depths unknown. Folks claimed spots of the Kentucky never had a bottom to begin with, that in certain parts a person could crawl across, and in other parts, drop and never surface again. Recent years of drought had changed that.

Lost things spilled onto the Kentucky's banks, into fishermen's hands, more than a few, revealing age-old secrets. The
usual trash: beer cans, bent fishing lures, refrigerators, and
other such junk. And a few scarier things: a rubber glove with
a person's bloated hand inside, and the red sneaker stuffed with
a human foot. The *Glass Ferry Gazette* ran a story, but no one
came forward claiming to be missing their nubs.

In the last few years, Mama'd told Flannery the local news-
papers and radio stations had been providing exciting updates
about surfaced treasures. One Glass Ferrian had found a Civil
War sword and a tinderbox full of old Indian artifacts, and another, a large tin of coins from a century-old bank robbery.

Someone else netted an emerald bracelet, mud-stuffed, inside
an ancient bronze goblet. Folks said that chalice was really old
and had traveled from Ireland, maybe even from as far away as
Japan.

A pretty maple violin in its tattered coffin case had been
discovered last year. And two years ago they pulled out Web
Sloan's garden tractor that had gone missing in the '20s. A partial human skull and one leather boot were wedged between one
wheel's rusted metal spokes. Mr. Sloan claimed his mama had
reported his daddy and the tractor missing in 1921, but no one
could find any records of such a report.

Quickly, Flannery poured Mama a glass of water and knelt
in front of her. "Mama." She nudged the glass gently. "Here.
Drink some water. Come on, have a sip; you'll feel better."

Mama took a trembly breath and nodded.

"Did you take your medicine this morning, Mama?"

Mama took a gulp and shook her head.

"You know Doc wants you to take it. Especially today. Let
me go get it for you." Flannery patted Mama's knee and stood.

"It's in the cabinet," Mama said, and bobbed her gray head
toward the hall bathroom. "Get dressed. You need to drive me
to Sheriff Henry."

Flannery hurried into the bathroom, opened the mirrored
medicine cabinet, and searched the stacked glass shelves. Her
daddy's old razor fell out, and she knocked over a bottle of

amphetamine salts the doctor had prescribed for Mama years ago. "No longer effective to boost her mood, or keep her mild depression at bay," he'd said to Flannery back then. "Let's try something new. For both of you."

Flannery scattered a few more half-empty pill bottles, iodine, old brown glass containers with rust-encrusted tops of dried-out paregoric and castor oil, and then snatched up the one that was new. It slipped from her grasp, and she bent over the soft-rose-tinted sink, trying to still her nerves bumping against the porcelain. That Patsy might be coming home, and like this, was something Flannery'd never dreamed, well hardly ever.

Flannery picked up Mama's medicine, read the instructions on the bottle, and pulled out two yellow pills. Her fingers buttered, and she dropped those too. Scooping the Valium out of the basin, she knocked Mama's frosted-glass bottle of rose toilet water over, spilling the pink liquid everywhere.

*Pink.* All this cupcake-pink. Mama and Patsy had insisted on smothering the room in it. The hue was everywhere, reeking from the tub to the sink, onto the commode and its matching roll of toilet paper, the blossomed wallpaper and rosy curtains. Flannery had begged Mama over the years to at least add some green, or a burst of red even, to break up the noxious crawl pink left under her skin.

It reminded Flannery of what she'd read about Jayne Mansfield and her Pink Palace with its pink champagne-flowing fountain and heart-shaped tub.

Mama and Patsy had fussed that the color was sophisticated, lovely like the silkiest nylons, or a pretty lacy slip worn under a dowdy duster. It fit Patsy and Mama fine, but for some reason, Flannery felt she hadn't, nor would ever live up to the expectations of that strong, womanly pink.

"Flannery?" Mama said faintly from the kitchen.

"Just a small spill, Mama. I'll clean it up," Flannery called back, dropping a towel onto the mess. "Be right there." She hovered over the sink, taking in tiny breaths of rose-filled air. She had to collect herself. Grabbing a washcloth, she pressed it to her nose.

Flannery looked hard at the bottle of pills. She'd been leaning on them, same as Mama. Years of this *new* medicine, that *old new,* and yet, *better new,* all the doctors promised, but never new enough to fully nip the pain from Patsy's leaving, from Flannery's losses, or to calm the shakes from what had happened back in the city.

She'd been a divorced woman for decades now, fancy-free in the fifties at that. Even though divorced meant the same as disgrace, a damnation in the eyes of small-town folks, being single suited Flannery just fine. Still, she couldn't talk about the marriage, not to anyone, ever.

Last year when she'd returned home to Louisville from "Patsy's birthday week," Flannery had stopped taking the pills. She'd cleaned herself up with the help of a nice psychiatrist, after having swallowed one too many and once again landed in Saint Anthony's. That hospital had kept her for two weeks. Two whole weeks. Luckily, it hadn't affected her teaching position at the elementary school because she had been on summer break, and the school was never the wiser. In some ways, bigger, more important ways, cities provided a shelter that no small town could.

Flannery hung the pink, wet towel over the tub and opened the window to air out the sickeningly perfumed bathroom.

Leaning over the sill, she looked out past the trees toward Ebenezer Road, inhaling the percolated winds from the nearby Kentucky River, forcing the calmness to root inside her. Mama and the news would have to wait until she pulled herself together. On a windy day like today, the river stole most of the angels' share, the old distillery's scent—lifted the sleeping bourbon's vapors from its aging oak barrels and carried the breaths down the river. Her daddy and granddaddy and most of the men in Glass Ferry had worked the bourbon all their lives. The Butler family had owned the finest stills in the land, and they had all breathed and worn that angels' share on their flesh and in their bones.

River breezes slapped against the house's brick façade, softly fanning Flannery's face. More than anything she wished to escape to the mud banks of the Kentucky—escape to the sweet times before her losses had started to pile up. Step onto her daddy's old ferryboat like when he was alive, sip the glass-eyed silence of the winding, stretching river, let the sweetness of its perpetual summer lap at her dangling bare feet and calm the tangled thoughts. Hear the lazy putting of the boat's engine as it scooted down the river. Going down there now for anything as horrible as that car, that Mercury dredged out of there—she couldn't bear it.

A cardinal landed on the willow tree in the yard, singing to its mate. Sunlight cast soft bands across the bird's black-masked eyes and standing red crown. A wonder lit Flannery, and she found herself holding fast to each rippled note, each light, painfully aware of the earth's workings. Its comings and leavings and pulling sighs. Patsy's and hers and others. It was as if she had suddenly knocked her funny bone against the sharpest corner of the world.

Flannery smarted at the realization that she, like the bird and those others who'd left the earth, maybe Patsy now too, were just blurs in a passing fury.

She could see it now and could almost welcome it without fear, and thought this would have been something fine to share with Patsy—a meaningful conversation like they'd had after Honey Bee died, a pledge given to each other before they'd given up on sisterhood.

"A dear sister," Patsy had called her, "my best friend. Always," on the eve of their daddy's funeral.

How she missed them both. Wished she could say those words back to Patsy, wished for so many lost years.

Plucking up the pill bottle, Flannery tapped it onto the ledge, dulling the marvel of clarity. She lifted it higher and shook the pills. Looking at the *new* like that had her thinking about the *old* and that last day with Patsy, Danny, and Hollis, and their final moments on Ebenezer.

She shuddered as she remembered standing in the dirt just outside this very window, right there by the long-legged willow in 1952.

*    *    *

That night, Patsy and Danny's double dates for the big prom canceled. Carol Jean's mama called at the last minute and told Patsy she had put her daughter to bed after her girl fell ill with a nasty rash.

Hollis and Danny pulled up to their house to collect Patsy a few minutes after Mama pulled away. Flannery kept checking her watch, eager to leave.

"Dad said I had to drive you two to the dance," Hollis said. "Guess I'll suffer playing chauffer tonight since you tots don't have your operator licenses." He grinned at Patsy. "But I expect a nice tip."

Patsy shot Hollis a hostile look, then just as quick sent Flannery an innocent shrug.

Flannery stood in the driveway like an ugly dogtooth weed amongst the bright sunny merrybells. An awkwardness gathered in her nyloned legs and had the gravel biting under her squeaking, grease-stained oxfords, while the party's dusty regrets slapped at Flannery's face and pride.

"We sure wish you could've come with us, Flannery," Patsy said again, brushing ghost lint off the skirts of her endlessly layered lemon-colored prom dress and fiddling with her dipping neckline. She peeked over her ankle-length skirts down at the flirty, round-toed Mary Jane pumps, daintily angling one of her cream-colored leather shoes, with the rosette bow Mama had fashioned onto the straps, to one side and then another.

The month before, Mama had driven the girls up to Lexington to buy a pair of dress shoes for Patsy's prom. They ate toasted cheese sandwiches at the crowded Woolworth counter and stopped at the inexpensive store, the modest Wennekers Sample Shoes.

But Patsy turned up her nose at the nice four-dollar heels Mama'd held up. Teary-eyed, begging, Patsy had wheedled Mama into trying the big store next door. Inside the fancy Purcell's department store, Patsy found herself a "dreamy" pair—a pair that cost Mama a whole eight dollars, twice the amount she'd paid for the two sets of saddle shoes the girls wore nearly every day.

That was the Patsy Flannery now knew. All dolled up like Suzy Parker on the slick pages of Mama's *Life* magazine. Patsy with the long, penny-glint, feathery-kiss curls and red bow-tie lips, in a tad-too-tight-to-be-polite sweater, looking all glam and glorious, while Flannery hid her knobby knees and flat tires behind baggy, rolled-up boy jeans and Daddy's old shirts. Her long drab tresses swept back and ponytailed.

"A tadpole in a pond of goldfish," Patsy had once said to another girl when she thought Flannery wasn't around.

Patsy got all the boys, too. It didn't matter how often Flannery stood in front of the mirror, suctioning her palms, pumping 'em, chanting, "I'm a lil' teapot, hear me shout; fill me up, and spill 'em out."

When Patsy turned twelve, she developed her curves. Mama had noticed and went straight out and bought a brassiere for the eldest. Patsy had her first kiss with a freshman, while Flannery was still trying for her first wolf whistle on the cobbled walks of Glass Ferry.

It used to be the girls would go to school and back on their bikes, but in the last year, Patsy caught her rides in automobiles with others.

Patsy complained to Mama that it was because Flannery's bicycle was too loud. That the clothespins and trading cards her sister attached to the spokes supposedly hurt Patsy's sensitive ears. "Real ladies don't bicycle and wrinkle their skirts like that," Patsy cried.

But Flannery knew the truth, always knew Patsy was more than happy about the boys lining up by the school walk in the afternoon, begging for the favor of toting her home, picking her up in the mornings down the road and out of sight of Mama's prying eyes.

Most folks said they didn't look like twins lately, and at that time it didn't feel to Flannery like they were even sisters.

When they were little, if the kids at school saw one of them alone, they would have to ask the twin to "grin and bare it." A school and town-wide joke and the only way to tell the girls apart. Flannery had a big dimple on her left cheek that showed only if she smiled, while Patsy's was tucked in the same spot, only hidden on the inside of her cheek. It was as if Patsy had been in such a rush to leave the womb to claim her firstborn status, her earliness, she couldn't even wait around long enough to let God finish filling in the muscly hole.

Lately though, everyone was stumped. Flannery had lost her dimple and couldn't find any reason to get her smile back. And it no longer mattered.

Patsy claimed she couldn't help it—couldn't help poking herself into all things ahead of Flannery. It was her birthright, after all, having made her royal entrance a full eight minutes prior. Her duty to be the queen and Flannery her servant.

But Flannery had her fill of it lately, especially since she was coming into her own—her womanhood. She'd noticed the boys' butterfly eyes lighting over Patsy, then skittering over her, before landing back on her twin. That in itself wasn't bad; that in itself gave her hope. She was sure one day those fleeting looks would light upon her and linger longer.

Flannery had been seeing it happen a little with Wendell Black.

Still, Flannery missed her sister, the one she'd known before troubles took hold, back when they shared the same skin in matching smocks, homespun clothes, smack down to the identical socks Mama would knit for them. They'd pile into bed together even, talking sometimes until early morning or until one of them lock-jawed herself silly into a sleeping yawn.

Patsy had stuck up for Flannery. She was protective of her younger sister, even against mean and scary teachers. Up until third grade, that is, when they were found out.

Flannery and Patsy's deal had been struck sometime during the third grade. Patsy would take Mrs. (Fussy) Fulson's vocabulary tests for Flannery, if her twin would take the arithmetic tests.

Patsy always whizzed through vocabulary tests, but failed miserably at all things arithmetic. She loved smart-sounding words, the bigger the better, which had gotten her into trouble more than a few times. Flannery had trouble with spelling bees, and didn't give a hoot about twisty tricky words, but loved towering numbers.

The two had it worked out. They'd ask to be excused to use the restroom halfway into any tests. Pestered into submission, Mrs. Fulson always let them go with the warning to hurry back. When they returned, Patsy and Flannery would switch desks and finish the other's test.

No one ever knew. But on one particular day when the students had wrapped up their tests, Mrs. Fulson went to "Patsy" and told her to collect the papers for her. Forgetting she was supposed to be Patsy, Flannery smiled a "yes, ma'am," exposing the telltale dimple.

Mrs. Fulson pulled her up by the ear. On the way to her desk, the teacher nabbed Patsy's ear and dragged them both to the front of the class. They stood there silent in front of their softly snickering classmates.

Mrs. Fulson took down the thick wooden paddle hanging on the wall behind her desk.

Patsy told the teacher it was all her fault, begging her not to whip Flannery. "Please, Mrs. Fulson, I stole Flannery's seat!" Patsy had insisted, stomping her little brown and white saddle shoes to make it true.

"*Cheaters,*" Mrs. Fulson scolded. "I should take you to Mrs. Moore's classroom and let her keep you."

Mrs. Moore was the second-grade teacher.

"God made us the same. And being the same ain't cheating, Mrs. Fulson. We're one and the same," Patsy argued.

Mortified at getting caught, then whipped, Flannery rubbed her welling eyes.

Patsy gently touched her sister's quivering shoulder. "Don't cry, Flannery. . . . Oh, you don't have to cry." Patsy patted and pulled Flannery to her. "I'll cry for us today," she said solemnly.

Furious at being duped, calling Patsy a trickster first, and then a swindler, Mrs. Fulson jerked the bolder twin away, giving her the first whipping and some extra licks, then turned to Flannery for the same. When the teacher was through, she handed the girls pointy paper dunce caps and sent them both scurrying to opposite corners to face the wall for the rest of the day.

Mrs. Fulson sent an explanatory note home with the girls, threatening to kick them out of third grade. They dared not give it to Honey Bee, knowing that he'd find out their wrong to its full extent, and that a lie added to the serious crime they'd originally committed would mean even double or triple their punishment.

After supper, Honey Bee called them outside. "Go pick your paddle." He pointed to the willow, expecting them to get the switches he'd tan them with.

Dutifully, the girls walked slowly over to the tree, broke off the smallest branches, and handed them to Honey Bee. After a few squirming seconds he asked the girls if they had been cheating.

Patsy pushed herself in front of Flannery and said, "Oh no, Honey Bee. Only me. Flannery was just caught smiling." Patsy yanked Flannery to her side. "See, Honey Bee?" Patsy poked Flannery, urging her to smile for him. "Show him, Flannery."

Flannery beamed the same as she had in school for Mrs. Fulson. Patsy lifted a sweet but dimple-less one too, and let a tear weight her lash for insurance.

"Well, hell's bells," Honey Bee chortled low, looking at his smiling daughters, shaking his head and dropping the switches. "I can't be whipping ya'll, looking all sweet and smart like that. Run on into the house and help Mama with the dishes, and no more cheating, or tricking poor Mrs. Fulson, or she'll send you to second grade, and I'll burn up your hineys with big fat switches."

"You get the dishes and set the table. I have to brush my hair," Patsy'd bossed Flannery, skipping off.

Mrs. Fulson had the two separated into different classes at the beginning of fourth grade.

Soon, Patsy began hanging out with other friends at school, picking pretty Laura Adams for a best friend over Flannery but dropping Laura just as quick when a boy came sniffing.

Flannery stayed after school more, hanging with her small

baton group, hoping for Patsy's favor when she was in between boys and friends.

But Patsy was never alone and only chummed with her sister when she needed something.

On their fifteenth birthdays, Patsy sweet-talked Mama into taking her to a *real* hairdresser. Mama took Patsy to Junie Bug's Hair Styling, where she had Miss Junie give Patsy a hair color bath like the coppery colored one that Suzy Parker wore. Patsy had been begging for the new do ever since she'd spied the famous woman's hair in the magazines.

"Get the blond," Patsy ordered Flannery. "Make her get blond, Mama."

As usual, Flannery agreed. It had always been Patsy who had her say, the first and final words between the two, content to lead and let Flannery puppy dog behind her.

Rather than hear the fuss, Mama'd always let her.

When the first drops of Junie's hair dye lit Flannery's scalp on fire and burned, Mama stopped the hairdresser cold, wouldn't let Miss Junie touch another strand.

Instead, Mama bought Flannery ribbons at the dime store to hide her mousiness in braids and ponytails. Flannery'd hid her platinum, skunk-spotted hair under an ugly old scarf Patsy insisted she wear. The only good thing about it all was when Patsy kicked Violet Perry for making fun of Flannery.

Flannery felt hurt and lost. If she had thought hard enough about it, she would've rightly guessed that it had really started the Easter before they turned ten.

Patsy had thrown a hissy over wearing identical dresses that year, insisting Mama let her wear something different. "Mama," Patsy'd demanded, "I'm almost ten. I want a different dress. A purple poplin one with a red satin ribbon like the one Cora Wallace's mama is making. One like my best friend's dress."

But Mama wouldn't hear of it back then, agreeing only that Patsy could wear a different color sweater over her dress.

"But *we're* best friends, Patsy," Flannery had chimed, embarrassed, thinking something was wrong with her.

"Cora is my new friend," Patsy told her. "And my best."

Hurt, Flannery lashed back, "Mama, I want a different dress, too. And prettier than those ol' ugly colors Patsy picks out."

Patsy snickered. "You'd still be ugly. Stinky, like Honey Bee's old whiskey and that nasty ol' fishy river."

Those digs cut, and after Patsy said enough of them, Flannery began to feel them in the worst ways. "At least I'm not a priss pot, always crying and—"

"Stinky pig. And *my friend* Cora says you can't put a ribbon on one," Patsy spat.

"I hate you!" Flannery screamed.

Patsy jerked hard on Flannery's braid. Flannery hit back.

Honey Bee caught them bickering and swatted both of their tails.

Flannery'd burst into tears, running up to her room. Later, Honey Bee called his girls to the porch and said, "Daughters, you'll make yourself a heap of friends and even lose yourself a might more, but you'll never lose what's in your blood, what belongs in that blood and to each of you. *Your sister.* Lose that blood, and you will become weak. Stay good to each other, so you can stay strong."

Flannery thought *she* should be Patsy's best friend. Told Patsy she was hers, even over her group of baton girlfriends nobody else hung with.

But Patsy liked her new friends just fine, and pulled to the attention they gave her, ignoring Honey Bee.

Flannery felt lost, halved, like an arm had been split off. After all, they were born together, *one and the same,* and that was about the closest friend you could ever have. And any less of a friendship was betrayal if it wasn't. *Wasn't it?*

Mama said there wasn't any harm in Patsy's wanting to make different friends and maybe Flannery should try it too. "After all, you'll marry one day, and have yourself a different life."

Honey Bee kept Flannery busy with chores in the barn, took her out on the river in the boat, and taught her more about his business.

* * *

Flannery snuck glances over to the Henry boys waiting to escort Patsy to the dance. Something was rotten, and she could smell it stinking and sticking all over those two.

Patsy said, "I'll be home directly after prom. Don't wait up, tadpole."

Hollis Henry stood there by the tree, shifting his eyes Patsy's way, stripping off tears from the willow's drooping branches.

Flannery looked at his head, fat, almost neckless, the way it sat stubbed too close to the shoulders. His hair prissed and looking better than hers, slicked up and pushed into a pompadour, styled to the middle, a loose strand slipping over a prowling eyebrow. It all looked odd on him. Like he'd borrowed himself from another for the night. Hollis didn't match the nice duds he'd picked out to escort Patsy and Danny to the door. She knew he was more suited for motor oil cologne, grease-stained T-shirts, and doing sweaty back-bending work. But lately he'd been wearing pressed shirts, dousing himself with his daddy's cologne every time he was around Patsy.

Flannery figured Hollis would try to pinch off the pair's date time by loitering in the school parking lot, smoking, drinking with the other troublemakers who didn't get approved by Miss Little until she'd open the gymnasium door and spot them and threaten Bible study for the rotten lot.

Hollis snapped off a bough and dropped it. She wanted to kick him, shove him away from the weeping willow, and yell at him for stealing the life of the tree.

There was something about him killing the leaves that just lit her nerves. She loved the old willow that she and Patsy and Honey Bee'd planted long ago. They'd found a sapling along the Kentucky banks a decade ago, and together dug it up and planted the tiny life here by the house. Honey Bee'd built a little wooden enclosure around it to protect its tender bark from deer, leaving the fencing up until the branches were high enough that the critters could no longer nibble on them and the trunk thickened.

Honey Bee'd declared it a fine kissing tree, maybe even a proper hitching spot for his daughters, and had pecked Mama's, Flannery's, and Patsy's cheeks with light kisses.

Flannery hated Hollis Henry yanking on it like that, groping it the way she'd seen him do the girls at school when the teachers weren't looking.

Flannery knew Patsy felt it too, knew the tree was special to both of them. When they were little, the two had played under the branches, dressed up in Mama's dresses, church heels, and made daisy chains to wear in their hair, pretending they were princesses marrying handsome princes, Patsy's favorite game.

Honey Bee had joined them, hunkering low to the grass, sneaking toward them, hopping like a frog, croaking, "Who wants to marry Mr. Toad?" They squealed and ran, and he caught them, pronouncing them each Mrs. Toad, leaving them all tangled on the grass, rolling, laughing in each other's arms.

The two pretend princes standing before Flannery today were toads.

Hollis threw down a wad of crumpled leaves and murmured an obligatory "Yeah, sure would've been swell if we both could've gone. If only I didn't have that damn detention on my back, we could've," but looking at Patsy in a way that only Danny should be looking.

*Liar,* Flannery thought. *You asked Violet Perry first.* Patsy must've read her mind, because she pinked a little and looked down at the ground.

"Least I get to take 'em. Stick around some until old bat Little runs me off," Hollis said.

Danny laughed. "Better not, big brother. Ol' Little catches you, you'll be reading the Good Word for a mess of weeks to come—four weeks to come, maybe more."

"Gee, then I'll be trapped hanging with the old folks forever, not just this evening," Hollis pouted. "Oh well, least I'm not stuck playing Cinderella to the royalty tonight. Dishing out ice cream and all those fun treats." He swallowed a snicker. "Gonna have *me* some fun."

Flannery's nerves itched a little more. She could sense a mean-ness, a cruelty of sorts in Hollis that had rooted years ago. He was "the disgusting part of a person" as her daddy would put it about bad folks. Flannery couldn't help but wrinkle her nose at the man Hollis was growing into.

"Going to be a blast." Danny grinned.

"Nifty," Patsy piped, then opened her little clutch and pulled out the compact of pressed powder to check her lipstick and eyeliner, sweep the thin velvet puff across her button nose.

Last Christmas, Flannery had saved to buy Patsy the gold-tone compact. She'd worked it out with Mama to secretly drive her to Purcell's in Lexington. Flannery'd spent her whole pay-check on the elegant compact with its filigree and inlaid rhine-stone clasp.

For Flannery's present, Patsy had tossed her a stale Chicken Dinner candy bar Danny'd given her months before.

Flannery dug into the apron pocket of the blue gingham-print uniform for her soda jerk cap. "I better hurry 'fore Chubby Ray has a hissy. Have fun." She waved a lame cheer with the paper-cloth hat.

Hollis stepped forward, pulling a stink of grass and woodsy cologne he'd pilfered from his daddy's medicine cabinet. Flan-nery smelled the drink on him before his words cut the air.

"We're going to Chubby's for treats before the prom," he said. "You can ride with us, peaches. Snug beside me." Hollis patted the side of his leg. "Ain't that right, Danny?"

Danny, who had been chugging on something that looked a lot like whiskey-brown water in a 7UP bottle, lifted the glass neck to his lips in agreement.

"It'll be swell. C'mon on, peaches," Hollis urged.

Patsy's cheeks colored, and she shifted her leg, silenced Hollis with a cold eye.

Flannery stepped back and pulled Patsy to the side, whis-pered, "Those boys are getting pie-eyed—"

"Don't make a fuss and don't tattle to Mama. Don't, tadpole. *Please,*" Patsy hushed.

"They're getting sauced, and you know it, Patsy—"

Patsy put a finger to her lips and grabbed her sister's arm, turning her around and out of the path of the boys' nosy glances.

"I don't like this one bit," Flannery said.

"Please don't," Patsy said, pulling Flannery into the sheaves of satin and netted tulle under yards of petticoat trappings that scratched out her echoing pleas. "I have to go tonight; *please,* it's important." Patsy fidgeted with the heirloom pearls collaring her slender neck.

Flannery pushed her off, popped a worried look over to the Henrys. "Mama'll have both our hides if you go off with those boys like that," she said, though she knew Mama never had an angry hand for such harsh matters. But Honey Bee had and would take a switch and light your tail in a short Kentucky second if you showed yourself or shamed your family in the slightest.

"It's not my fault Carol Jean got sick!" Patsy swept her fingers under the pearls and scratched the small, rising bumps she got whenever she was upset. The boys stood back watching.

Clutching the bottle to his frumpy tuxedo, Danny pretended to inspect his trousers and black dress shoes, run a hand through his light brown locks. Hollis leaned against his shiny red Mercury, holding his silver flask, brooding over something.

"You can't go off with them like that," Flannery insisted.

"I'm going," Patsy declared.

"You know how Mama feels about liquor. Don't get into that automobile," Flannery warned.

Patsy raised her chin.

Flannery gripped her arm, and Patsy jerked away. Flannery tried to yank her back, missed her arm, but caught her shoulder and neck.

Patsy kicked Flannery's shin hard enough to make her let go, and then ran over to the Mercury, hopped into the backseat, and slammed the door.

Danny and Hollis jumped in after Patsy.

Flannery stooped over and rubbed her leg and saw a running snag. "Patsy Butler, you better get your butt back here," she yelled, and then caught a glint in the dirt. It was a silver clasp. Not a foot away lay the family jewels.

Snatching up the string of pearls, she slipped them into her pocket before Patsy could look back to notice.

"You're going to be sorry," Flannery hollered as Hollis goosed the engine and lit off, spraying gravel and grit on her freshly starched uniform. Danny's bottle flew out the window and hit a rock, rolling its broken, toothy neck her way.

The automobile's radio mewed Patti Page's "Tennessee Waltz" into the countryside.

Old winds snagged Hollis's and Danny's chorally whoops. Patsy's nervous giggles spilled into the jeers, their laughter trailing into the exhaust's smoke, slashing Flannery's skin, cutting deep into dark, tender spots.

Sweeping a hand down her dress and nylons, Flannery dusted off the hurt and dirt.

Carefully, she dug out the string of pearls and inspected them. The clasp had broken clean from the small loop at the end of the string.

Flannery dropped them back into her left apron pocket, the one that was always the cleanest at the end of her shift. She wasn't about to give them to Patsy now. Those two drunken fools would have them off her sister before the night ended, or Patsy would try to fix the old clasp herself and then lose them again.

Flannery stroked her smarting leg again. *In the morning and in front of Mama I'll give them back. That's the right thing to do. Mama needs to know the whole story too.*

She glanced at her wristwatch. *Look at the time.* Patsy didn't have the desire to keep it and thought she didn't need it, having been declared the firstborn by a few measly minutes. Never on time, and mostly never caring, Patsy had always run others late, secretly enjoying the luxury of milking time and making others lose their own precious minutes, even hours, over her.

Flannery headed down the drive toward Ebenezer Road, picking up her step and pocketing Patsy's time. *She'll be late just like me,* Flannery soothed.

# CHAPTER 4

*Patsy*
*June, 1952*

At the end of Ebenezer Road, under a thinning day that rubbed itself against the bark of a spreading elm, a murky light laundered saw-toothed leaves, splashed down onto the gnarled feet of the old tree, the 1950 Mercury resting in its puddled path.

Patsy inspected her new prom shoes, worrying about them getting dusty. *At least it's still daylight,* she comforted, standing under the elm, wringing her hands, stroking her arms. The early evening light slashed coppery-gray streaks across her pale skin.

*The leaving hour.* She feared this time of day, hated that the last hour always felt like it was snatching a vital part of you with its leaving—could pull you into its sneaky shadows and disappear from the world without a trace. Frightened by the way the bats swooned for skeeters, cartwheeling, dipping a little too close to your head, and hated the way chittering birds hurried to tuck themselves in. Hated this place, too, lately fearing it more than ever. Though she didn't understand why the old spot had set its tentacles onto her like that. That was the reason she'd stopped riding her bike and started catching rides with Danny and his brother down the road in the mornings, begged for the totings in the afternoon.

Sometimes Flannery stayed after school to practice her silly baton twirls. If Patsy couldn't hitch a ride, she would get stuck walking weedy Paintlick Field. Bad enough, but there was Ebenezer Road too, the only cut-through to home and all by herself—something that gave her the willies.

Old Ebenezer snugged alongside a cemetery and was an occasional private nest for lovers and rumored to be haunted. Walking the dirt-packed road, under a canopy of sleeping elms, she'd have to keep a sneaking eye behind and ahead, loudly humming to get out of that pocket of fear she carried.

Patsy snapped her head away from the cemetery gate. A shudder climbed up her backbone and slid around her scalp.

Others felt the same way, and, over the years, more than one stranger's automobile had broken down on that dead-end road. Some in Glass Ferry said the town should build a filling station out there.

Just last month, one carload of out-of-towners swore they'd seen what others had over the years. A small family cemetery crooked across from a white clapboard house. Children yelled out of its two-story panes, and in the yard below, a long-skirted woman wearing a bonnet called back to the youngsters.

The woman turned to the lost travelers, beckoning them up to the white picket fence. The stranded folks walked the fifty-odd feet and looked over at the graveyard and back to the house. But no one was ever there, just a church-quietness that licked at the home's laced curtains, and a gift resting outside the somber cemetery's wrought-iron gate—a full gasoline container for the frustrated strangers' empty automobiles that had mysteriously gone dry at the end of Ebenezer Road.

Late into the blue hour, the weary travelers hurried and tended to their automobiles before full dark took hold. Some ended up renting one of the vacant rooms above Lenora's Dry Goods & Notions, the only resting spot and motel of sorts to be had in a circle fifty miles across.

Most felt the urge to drive back to Ebenezer Road the next day to thank the charitable family. Pulling up alongside the cemetery, they found only a half-broken picket fence that had rooted itself into the black earth, and the crumbly remains of rubble and chimney rock where a house once stood.

Folks said Ebenezer Deer and his three children had perished in the farmhouse fire decades ago when the midwife, Joetta, left her husband and small boys to tend to an ill neighbor. Others called her a witch and said she'd done the deed herself.

Driven to madness, the widow hanged herself under the elm, folks rumored. She'd been walking Ebenezer Road ever since.

Flannery didn't mind being on Ebenezer, she'd told Patsy. Said the old place reminded her of a lullaby that was always tucked sweetly in your chest. And that the parting hour made Flannery think of Honey Bee and their old whiskey boat on the river heading home in the sunset.

Patsy couldn't understand why Flannery would like this horrid place, especially in the hour that calls to the darkness. *Why couldn't her twin feel what she felt? What Honey Bee knew, same as her: The place was bad.* Though her daddy'd never said *why,* Patsy had known his look enough not to push, the tilt of the head; what with that and the cut in his eyes, he'd warn his girls he was through talking about Ebenezer and was ready to let go of any further discussion.

"Flannery, you got to feel something too," Patsy said one day as they walked home from town. "This old place is ugly, and you know it." Patsy urged her sister to change her mind, prove Patsy had sound reason to hate the place.

"It's not too bad," Flannery'd said.

"Even Honey Bee told us it was. Said we couldn't play here when we were little. That we shouldn't tarry in this spot. Not on the way to school, or on the way home either. That there was evil soaked here. Mama said so, too," Patsy'd reminded her sister.

"Mama just doesn't like to talk about Joetta. Any bad things." Flannery had shrugged. "They probably just said that 'cause of the cemetery. And those hoodlums who cut loose once in a while out here and trash it up. That's all."

"Flannery!" Patsy said, exasperated. "Remember when Honey Bee took a switch to us?"

"'Cause we were poaching Joetta's flowers here," Flannery said. "Simple as that." Then quietly, "Okay, I might hate it some," she admitted, "but mostly I think it's sorta interesting. Kinda pretty in a strange, sad way."

Now soaked with the hour, those rumors, the feelings, and that history, Patsy looked anxiously over to the Henry boys, tapping her heel against a buckled tree root.

No sooner had the three sped off from her house, Danny got sick, begging his brother to stop. Hollis pulled onto Ebenezer to let him empty his stomach.

The Henry boys had stuck her in this dreadful place. She didn't care what Flannery thought, and knew Mama and Honey Bee were right. This place was evil. Patsy cast another wary eye over to the cemetery. A swarm of gnats hovered above one of the tombstones like a cloud of swirling black snow.

Standing here with the Henry boys she found herself feeling it more, a flame biting under her raring-to-go feet.

She could hear Danny on the other side of the Mercury throwing up. "Danny," Patsy called out again, "we're going to be late."

Patsy stole a quick glance at the pile of chimney ruins, then back over to the automobile. It had a full tank, Hollis assured her, and her date did too. More than what she'd first thought.

Patsy slipped behind the elm, took her stare to Paintlick Field, waiting for Danny to finish. In a few minutes it got quiet, and she poked her head out and saw what she'd feared. Danny was splayed out in the backseat, passed out from all the hooch he'd been drinking. Hollis leaned against the hood, sipping from a flask.

Flannery had been right after all, Patsy thought.

Patsy rubbed at the rash heating her neck, patting its flaming flesh once, twice, and cried out, "My pearls, *oh, my pearls.* They're gone!" Patsy looked down at the ground, twisted and turned, glancing all around. "Help me find them. Please!"

"Sure thing, doll baby," Hollis slurred, sauntering toward her.

Hollis had set his looting eyes on her from the moment he pulled up to the house. Most of the girls in town thought he was charming in an odd, dangerous way. But Danny was who she wanted; he had wooed her with his book smarts and mostly good grades—something Hollis didn't know. Hollis's brain was soaked from bourbon, grease-lightning automobiles, guns, and smutty girls. For two years Hollis had been working as a broom boy down at one of the distilleries, sweeping dirt and stacking barrels, and for weeks now he'd been trolling for another chance with Patsy.

Patsy tried not to give much thought to the older brother, now and oftentimes before this evening, showed contempt for his oil-spotted shirts and dirt-stained hands. When Danny was near, she did it for his sake too.

It was unnerving, the way Danny made her feel protected and certain while Hollis alarmed her and left her confused and out of control. Aside from Danny's growing fondness for liquor, the brothers were anything but alike.

The three, she, Danny, and Hollis, had been pals when she and Danny were in third grade, and Hollis in fourth, all of them hanging in the school yard, skipping rope, playing tag. It had been an easy choice since Flannery wasn't much interested in being with the threesome, preferring to twirl her baton with the group of girls called the Battling Bats.

Patsy and Danny had looked up to Hollis, especially when he got himself a huge growth spurt and filled out some. And through the years, Hollis'd looked after them, too, making sure bullies kept their distance from Patsy and Danny.

One time in third grade, out in the school yard, Patsy had a sudden nosebleed. Danny had paled and squealed, but Hollis didn't. He patted her shoulder, telling her he'd get help.

Then Hollis tore out for the school building, slipping inside to find something to stop the gushing. He'd raced back out with a heap of tissue in his hands, helping Patsy press the wad to her nose, slowly walking her inside to the school nurse.

But when Hollis hit seventh grade, and Patsy was in fifth, he'd ruined their friendship after he'd tried to snatch a kiss from her when no one was looking.

Embarrassed, Patsy stopped hanging with Danny and Hollis when the brothers were together, keeping her distance from the older brother, who became an even bigger pest after the stolen kiss, teasing, dogging her off and on over the years, and usually in between his other girlfriends.

Danny and Patsy'd paired off quietly and left the boisterous Hollis out. Danny was the one, and she had known it when he'd first shown up at her house with some magazines when she turned fifteen, and then brought her a handful of wildflowers the following Sunday. They'd have themselves quiet visits on the porch. She loved the way Danny talked about getting out of Glass Ferry, stepping out of the shadows of his lawman daddy and big brother.

Danny'd told Patsy he'd always had himself a fancy for one of those modern kit houses like the ones that used to come straight from the Sears, Roebuck and Company catalog. Had his eye on the Liberty ready-cut homes that cost less than one thousand dollars and could be mail ordered and shipped by rail to any-where you laid down roots. Like old Willy Nickles's house that he'd bought for three hundred seventy-two dollars in the twen-ties and put together on Turkey Hill.

Danny had himself some fine aspirations of owning a real castle, becoming a real businessman someday, away from the stinking bourbon town. Many Sunday afternoons the two had spent pouring through his catalogs and old copies of *Harper's Bazaar* and the *Screen Romances* magazines that belonged to his mama and he'd be sure to sneak over.

Patsy pinched at her sticky prom dress, lifted the fabric away from her sweaty chest, looking down at her breasts to see if the pearls might have fallen there.

"I can't find them," Patsy said, wild-eyed. "My *pearls.*"

Hollis lumbered around, kicking at the dirt and leaves. "Me neither," he mumbled.

Patsy begged him to search some more just as footfalls up Ebe-nezer Road sounded behind her, closer and closer. Flannery's.

Flannery ignored them, trudged right past the automobile and her sister, but Patsy latched on to her arm. "You need to help me."

"Fat chance after you ruined my nylons," Flannery said, and

glanced at the Mercury and Danny's head plowed against the backseat, mouth ajar. "Patsy, you better march your butt back home if you know what's good for you. Look at your date, him near dead drunk like that. He'll embarrass you and me and Mama, too—"

"Tadpole, not now. Oh, I've lost them," Patsy said. "Did you see my pearls back at the house?"

Flannery pulled her glare to Hollis. "These Henry boys are no dates for a prom."

Patsy followed her sister's gaze. Hollis held a smirk on his whiskey-glossed lips. "Flannery, my pearls, have you seen them?" Patsy asked again.

A flicker of anger lit Flannery's eyes. "Gee, no."

"They're not here, doll baby," Hollis said to Patsy, sounding bored.

"Help me find them," Patsy pleaded tearfully, struggling to stay pretty and fresh as a rain-splashed daisy. Something she was good at too—the faucet she could switch on with no more than a blink. The tears had worked mostly on Honey Bee, always on Mama, and some on Flannery.

Patsy couldn't bear to see anyone else's tears, though. Especially not Flannery's. It was as if her heart was being handed back to her broken.

"Check in the Mercury," Patsy told Hollis. "Flannery, help us. I can't lose them."

Flannery swept her hand down her wrinkly uniform and the torn stockings from Patsy's earlier kick. "What about these? These cost me a whole forty-nine cents, Patsy Butler."

She winced. "Not now. Help me find them."

Again, Flannery pointed at her own legs, then tugged at Patsy's dress. "You need to fix this."

Patsy brushed off her sister's hand.

Suddenly, Flannery kicked off her shoes. "You know the rules. Chubby Ray'll send me home if he catches me like this." Turning around, Flannery reached high under her dress and unsnapped the garters. Hopping on one foot and then another, she bent over and peeled off the ruined hosiery.

"*Flannery Butler!* Stop it . . . Oh . . . What are you doing?" Patsy's eyes popped.

Flannery threw her stockings at Patsy's feet. "Give me your nylons."

Hollis picked them up and struck a low catcall.

"Give 'em here," Flannery demanded. "They're hidden under your skirts. They ain't no use to you."

Patsy pressed her hand to her heated neck. "I will not!"

Flannery growled.

"I won't be able to dance," Patsy argued, knowing there were strict rules about the dancers scuffing up the polished wooden floors. Shoes came off for dancing, and any bare feet had to be properly covered with socks or hosiery.

"Come on, Patsy, hand them over."

"No. You know Miss Little won't let me on the floor, and it won't be any fun unless I can dance. I'll miss all the fun—"

"That'll make two of us." Flannery thrust out her palm, waiting.

"I won't."

"You're making me late." Flannery looked at her watch and scowled. Disgusted, she shoveled her feet back into her shoes.

"*Flannery,*" Patsy pleaded, "where do you think you're going? You can't go. You can't just leave me here like this. Please, Flannery? Don't go."

Her sister turned away.

"Come back here, now. Mama's going to be real mad at you," Patsy said, fuming. "Real mad, you leaving me like this, undressing like that in front of the boys, going into town naked-leg," Patsy threatened. "*Please,* I'll be late for my prom. . . . Help me now, and I promise I won't tell a soul what you—"

Flannery snapped up her sweaty arm and kept walking. She struck a finger to her wristwatch, tapping. "Can't," Flannery hollered back. "I'm eight minutes late for *my* nifty night." She picked up her feet and broke into a light jog away from Patsy and the boys. Away from Ebenezer Road.

# CHAPTER 5

*Flannery*
*1972*

Flannery slowed down as she drove past the old vacant Butler distillery and wound her way alongside the Palisades toward the location where the wreck had been pulled from the river.

At the last minute, Mama'd been so fraught with the nerves over the news, Flannery feared her heart would surely give out. Flannery called the doctor. He dropped by and gave Mama a sedative, ordering her straight to bed.

Flannery cranked the car window all the way down, letting the cool mountain breezes soothe her nerves. Memories flooded back to her like the great Kentucky after spring rains, thoughts of her daddy and what he did on that river and in that distillery up the bank a ways. The old 950-gallon submarine still Honey Bee and his own daddy had built shortly before her granddaddy passed, nailed and riveted and welded together from hammered sheets of copper and stainless steel and planks of wood.

Each year in the fall, Flannery and Honey Bee would travel up north to Fort Thomas, Kentucky, to purchase sorghum. He'd let Flannery help load up the grasses. "What sweetened the child's tongue will liven the old," Honey Bee told Flannery as she chewed on the sorghum stalk, sucking the sugary liquid he sometimes used for his whiskeymaking. Same as his daddy and granddaddy had done.

Flannery loved everything about whiskey, loved that Honey Bee had taught her the secrets of its doings. Loved the dark earth and the mystery of its scent that tucked itself into a strange sweet growing time.

She learned that where they lived was a perfect spot, and a "Heavenly home for the whiskeymakings," he'd told her. "God's sweet breath blows through these old rocks," Honey Bee said many times. The purest waters were found in their neck of the woods because of the limestone and the twisty Kentucky River, the streams and creeks that coursed through the rock-heavy landscape filled with the precious bluish-gray rock.

The waters doing that, running through the rock the way they did, made for the finest tasting bourbon around. "The limestone pulls out the stink of iron and sulfur, makes it pure and innocent," Honey Bee'd said. "Then my 'tucky River does the rest." He'd winked.

But her sister was more like Mama, and couldn't stand the business. "Devil's stinky hind quarters," Patsy and Mama called it for as long as Flannery could remember.

"This ain't your rotgut *corn likker* those old bootleggers try to pass, Jean. Ours is even better than ol Jeptha's." Honey Bee took honest offense.

Jeptha Jones was a moonshiner known for the smooth liquor he made from Bloody Butcher corn. Jeptha's family had been growing the blood-speckled grain for generations. Every year he'd save Honey Bee a bag of grist so Jean Butler could use it to make the cornbread Honey Bee fancied.

"I use fine grains, the finest touch," Honey Bee said. "That stuff some of those counterfeit pea-brains make will burn the hairs off your tongue, scald your gums, and leech out your ass, and light your skin afire. Leave you nothing less than mean-dog, knee-waddling inebriated. But, mine—"

"The devil's water," Mama insisted.

"Now come on, Mama. My 'tucky River Witch is respectable. It's licensed. A true gentlemen's whiskey. There's no cut of bath water or cheap sugars in my spirits. No, ma'am," he'd said.

"Respectable? Only because we have to keep that sheriff's pockets full with his granny fees," Mama complained.

"Taxes," Honey Bee said.

"Sinful bribery by the Henry brood," she booted back. "Smelly."

"An angel's sweet hand and what your pastor has said, and what your 'respectable' card club ladies come a'calling for when their menfolk's leashes unspool a bit. *Heaven*." Honey Bee would rile back and point to the family's fine two-story that overlooked the river and was had from the whiskeymaking.

Mama would fuss a little more until Honey Bee reminded her, "Woman, it saved us through the '37 flood, and more than once during the hellish Depression and Prohibition. Those government men only allowed four of us distilleries to stay open in Kentucky. Only handed out four measly licenses to produce medicinal whiskey"—Honey Bee had wriggled his fingers—"and sure enough granted me one, same as the fancy Colonel Albert Blanton up there in his Stony Point mansion on the hill."

Colonel Blanton was the president of the fine George T. Stagg distillery down on the Kentucky River. Folks said that when Blanton was sixteen, he became an office boy at the Old Fire Copper distillery, toiled like the devil, and eventually worked his way up to president of the company when George Stagg bought it.

Flannery had heard the whiskey stories many times, and of the hard times that fell upon the business. "Men seemed to be accident prone during those times, convalescing a lot longer," Honey Bee'd recalled. They would come to her daddy, show him their note from the doctor, which stated something along the lines of *Mr. Brown's convalescence necessitates the infinite use of alcoholic spirits.* Then the doctor would add the instructions that the patient should take the drink at all meal times, quantity indefinite. *Carry this at all times* was stamped under the physician's signature.

Flannery never understood the big fuss about any of it. But Patsy and Mama claimed the whiskey made them sick—the way the vapors settled into seams, soaked every crevice, darkening, seeping onto cornerstones, blotching rooftops and skin. It had to be the devil's imbibing to do all that.

In the summer of '43 when Flannery and Patsy turned seven, Patsy'd begged Honey Bee to let her quit her simple chores at the distillery. The sweeping, and the dusting of the old stills in the barn.

Honey Bee ignored her pleas until late summer. He'd found out Mr. Glass was selling the family ferryboat because the government men were finally going to build the bridge that would connect Glass Ferry to other counties and the rest of the world. Despite Mama's complaints and the cost to keep it up, Honey Bee bartered with Mr. Glass and brought the ferry home, docking it on the river bank down from their house.

Soon the government called on Honey Bee, offering him a small fee to keep the old boat in service for the sake of commerce and goodwill. But Honey Bee turned them down. The state pleaded with him to at least consider providing service a couple of days a week for those stranded folks needing to conduct business and family matters up and down the river.

Honey Bee settled on Saturdays for passenger toting, and pocketed the small change, gaining the sleepy but approving eye of the government for his *other* totings, he'd told Mama.

Flannery was so excited to ride in the boat she nearly burst. "Can we go to the city? Will we see oceans? Can we visit China?" she asked Honey Bee. But her sister sulked. On board, Patsy'd fretted about her pale skin burning, then turned green at the gills from the motion. Patsy didn't want to help clean the boat, saying she would surely be the boat's Jonah and jinx Honey Bee's ugly old ferryboat.

At that, Honey Bee sent Patsy straight back to Mama's apron, then gave Flannery her sister's duties, making her helmsman of the old scow that had once belonged to the original ferriers and first settlers of Glass Ferry, Kentucky.

Fall arrived, and Honey Bee had the boat hauled out of the river and stored in his large pole barn near the banks.

Honey Bee and Flannery scrubbed the ferry's wooden sides,

rubbing pine tar into the hull's plank seams, weatherproofing the old bucket. Flannery'd polished the wood railings and shined the brass, mostly inside the wheelhouse, until it gleamed, while Honey Bee took out the four passenger benches below to make room for his firewater.

It wasn't long until Honey Bee took a bottle of his good bourbon and christened the old boat *The River Witch*.

In early spring and every spring after, Honey Bee would roll out old bourbon barrels he'd made from white oak staves. He and Flannery would char them by rolling the barrels on their sides and taking fire to the inside, charring for a good three minutes, as much as five even, until Honey Bee thought the staves had a rough, shiny texture that looked like alligator skin.

Once in a while she and her daddy would lightly rub the casks with salt, pinches of coarse pepper, and sometimes tobacco into the lids. After, Honey Bee'd fill the oaken drums with spirits. Other times he might distill a special whiskey by having Flannery press and squeeze the sorghum stalks to use the syrup in his spirits. But most times, Honey Bee had claimed the river could do better than any of those things.

Finished, Honey Bee lugged the barrels on board, locked them inside on wooden racks he'd built under the refinished bench seats, and daily, weather permitting, he and Flannery would carry the whiskey up the river a ways and back, letting the motion rock the spirits, caramelizing, aging it until late fall.

For eight months Flannery's daddy let the Kentucky River breathe into his hooch until the spices and sugars turned to fire.

Folks from as far north as Cincinnati and as far south as New Orleans and as far west as St. Louis would come and pay top dollar for Honey Bee's Kentucky River Witch Whiskey— beg his secret, beg to know its cut. Every time Honey Bee Butler swore it was the river, his beloved Kentucky River giving it life, cutting the whiskey with its glory. "Mother river whips it with its gentle paddle. You know there's a paddle for every ass, and my beautiful 'tucky River spanks the very fires into my whiskey."

Flannery flicked through the memories. For generations the

Kentucky River had given the Butler family a grander life than most in Glass Ferry, lent Flannery a buoy to make her feel safe for a precious thirteen years before snatching it all away.

It was hard for Flannery to believe a crueler river would be her sister's paddle. That the same river that had given her so much would take yet another from her.

# CHAPTER 6

*Patsy*
*June, 1952*

Hollis sidled up to Patsy, leaned in, and snaked a traveling hand around her waist and to her backside, pressing down tulle, digging into the pile of dress fabric for a pinch of flesh. "She's a wet blanket; let her go," Hollis said. "We don't need Flannery. Hey, I didn't get to tell you back at the house, but you look like a living doll."

Patsy elbowed his hand away from her bottom and glared up at him. "We have to find my pearls, get Danny sobered, and get to my prom!" She snapped her arm toward the automobile and a lifeless Danny inside.

"Relax, doll baby. Let junior nap; you got time. Lots of time." Hollis pushed Patsy back against the elm, crowding.

"Don't, Hollis—"

"C'mon. I really like you. Don't tell me you didn't like the last time, haven't wanted to like it again," Hollis said, leaning in to kiss her. Patsy turned her head. His lips brushed against her ear. "You're as pale as a ghost, as white as that ol' ghoul Joetta. C'mon, doll baby. C'mon over here and let big ol' Hollis give you a special something that'll make you glow. Something you can wear proud to that prom. You'll put them other pretenders to shame. Let a real man love you right."

"I love Danny. You know I love Danny." Patsy shoved Hollis

with her elbow. *No way. Not here, not now, not ever again—oh, if only things hadn't turned out this way. If only—*

Hollis grabbed her breast. "Aw, c'mon. Don't play hard to get with me. I know what you like. Remember? We can even kiss like them movie stars you're always blabbering on about if that's what you want." He laid a sloppy, booze-coated one on her lips.

"Get off me, you damn fool," she cried, pushing, swiping a hand over her mouth. "You dumb oaf!"

Inside the automobile, Danny stirred. Hollis and Patsy turned toward the noise. Danny grunted and groaned again and then, just as quick, he quieted, fell back into his stupor.

"Danny," Patsy called, edging herself away from Hollis.

"We got time." Hollis sidestepped and blocked her retreat, pulled her in tight and kissed her hard.

*Time.* Something Patsy had been running out of ever since she'd accepted a ride home alone with Hollis on that school day nearly three months before.

That day it was Danny who had promised Patsy he'd see her home after classes, but when she came out of the building late, she caught him flirting with Violet Perry and saw the pretty pastor's daughter dishing it back.

*That is just like Violet,* Patsy puffed, *a Goody Two-shoes in front of the adults, and a trollop behind their backs.*

"Ain't I just the prettiest violet amongst all these old boring grasses and weeds," Violet liked to tout herself to any boy who raised a sniff. Patsy hoped the floozy got her comeuppance one day, got her pretty, nodding head chomped off by a hungry passing ass.

Fuming, Patsy had slipped by the two, unnoticed.

Nearby, Hollis sat in his Mercury, happy to see her last straw. He had seen what was happening, encouraged it even, then called Patsy over to his window, urging her to leave Danny behind, spilling on and on about his brother's cheating ways. "Those two"—he pointed over her shoulder—"have been at it a week. Awful chummy. Looked like he even kissed her on the lips right before you came out."

Patsy glanced back over her shoulder and seethed.

"Come on, doll baby. It's after four, and it's Friday," Hollis wheedled. "I'm not working this weekend. Give me them lesson books and hop in. I'll tote you home safe 'n' sound. Get in, and ya won't even have to worry about ol' Hal Hardy's rabbit getting ahold of you." Hollis chuckled in a way that, looking back, should have set off alarms, grinning at her with those tom-prowling eyes of his.

But Patsy shuddered at the thought of Hardy and his crazy grave rabbit on the loose out there. It was bad enough worrying about Joetta, but the thought of that horrid rabbit lit her full of the biting nerves.

More than once Patsy'd spied a fat hare on Ebenezer, nibbling grasses inside the cemetery, and each time she'd stumbled and fallen trying to run away from what she thought she saw, or imagined.

Flannery had chided her for being a scaredy-cat of a little bunny. One day the girls were walking home when they saw the awful creature over by one of the Deer tombstones.

Flannery had pulled out an apple she had saved from her school lunch and tried to prove to Patsy the creature was gentle, harmless. Crouching down, Flannery wetted a ticking on her tongue, held the fruit out to the bunny. But the creature laid back its long ears and let out an ear-piercing squeal, before scrambling away.

Patsy screamed out, "Run, Flannery! It's Hardy's rabbit!"

Old man Hardy had lived on Blind Neck Hill up in the Palisades. He was a fine rabbit hunter, and before going off to battle in WWII, he'd taken great pains in order to snag himself the luckiest charm known: a bona fide rabbit's foot taken in a Kentucky graveyard.

Two weeks before Hal Hardy went to war, he took up camp in Ebenezer cemetery, waiting patiently to catch his lucky grave rabbit. He said he met up with the kind-natured Joetta, claiming it was her who'd helped show him where the hare was hiding.

Hal got his lucky foot, snaring the biggest rabbit around

those parts, carrying that lucky hind leg across the big oceans and then back to Kentucky, and doing it all with nary a scratch.

Later, one of his two sons took off for the Korean War. Before the son left he asked to borrow his father's lucky rabbit foot. But Hal was superstitious, partial to his old good luck charm, and selfishly said no. When his son came home in a pine box, Hal blamed himself for letting the boy go off without a charm for protection. And when the government called Hal's other son to war, the father insisted his boy get himself his own piece of good fortune, sending him out to Ebenezer on a cold, snowy night.

Inside the cemetery, Hal's son lost his footing, tumbling down that version of his own rabbit hole, and died when his head hit an old jagged tombstone. Months later, when old Hal was found dead outside Ebenezer graveyard from his own self-inflicted gunshot wound, most whispered that it had been Joetta's ghost pushing him into a suitable punishment for not protecting his boys.

Patsy snuck a peek back toward Danny and Violet.

"Come on. Let's go, Patsy." Hollis tugged on her arm and patted the seat beside him. "Oh, c'mon, doll baby. You're too pretty to walk home all on your lonesome. Look at your pretty dress. Why, you'll get all dusty, and be all sad, while Danny boy and Violet are having all the fun," he said, reaching for her books, winking.

Violet Perry leaned into Danny's ear and whispered something. Something sweet, Patsy was sure. Because Danny smiled at whatever the shared secret was, then snugged in close to Violet's bent ear. Then a tease sparked in Violet's eyes, and she passed another back to his tilted head. A secret he'd never share with Patsy, and one that looked a lot like the ones he and she had split between themselves when they were last together on her darkened porch. The talk they'd shared about getting hitched one day in the not too distant future, getting out of Glass Ferry, and never ever coming back.

Anger fueled her, and a half-baked *good riddance* slipped off her tongue. Patsy handed Hollis her schoolbooks through the window. Grinning, he tossed them into the backseat while Patsy rushed around to the passenger side.

By the time the two reached Ebenezer Road and parked, Hollis had convinced Patsy his brother was two-timing, and sweetened the telling by offering her his flask. He'd turned on the radio, letting the Ink Spots float into the early spring air with their soft crooning of "I'll Get By."

For a moment she regretted climbing into that automobile, sharing that front seat with the older boy and alone, leaving with Hollis in the first place.

At first she refused him. But he wheedled and begged so sweetly for her to try a sip. "It'll help with the female nerves some," he promised. "My ma has a nip or two every afternoon. Never misses her four o'clock sipping."

Cooling, Patsy tried the whiskey for the first time ever. She coughed and sputtered. Hollis patted her back. "That's right," he said. "Let it get down there good and warm you up from the middle. Breathe its good fire into ya."

Surprised, she found the sensation exciting, almost enjoyable. It numbed the pains of betrayal, so she took another sip, this time more quickly. And when Hollis placed a hand on her knee and pushed up her skirts, sliding his fingers casually along her thighs, after the third, she was all in, almost, and only pretended to halfheartedly push his hand away.

She didn't half mind him doing that. A senior boy liking her in that way, feeling her in that way, having the manly touch that his younger brother didn't have.

Most girls swooned over Hollis too, and the boys thought he was a regular Casanova, him with his weekly paycheck and fine wheels. The looks, a reckless bang slipping over his big sleepy eyes, the always-present pout on his full lips.

Feelings welled. For a few racing heartbeats she let his hand stay. She knew she had to stop, knew she had to and right now. *What if someone passed by? If Flannery changed her mind about baton practice? Or a classmate from school came snooping? What if Hollis bragged?* Though she had never heard Hollis, some boys, especially the younger ones, crowed and told till the cows came home. Hollis always said to his friends that he didn't bite the feeding hand. Still, he'd sneakily tease his pals, let them come up with a few good guesses about his latest squeeze.

"Stop now, Hollis; that's enough. You need to take me home." Every second that she lingered here with him half draped over her could get worse, or better, or . . .

He looked at her breasts, and on down at her legs as if he hadn't heard a single word. "You know I'm crazy about you. Just have yourself another small nip, Patsy. Let's have us a bit of fun, same as ol' Danny boy."

*Danny.* Revenge stoked inside her.

Hollis gently forced the cool metal flask into her hand, lightly tapped her button nose. "Come on. Take my batwing. Just one more drink, and I swear on a stack of Bibles if you still want to go, I'll see you right home, or wherever you want to go, doll baby. Do whatever you want."

She giggled at that and grabbed his wandering hand. It was true Flannery never missed baton practice and wouldn't be home till six—nearly two hours from now. And since it was Friday, most kids would be meeting at Chubby's after school. Mama had canasta club tonight and would be busy with that. "Okay, one more. But you promise, right?"

He breathed against her neck, traced a small invisible X on her breast. "I told ya already. Promise."

She snatched up his palm, let her fingers flutter against it a few seconds before breaking away, reaching for the flask. Patsy asked him to swear again, spilling some of the booze down the front of the green-striped spring dress Mama had sewed. "Gee, Hollis, look what you made me do." She laughed and swiped her damp breasts.

Hollis dropped his head close to her chest.

She nudged him away. "Give me something to dry this mess, or I'll be in trouble."

Hollis clicked the button on the glove box, and the little door swung down. "In there," he mumbled, closing in on her neck for another snuggle.

Patsy lifted out a stained, smelly rag and saw the small gun underneath. "Sure is a fancy gun," she said, touching its barrel, curious. "Oh, I want to hold it. Looks like the one my daddy taught us girls to shoot. He said I was a crack shot." She stared at the black barrel, blinked, then peered at the scrawny, crude letters carved there, trying to make them out. Rubbed her blurring eyes, looked again at what someone had tried to scratch out. "Hey, this looks like—"

"Don't touch it." Hollis clicked the glove door shut and turned back to her, nuzzling her shoulder. "I don't want it to get scratched. I waited a long time for my daddy to pass me his prized gun, this fine Henry pistol."

Patsy knew Hollis was crazy about this new gun of his, and she knew it had been getting him into trouble lately. A month ago Patsy had been walking to work, hightailing it through Ebenezer, when she heard a farmer yelling at Hollis for brandishing the pistol. The old man had lit into him good for shooting off rounds from his new plaything, threatened to take Hollis's gun away and send for the sheriff. Hollis had begged the farmer not to tell his daddy, promising to atone by painting his fence this summer.

Soon after, one of the teachers did send for Sheriff Henry, the school gossiped. Mr. Dirkson had confiscated the pistol when he caught Hollis in shop class engraving his initials on the wooden inlays in its handle with the school's woodworking chisel. The teacher made Sheriff Henry and his missus come in for it, and the principal gave Hollis a big fat detention.

Hollis's hands slipped over Patsy's, pressing into her chest as she tried to clean up the spill.

Patsy batted at him lightly, then wiped the front of her dress with the stinky rag one last time. *At least the smell would cover the drink.* She tossed the rag onto the dash and glimpsed down at the stained boots he wore, soaked in mud and whiskey.

Patsy wrinkled her nose. "How do you stand working in such a smelly place?"

"It has its perks." Hollis nibbled on her ear, tickling. "Go on,

Patsy, have yourself another swill of the latest I pinched off the distillery. I don't share my best with just anybody. You know that, don't you, doll baby?"

"Hollis. You gotta *swear* to tote me safely home," she reminded, all wide-eyed innocently, patting her hair. She knew she shouldn't tease him like that, but it was kinda fun, making him promise like that, knowing a senior boy wanted her in that way.

"I swear it, doll baby, swear on my dear ma."

Patsy took a sip, felt the tingling from his fingers and had herself a bigger swallow. Hollis whispered into her ear, and more easy promises spilled as the flask emptied.

By the time they'd finished the flask, along with nearly another half bottle of bourbon that Hollis had pulled out from underneath the seat, Patsy found herself out of the Mercury, lying on the ground, pinned beneath Hollis under the old elm, her mind muddled, cares slipping more.

She'd gone in and out of a terrible, sweet dream, afraid but all alive and heated in a way new to her. Patsy hated his rough touches, but wanted more of this brother who wanted her, surrendering a purr for all of him, coming around long enough to want none. Soon a deep sharp pain lashed at her, had her crying "no."

Hollis covered her mouth with his hand, while she squirmed and tried to buck, rear up, and fight.

A few more pumps and he rolled off her with one last braying groan—his bathed boots scented from the angels' share, sooted, and pointing his victory to a blinding-blue sky.

Nearly dead from the drink, close to passing out, Patsy lay numb, listening to his snoozing, nursing inside herself, eyes fixed to the swaying tree branches, the sunlight rippling through singing leaves, waning.

Something nearby stirred, and she turned her head to the noise. Patsy was sure she caught a movement. Something, someone. She squeezed her watery eyes shut and popped them back open. She could've sworn it was someone sneaking—maybe even ol' Joetta leaning against the tree, motioning to her. Though

Patsy had never in her life seen her, she could feel a presence. Something she knew was off.

Patsy blinked and bolted upright. Sitting still, she soaked up her surroundings. Branches and clusters of leaves sent shadows across the trunk, spilling a skirt of light tricks across the dirt bed that Hollis had made for her. Satisfied nothing was really there after all, her vision blurring, her head fuzzed, she lay back to rest her eyes a bit.

But then the sky began spinning. Off-kilter, her stomach clenched and rolled. Wobbly, Patsy pushed herself up, knee-walked around the elm to a spot of velvet moss, and threw up until her stomach lining burned and there was nothing else left to heave.

Moaning, she crawled away, sickened and scared. Falling back onto the grass, Patsy closed her eyes. "You okay, Patsy? Doll baby . . ." Hollis called out, foggy, reaching for her hand, patting before drifting back off.

She let herself surrender to a turbulent slumber. By the time Patsy pulled herself out of the hazy sleep, Hollis was straddling her again. Catching sight of her ripped nylons and pink panties strewn to the side, she pushed him off, jumped up, crying, shouting, "You . . ." She caught her breath. "You son of a bitch." She straightened down her skirt that he had rolled up to her stomach. "*You no-good low-down son of a bitch!*"

Quickly, Hollis pulled on his trousers and buttoned his shirt.

She wriggled into her pink polka-dotted underwear Mama'd bought her girls at the fancy department store in Lexington, then to her sobering horror stripped back out of them when she saw the telltale sign of her now lost-forever virginity.

"*You.*" She stabbed a shaky finger at him, threw down the panties. "You got me drunk. You violated me!"

"I—I thought you wanted to be together. Listen, Patsy, I've always had a thing for you—"

"You're a pig."

Embarrassment crawled into his eyes, and then just as quick, boiling anger took hold. Hollis swore she'd asked for it, *begged even.* "Shit. You wanted it same as me." He rubbed his crotch for the truth. "I tried to stop, but you wanted it too bad. Couldn't disappoint you, being all sad over junior boy like that—"

Patsy shook her head, screaming, threatening to tell Sheriff Henry. "Liar! Filthy *liar*. You raped me, Hollis Henry! And your daddy's gonna hear—"

"But you wanted it!"

"You'll go to jail—"

Hollis cursed and smacked her, a fear creeping into his eyes.

"You sonofabitch. You brought me here to . . . to do this." Patsy cursed back, swung and punched his broad shoulders, slapped at his head.

He staggered, snatched the belt from his britches and smacked her arm with its buckle.

She cried out. "Mama . . . my mama's going to have your tail for messing with me. Messing with an underage girl—"

"I gave you just what you wanted, slut. You're whining now? Hell, you weren't whining when I gave it to you."

"You took—"

"You *liked* it." Spit blew out of his mouth.

"I hate you, Hollis Henry."

Hollis looked like he'd been hit. "I gave you something you liked. You know what, bitch, I can easily give you something you don't—" Hollis drew back and snapped the leather across her shoulder once, then struck her arm, drawing a trickle of blood. He tried again, just barely missing her jaw.

Patsy raised her arms over her face and stumbled back against the tree, sniveling.

"Just try to tell. I swear I'll make you sorry, Patsy. *Swear*," he hissed in her face. "You tell a soul, you'll find yourself living in a Hell worse than my daddy's jail."

"You . . . you . . . sonofawhore! You vile—"

Hollis grabbed her arm, dug his fingers in, squeezing until he had her on her knees, cowering. "Nobody, ain't *nobody* going to believe a common tramp over the sheriff's son. The ol' moonshiner's spit." He raised the belt again. " 'Specially when I have my own *brother* to vouch for me. You hearing me, Patsy?" He knocked his leg against her head and shook his belt.

Patsy gasped. *Danny would never have her if he knew.*

" 'Cause our Danny boy's going to hear a lot if you so much as—"

"You sorry—"

"*You!*"—he jerked on her—"You ain't gonna tell nobody about the disgraceful way you came on to me, dropped those drawers real quick for me, Patsy." He towered over her, dug his fingers even deeper into her bone, bruising, threatening until she cried out, broke down sobbing.

Hollis straightened his tall, thick frame, then nudged a foot at her soiled panties and shredded nylons. "You best clean yourself up and hide your whoring—bury them things in the dirt there." He kicked a fallen branch for her to use, grabbed the nearly empty whiskey bottle, and sauntered off to the Mercury to wait.

Weeping, Patsy began digging a hole to bury her undergarments beside the tree, silently promising never to mention the indiscretion to another living soul.

Now, here she found herself, again, pinned against the elm with the wrong brother on her prom night. How did she let this all happen?

"Give us a chance. We can start now while the boy takes his nap." Hollis hitched a thumb over to sleeping Danny in the backseat, pressing in with another rough kiss to Patsy's lips while holding down her batting arm.

# CHAPTER 7

*Flannery*
*1972*

Flannery pulled her Chevy off the road next to a guardrail and rested her forehead on the wheel, pinning her runaway thoughts and wanting for more time.

She thought about turning around, turning tail and leaving Glass Ferry like the day she had turned her back long ago.

There were places, she knew, that you could drive to, where you could round a winding bend, breeze by a yawning pasture, and feel safe, happy, and your bones would get a tiny itch and scratch out a Hallelujah. But such a place wasn't in Glass Ferry. Had never been in Glass Ferry for her after Honey Bee passed and Patsy split on her like that.

Flannery had found that kind of rejoicing in the doings of the city. In Louisville's night lights and stretching streets, tall cradling buildings, and sharp-rounded corners.

The university had been a place to start anew, a wonderland to escape troubles and forget her sister's abandonment.

Reluctant to let her baby girl go, Mama finally relented and sold Honey Bee's old car, his tools in the barn, and the old tractor to pay for Flannery's college.

Flannery had been homesick the first two weeks, sick about leaving Mama like that, worried for her well-being. They talked on the phone every day, sometimes calling each other as many as three, four times in one day.

Then Flannery met a guy on campus the third week of school, her first real steady, a senior boy named Thomas Gentry, the son of a druggist who took her to the lavish Seelbach Hotel. Inside, he'd led her down the marbled staircase into the Rathskeller, a Bavarian-styled cathedral cellar with colorful Rookwood pottery tiles lining the walls, columns, and graceful arches, patiently telling her details about the famous architecture.

Thomas had pointed to the Rathskeller's ceiling covered in fine-tooled leather, and then to the noble columns where pelicans made from the Rookwood were perched. Disturbed, Flannery looked away, remembering she'd read about the strange pelican symbols. The legend said a mother pelican would stab herself in the breast with the beak to feed her starving young the blood from the piercing, only for the mother to die herself.

It was still a sight to sit in the fairytale room. They'd listened to the latest jazz recordings.

Thomas showed her where F. Scott Fitzgerald and king bootlegger and gangster, George Remus, had once sat, sipped bourbon, and smoked expensive cigars together. He told her Fitzgerald had used the beautiful hotel for a model in *The Great Gatsby,* and talked about the secret gangster tunnels that had been built inside the hotel.

She and Thomas talked over drinks. Later, he swept her up to the Grand Ballroom where they danced.

There were kisses, many, and in many places—the overlook atop Iroquois Park, an alley behind campus, inside dark movie houses and other shadowy hideouts where those kisses caught fever, and Thomas's hands burned, leaving them both with bigger wants.

Still, Flannery vowed to bring chastity to her marriage, and soon Thomas moved on to a girl willing to bring more to his bed and sooner.

The city was busy. Her dorm loud. She'd made friends, and it wasn't long until she had a bunch of sisters. Sisters who didn't compare her with a twin they'd never met, who made *her* their "one and only."

Weekend nights brought panty raids from across campus when the boys would sneak over to the girls' dorm after the resident director went to sleep.

More than once, her roommate, Gina, talked her into going to the big Ben Snyder's department store downtown and buying scanty bloomers.

Flannery bought herself a shocking-pink, silky pair trimmed in lace. That night the girls gathered in the darkened halls to throw their underwear out the windows to the hooting boys waiting below.

Some girls wrote their telephone numbers on their underwear, but Flannery didn't dare. Still, she managed to drop hers into the hands of a hulky football player who'd knelt down on the grass, whistled up at her with prayerful clasped hands, begged the favor of her prized undies.

Everyone in the dormitory squealed at that, teased her good-naturedly. And when he came calling the very next day to ask her to the Woolworth for lunch, the girls shared their makeup and clothes with Flannery, sending her off with congratulatory kisses.

She found all kinds of wonder in the beginning when she'd moved away after high school. Lost it for a while too, but lately she'd been trying to grasp it back, was sure she'd gotten a good hold on the tail 'til now and news of the wreck in the river.

Here in Glass Ferry there was nothing but buried truth and the beginning of a desperate prayer from what had been birthed on Ebenezer long ago. And now, she could again feel her safety slipping away if she wasn't careful.

Today, Mama had made Flannery promise to bring her sister home.

Flannery raised her head off the steering wheel and once more looked over at the river stretching below. Needing air, she stepped out of the car and over to the rail, leaning against it, gnarling her fingers over the rusty metal.

Flannery wondered if the old Mercury might have plunged

down here, rolled down the craggy side and crashed through the spindly trees. She studied about just where, knowing it could have been anywhere along here, but no telling how far the mighty river had tugged that death car downstream—no telling if a guardrail had even protected this stretch of the Palisades back then.

Images, not of the car, but of her daddy, surfaced again. She could use some of that River Witch whiskey about now, should've gulped it down with one of Mama's Valium while she'd had a chance.

She had saved that old bottle Honey Bee'd corked just for her. Toasting him on his birthdays with a small nip each and every year.

Her daddy had introduced her to whiskey before he died in the spring of '50, not long before her fourteenth birthday, passing her the special tulip-shaped glass, one of his mother's old sherry glasses he and his taster always used.

"We got to test this new barrel, you and I," Honey Bee said. "If this is good, then we know the whole batch is good."

"Me?" Flannery said, looking around for Merrick Jackson, her daddy's best friend and master taster, who everyone called Uncle Mary. When folks began to kick off the *ck* at the end of *Merrick,* the old-timer insisted that they at least starch it up some and fasten an *Uncle* to his nickname.

Flannery thought Uncle Mary looked like God, or at least the closest image to Him that she could conjure from pictures. Not from around Glass Ferry, Uncle Mary told folks he'd slipped in from "over yonder somewhere in the winter of 1930." A bit of a loner, he was even old-like, the way God was, always cutting an angry, cold brow that might cool in the second you used to lift a foot to hightail it from what you believed was going to be his wrath coming down on you.

Uncle Mary had a shock of white hair that matched his right brow and eyelashes. But on the left side of his face, a bushy orange arch sparked above identical colored lashes, making him pop like a mad marigold. Flannery heard folks speculate that God had battled Satan for Uncle Mary's soul and won, but not before the devil swiped his fiery thumbprint across Uncle Mary's face.

Uncle Mary could strike a look to the most feral of Kentucky blackhearts and was strong enough to fight off the meanest dog barehanded. But he also reserved a gentle touch that could lift a fallen chick back into its nest and coax the thirteen potted granny violets he had growing in his small cabin into bloom. He knew his whiskey, knew Kentucky, and knew the river. He liked Honey Bee's way of thinking and decided to pal up with him long ago.

Flannery asked Honey Bee, "But what about Uncle Mary—"

"Pay attention, Flannery girl," Honey Bee quieted. "We'll know in a minute. If it's not ready, you might let it sit for a bit longer and see what that does." Honey Bee pulled out the bung in the chest of the barrel, just far enough to let the liquid drip two fingers' worth into the glasses, then plugged it back.

"We'll start with the nose on this batch," he said. "Test the aroma first."

Flannery held her glass up and thought the color was pretty enough, like the sun-bathed bark of a tree that had lived an old life.

"Smells like a fine one—fine witch water," Honey Bee said. "Here, just pass it under your nose and breathe it in."

Flannery didn't understand exactly why he wanted her to do all this, why he didn't go get Uncle Mary, but she was so curious that she didn't ask more. Here Honey Bee was treating her like a man, a grown man with the smarts for such things, letting her taste the very first batch of the season right along with him, though she had, in her mind, no idea how to judge the whiskey.

Flannery sniffed the bourbon and smelled oak and hints of maybe caramel candies like her grandmother had made. She looked at Honey Bee.

He jiggled his wrist at her, and then Flannery remembered to hold up the back of her hand, take a breath of skin first.

When Honey Bee nodded, she decided to make extra sure, so

she prepared her nostrils again for the first smell by sniffing her flesh again, cleansing, to get a true whiff of the batch.

Flannery stuck the tip of her nose into the glass. Now it smelled of pepper, faint, but present, sure enough, with the oaky scents of the barrel that had picked up the soft pinches of vanilla and a slip of salt. Flannery told him what she smelled.

"Good." He raised a surprised brow. "You've told me about the nose of the whiskey. Don't you know, I think I may've grow'd myself a real Catherine Carpenter," he teased proudly.

Catherine Spears Carpenter had been a widow, a mighty brave and fierce Kentuckian who'd lived in Casey County in the late 1700s. She'd lost two husbands, but not before she'd birthed nine children, remarkably all healthy babies who lived long lives in the harsh wilderness. Mrs. Carpenter had been well-educated, and worked her dead husband's distillery, raising her children alone with the money she earned from her famous sweet and sour mash recipes. She was legendary for that, and for surviving the savage Indian attacks and brutal existence the land offered.

Flannery split a wide grin and glanced at her daddy who'd poked his nose the same as she had. Then Honey Bee tilted his face to the sky and exhaled. He pressed the back of his hand to his mouth, smelling, and then pushed his nose back into the glass and parted his lips to inhale the fiery fumes, and then sniffed again. She copied him, mimicking each and every little movement.

Honey Bee set his glass down and said, "Put some on your tongue, let it sit a spell, then spit it out. Go on, now."

Flannery had been confused. *Why wasn't Honey Bee tasting it too?* Still, she took a drop, let the whiskey warm her tongue, then spit it out, coughing. It had tasted like the river flowed today, a rough lapping across flesh with a peppery bite of other savory and unsavory things she couldn't yet name.

"Take yourself a small pull this time," he ordered.

His daughter did, then wheezed and coughed as the liquid bumped down her pipe. Flannery wiped at the sudden heat lighting her brow, fanned her neck.

Honey Bee handed Flannery a wooden cup filled with water and told her to take a gulp. After she did, he said, "Dip your fingers into the water and let the droplets stream down into your whiskey glass, soften the spirits a bit. Now take a bigger pull of the witch water, but don't swallow. Let it work its way to you."

Flannery filled her mouth, choking back an urge to cough.

"Not yet . . . Chew it," he said. "Let it nip at your tongue and cheeks. Now swallow it, and see how just a few drops of water can straighten it right and tight."

Flannery did as she was told, swishing, fighting the bark rumbling her throat. Soon the liquid poked and gently picked up a sweet fire as it passed down and slid into her belly with a satisfying, spreading heat. She gasped, coughed once, and a moment passed before she grinned, leaned back into the chair, and held up her glass for more.

Smiling, Honey Bee lifted his still-full glass and said, "Flannery girl, when the whiskey's just right, the hand will beg for more. That's how you'll know." And then he passed his drink to her.

The smell of dark river, mud, and strange growing things crowded into the memories of that moment. Flannery gripped the guardrail with both hands, dropped her head, and looked down the cliff toward the water. A trembling took hold of her shoulders.

That first-tasting memory had come back so strongly and so sweetly, but she knew it couldn't be held for long, the bitter piling, a grief pulling her in. It wasn't but a few weeks later when, just as she got home from school, Honey Bee'd said, "Flannery girl, walk down to the barn with me. I need you to help with something that takes two pairs of hands."

Patsy had barely acknowledged her daddy, brushing quickly past him and up the stairs, calling over her shoulder, "I hope I don't have to go, Honey Bee. It's muddy out there, and I can't be getting myself all dirty and—"

"No, Queenie," her daddy said quietly, looking at Flannery. "Takes a worker bee for this."

Flannery set her schoolbooks down on the kitchen table and followed him out the door.

When Honey Bee took her hand in his on the porch and walked her toward the river to the barn, something inside told Flannery that her daddy needed more than help with a chore.

A blue heron glided past them, its neck tucked tight into an *S*, long, arrowed legs trailing behind its bluish-gray tail feathers. It landed on top of a nearby sycamore, squawking its landing call. On a branch below, young chicks poked their heads out of a bulky stick-saucered nest, ticking furiously for food. The big crane settled statue-like on the high perch, watching.

Flannery looked away, remembering the boy in her history class with the glass eye. He'd shot one of the birds out of its tree, and when he went over to pick it up, the feisty bird had lit into him with its long, daggered beak, poking Calvin's eyeball clean out.

Flannery and Honey Bee walked silently into the old pole barn, the coolness washing down oak boards and onto the dirt floor, an earthy dampness rising into the stretching quiet between them. Honey Bee stood there not saying a word and Flannery daring not to ask.

At long last, Honey Bee said, "Your mother is going to talk to you, tell you something very important. But I wanted to tell you first, Flannery girl. . . . I've been mighty sick for a while now. And I'm going to get a lot sicker."

Flannery gasped. "Honey Bee, what's wrong? Is it your sugar, the diabetes sickness? Oh, Mama said you've been sneaking bites of her pies and—"

Honey Bee took hold of her shoulders. "Promise me something, daughter." A kind sadness filled his tired eyes as he held her tearful gaze.

Flannery mewed a protest.

"Listen to me, Flannery girl. Ol' Kentucky River is calling me home. Do you understand?"

Flannery managed a weak nod.

"Your mother . . . When she tells you, promise me you'll pretend she told you first, that I didn't tell you what's really wrong with me."

Over the years Flannery had heard her mama's protests about her daddy's drinking: "a killing-type-drinking and will kill you quicker than your diabetes," Mama'd cried; "the same-old, same-old harping," he'd denied.

One night had been different, strange in a scary way. Their voices, Mama's and Honey Bee's, had startled Flannery in the middle of the night. Unable to fall back asleep, she had wandered downstairs and from the hallway saw her parents sitting at the kitchen table with only a candle lighting the room. Something in their voices made her step back and eavesdrop, poke her head out from around the corner and sneak glances.

"But you never drank until that night," Mama'd said. "Only sampled for the business. Even made Uncle Mary do most of that."

"Quiet, woman," he snarled, and poured himself a bourbon from his River Witch bottle, taking a long swallow. "I never had the need till then."

"It's not your fault," Mama said softly. "And drinking like this won't bring them back."

"If only I'd gotten there sooner." Honey Bee fattened a fist.

"Oh, Honey Bee. I don't want to lose you like this. We have our girls. Our girls need you. I do too. You've got to let go of this anger. You can't be smart *and* angry—"

Honey Bee grunted something Flannery couldn't pick up.

"You know our babies are safe now. With God," Mama whispered, reaching for his hand. "God's been looking over them. . . . Nobody can hurt them anymore. It happened so long ago. You've got to stop this, and accept our Heavenly Father's—"

Honey Bee growled and took another drink.

Mama cupped her hand over his. "Come to church with me Sunday."

Honey Bee sighed tiredly.

"You don't pray anymore. Seek His truth and listen to God's Word—"

"God is a long-tongued liar." Honey Bee pushed himself from the table and escaped out the back door with his bottle.

The next morning, Flannery tried to ask Mama about her brothers, snooping for more, though her parents had said the summer diarrhea took a lot of babies that year. "Did they look like me and Patsy? What was the color of their hair, their eyes? Who hurt them, Mama? Did someone—?" Flannery dug until Mama held up a hushing hand.

"Your brothers were only with us a short time before the Good Lord took them. And be mindful. A young lady doesn't talk about private matters, shouldn't go begging for impolite conversation. It's ill-mannered, Flannery Bee Butler, and I won't have it," she said in a faltering voice. "Now go and get the wash off the line; there's a storm coming," Mama shamed.

Flannery had never thought it was anything more than just missing the babies, that adult fussing, the fretting most kids see in grown-ups from time to time.

And she'd never worried about Honey Bee's long sugar tooth for the whiskey. Didn't think she needed to until that day down at the barn with her daddy proved different.

In 1950, Honey Bee had looked at his daughter and said, "Listen to me now."

"No. Don't say it." Flannery pounded his chest, collapsed in his arms. "No. Don't leave me, Honey Bee, don't leave me, Daddy. Please . . . *no.*"

Holding her, he found a strength in his dying arms and dis-eased body to gather his younger daughter closer. "You take care of your mother and sister, Flannery girl. I need you to be a strong worker bee for the queenies, a strong guard bee for our whiskey recipe."

"I can't—" Flannery cried.

"You already have," Honey Bee said, and then whispered, "Now remember this: The sheriff gets the first barrel—always. He gets a fussy croup that acts up a'might if he doesn't get his medicine. And he gets a might fussier if his granny fee ain't in on time. You hear me?"

"Yes-yessir."

"Let Mother River and her witch water give you, Mama, and your sister a good life. Just know you'll have a longer one if you leave the partaking to your customers. Do you understand what I'm saying, child?"

"I . . . I don't . . ."

Honey Bee grasped her tighter. "*Understand.*"

"I th-think so."

"Daughter, *know* these words I've given you." Her daddy pressed his forehead to hers and in a low gravelly voice passed on the sins of his soul and their family business to thirteen-year-old Flannery.

# CHAPTER 8

*Patsy*
*June, 1952*

Patsy worked her hands free, bumping Hollis away from her, calling out for Danny.

Hollis laughed low and clutched her back.

"Get off me, Hollis," she hissed, jerking away. "Get your filthy hands off me. You'll get my prom dress dirty."

He grabbed her around the waist and pulled himself close again. "C'mon, Patsy."

"Stop right now."

"Hitch them skirts up for me again."

"No!" she screamed above the mounting cry of crickets, cicadas, and other bugs, drunk from their own nightly forage to find mates.

"We got time." He rubbed his hip against her dress, pressing her tulle-covered thighs. "You can't tell me you haven't thought of me and you. Haven't had the hurt for more of my good loving."

"I can tell you this, Hollis Henry: I hate you. I hate the way you're reckless and cruel. Hate that I'm gonna be stuck . . . stuck with your . . . *your bastard!*"

"No." Hollis knitted his brows, looked down at her belly, and took a step back. "No way."

"It's true," she cried.

He grabbed her hand. "If it's so, I will make it right and marry—"

"Never." She jerked free.

Cut, Hollis looked away. "You're not going to pin that on me."

"You took me against my will." Patsy swung her hand to the tree. "Violated—"

"You wanted it. Don't you lie."

"You made me take your rotgut whiskey and—"

"You're a gawdamn moonshiner's daughter. You can't tell me your ma didn't nurse you with her titties full of the stuff—"

"I can tell you this: It's yours. And you took what isn't. But you'll never have me—"

"Ain't my brat, and you're not gonna get my good name for it."

"Then know that we'll both hate your heathen bastard inside me," she said coldly.

He backhanded her hard across the face and pushed her away.

Patsy yelped and touched her mouth and then pulled back her hand, peered at the blood from her split lip. She looked over Hollis's shoulder and hollered, "Danny, help!"

Moaning, Danny awakened and pulled himself up in the backseat. He swung his legs out of the door. Rubbing his head, he grumbled, "What's going on here? Hollis, w-what the Sam hell—"

Patsy backed farther away from Hollis and pointed at her lip then back to the older brother. "Your brother," she said, breathless, "he did this to me. Tried to have his way with me, and . . . and when I wouldn't, he clobbered me. Look at me, Danny. *Look at what he did.*" Patsy's eyes filled.

Danny startled and jumped out of the Mercury. "Wh-What the hell did you do to her? Patsy, you okay?" Danny looked at her bloody lip. "What the Sam hell, Hollis—"

Hollis held up his hand and took a step back. "Now hold on there, Danny boy. She wanted me, lil' brother. Teased and threw herself at me, a shameless mess."

"You're drunk, Hollis Henry," Patsy said.

"A shameless mess, I tell you," Hollis went on. "Teased same as that day I gave her a lift when you were all cozy with Miss Violet. I gave her what she wanted real bad, Danny boy. Calm down. Think some. There's plenty for both of us—"

"You dirtbag." Danny raised a fist. "She's mine, you lying bastard. Get your dirty hands off of her. I'm sorry, Patsy—"

"Come on, brother, we can keep this in the family. We'll flip to see who takes care of what's she's got cooking in there." Hollis laughed, pushed out his belly, and patted.

"You shut your rotten trap, Hollis," Danny said, reddening. He looked at Patsy. "That true, Patsy?"

Patsy tearfully shook her head and instinctively raised a lying hand over her stomach. "Oh, Danny, let's leave." They could finally run off, and it would solve everything for her. "I'll go anywhere with you, Danny. I love you. And only you." Patsy held out her trembling hands to him. "Let's go, please—"

Hollis paled and turned to Patsy. "You love my brother? Only him?" He cast a doubting eye to Danny.

Patsy nodded at Danny.

Hollis tightened a fist. "Now why do you suppose she dropped them panties for *me* then, brother?"

Danny spit at the ground and rushed Hollis, pummeled his face.

Hollis staggered backward and fell against the tree. He shook his head, and in an instant lunged forward and tackled Danny, sending them both to the ground.

Danny got in a solid blow to Hollis's jaw.

Hollis threw him off and scrambled to pin Danny down.

Danny cursed.

Using an arm, Hollis forced his elbow into his brother's throat.

Patsy grabbed Hollis's hair, tugging. "Stop it . . . stop it, you drunken fools! Get off him, Hollis!"

Hollis threw out an arm and knocked Patsy in the head, sending her back and stumbling.

Danny righted a fist and plowed it into Hollis's cheek.

But Hollis landed a punch back to Danny's head and then another. And a third, hard on Danny's nose.

Patsy thought she heard a sickening crunch. She ran over to

the tumbling brothers and tried to pull Hollis off Danny. "Stop. Hollis, stop. You're going to hurt him, you brute!"

"Get back, Patsy." Hollis whipped out an arm, hitting her hard in the chest, knocking the wind out of her.

Danny stuck up his fist and jabbed Hollis square on the jaw, then once again, cutting his cheekbone.

Hollis blinked and grunted, then clamped his hands around Danny's throat.

Patsy looked around for help, for a rock, for anything that could stop crazy Hollis. Her eyes lit upon the automobile's open window. She rushed to the Mercury and leaned inside the passenger side, looking for anything to hit Hollis.

Hollis's flask lay on the seat, and then she remembered, remembered spilling her drink, remembered the oily rag in the glove and what it covered.

With the bottom of her fist, Patsy pounded open the glove box, dug under the dirty rags, and pulled out the pistol. She turned back to the brothers, and cried out, "Let him go, Hollis!" She pointed the gun his way. "So help me God, I'll shoot."

Hollis snarled. Pulling himself off Danny, he held out an arm, stood, and took a step toward her. "You hand that right over," he ordered, slicing a hand in the air. "Right here."

She wagged her head.

Danny rolled in the dirt, rubbed at his neck, trying to pull off his bow tie.

"Give it here, or I'll take my belt to you again," Hollis growled, and in one step was upon her, snatching it away.

Danny got his footing and charged Hollis, grabbing for the weapon.

Hollis held on, the brothers' arms locked high, gripping the gun and each other. Danny kneed him, and Hollis yelled and loosened his hold long enough to hit Danny on the side of the head. Raging, Danny only jerked a little, fought hard to keep his hold.

The weapon discharged, sending the bullet into the air.

Hollis fumbled. Danny's grip loosened, and the snub nose dropped to the ground.

Patsy crouched and closed her hands over her ears while the boys scrambled and grabbed for the gun.

Hollis was quicker.

Still Danny latched his arms around his brother's chest.

Hollis easily broke Danny's grip, twisted his arms, dug in with his fingers, and the gun went off again.

Patsy tried to scream, but nothing came out, just empty rushes of frantic air. She glanced around for something, anything, to bring Hollis down.

Danny staggered over to the elm, leaning on it for support.

Anger washed over Hollis as he closed in on his younger brother. "I should kick your scrawny ass." Hollis breathed heavily, inspecting his gun. "I warned ya never to touch my pistol." Hollis stuffed the gun into his trousers and pulled up his britches, adjusting, covering the gun with his long-tailed shirt. Lifting a fist, he shook it at Danny. "I should break your arm just for that."

Frantic, Patsy searched again for something to help, and gasped when she spotted it, something she hadn't seen before: a hefty, hand-sized rock over by the cemetery gate. She scurried to the fence, picked up the broken piece of headstone, and ran up behind Hollis.

Danny cried out and slowly moved his right hand up to his left arm, cradling the injury, unable to stop the growing stain of blood darkening in the early evening light.

Unconcerned, oblivious, Hollis nursed his own self, swiping at his cut face and swollen eyes, spitting blood into the dirt. "Ought to clobber you another good one, Danny boy. You don't deserve her. *Sissy*." Hollis brushed the dirt off his sleeves.

Horrified, Patsy watched Danny wobble, before sliding down the tree trunk, plopping onto the trunk's bark-legged skirt.

She let out a startling scream and threw back her arm.

Hollis blinked, then snapped his neck at Danny's wound, gaping before doing a half spin into Patsy's war cry.

With all her might, Patsy tightened her grip and smashed Hollis in the head with the rock.

# CHAPTER 9

*Flannery*
*1972*

Flannery stared down the steep cliffs, past the litter of broken bottles and other bits of trash. A breeze of angels' share and murky waters drifted from the Kentucky, skittered up mountain rock, rippling across the sun-stretching arms of trees. She took a breath, dreading going down there to see what they had pulled up from the river today, the bite of the old land coating her tongue, an aftertaste of stale whiskey caught in her throat.

Thoughts of Uncle Mary surfaced, and Flannery remembered his bite, the whipping he'd given her on the day they buried Honey Bee in the spring of 1950.

Honey Bee'd promised Flannery he would wait to push off into the river until after school, but when she got down to the bank, she saw he'd left in the boat without her. She sat there hours, waiting on the grassy slope, knees hugged to her chest, wondering why, worrying how he could leave without her for the first time.

When it was close to sunset and he still hadn't returned, Mama called Uncle Mary. He went looking and found Honey Bee collapsed on his ferryboat, stuck on a sand bar a mile downriver.

By the time Uncle Mary dragged Honey Bee up the bank, her

daddy was dead. Flannery and Mama kneeled on the ground beside Honey Bee's body, praying over him.

The doctor arrived and told Mama that Honey Bee's body done broke from the disease he'd been fighting. "Yellowed up like the sun and burned out." He shook his head.

Mama cut him off, blaming herself. "If only I'd locked up the sugar. If only he hadn't had the long tooth for it," she added bitterly.

The doctor and Uncle Mary looked away, not saying a word.

Flannery wrung her hands with a full knowing of her daddy's true demise. Patsy, who had just walked down to the river to find Mama to help her with something, dropped to the ground in a faint when she spotted Honey Bee.

The morning of the funeral, Flannery, Patsy, Mama, and Uncle Mary sat in the front pew inside the small, packed church soaked in the stink of burial flowers. Folks Flannery knew and those she'd never met came to pay their last respects.

Men from out of town, dressed in wide, chalked-striped suits, sporting pocket squares on jackets and sharp-creased fedoras atop their heads, sat knee-deep with spiffed-up locals wearing clean, pressed Sunday collared shirts and pink scrubbed faces. Other mourners spilled out of the church house and onto its wooden porch and grounds.

Mama, shock on her sagging face, stooped in misery, moved turtle-like.

Flannery and Patsy held hands during it all, soldiering strength from each other until the end when the preacher called for silent prayer. At that moment Flannery felt a soft rumble in Patsy's grip that leeched into her own hands, battering her heart.

"No, don't," Patsy'd mewed low. A deep coloring filled her cheeks as she stared at Honey Bee's casket. Then her voice grew stronger. "Don't leave me, Daddy. Please don't go, Honey Bee," Patsy cried loud. "Don't, oh, don't go," she'd screeched into the hushed crowd, sobbing until Uncle Mary took Patsy's hand and led her out of church.

Flannery had buried her tearful face on her mother's shoulder.

The preacher gave a fine service, one grander than Mayor Dillard's, who'd died two years before.

From the doorway of the church, Flannery watched Uncle Mary say a private word over Honey Bee's coffin, lift a bottle of River Witch from inside his jacket, and place it inside his casket.

After, they held an early supper at the Butler house. Strangers stopped in and discreetly left fat envelopes of money on Honey Bee's cellarette in the parlor for Mama, handing separate ones to the preacher.

Later, when most of the guests had left, Flannery found Patsy up in their room. She sat down on the bed where her sister was curled up, crying. "Hey, Patsy, come down to the barn with me. I think that old mama cat had her kittens a few weeks back. We can go find where she's hidden them. Take them some scraps from the supper."

Patsy shook her head. "I can't," she said. "Can't stand to go into Honey Bee's place and not see him. He's gone, Flannery. Gone! Who'll care for us now? *Who?*" Patsy wailed.

"Honey Bee taught me how," Flannery said, rubbing her sister's shoulder, her last promise to Honey Bee taking hold, the worry sawing across her bones. How would she bear it all, now that Mama was wrapped in her own silent grief, Patsy coiling inside her own? Who would see to her?

"Our Honey Bee took good care of us," Patsy whispered.

"I will too," Flannery said solemnly.

Patsy looked at Flannery, doubt pricked across her brow, but a yearning to believe flickered in her eyes. Flannery sensed that Patsy wanted to be excused from her duty to her sister, the one that comes from obligation as the oldest.

"I always wished I was born after you," Patsy said quietly.

"Then I'd be the prettiest." Flannery tried to make light.

"I'm not as strong as you, Flannery. Like you and Honey Bee."

"Only 'cause Mama says it." Flannery brushed a curl away from her sister's wet cheek. "You're strong *and* pretty enough."

"You and Honey Bee were so much alike. I can't lose you."

Flannery squeezed her hand. "Shh, I'm here."

"You've always been braver. I wish . . . I—"

"Patsy, I'll take good care of us." At that moment Flannery knew. Saw a measure of relief in her twin's red-rimmed eyes.

"A dear sister, one as good as any friend," Patsy said. "You'll always be my one and only." Patsy pulled Flannery's hand to her cheek, kissed it. "I love you, sister." Patsy sighed, a relief in her breath.

"I love you too, sister. I'll take care of us. Promise." Flannery crawled into bed beside Patsy and held her until her twin cried herself to sleep.

It was still light when Flannery went into her parents' room and found Mama asleep on the bed. "Mama." She gently shook her shoulder.

Mama stirred, fluttered her grief-stricken eyes.

"Mama, I'm scared," Flannery said. "Can I stay in here tonight? Please. I—"

"Go to your room. Your sister needs you," Mama said, turning away and onto her side, a sob thickening her breath.

"She's asleep. Mama, please. It's only seven. I'm so lonely. I miss him so much. Can I just sit on the bed beside you for—"

"Don't be selfish." Mama's words were strangling, biting.

Flannery went downstairs and sat by herself at the kitchen table. Neighbors and friends had cleaned up and put away dishes. After a few minutes, she snuck out with some fried meats and ran down to the barn. Inside, the feral mama cat slinked past her in the shadows. She watched it disappear behind a crate.

Needing to love and feel that in its wholeness and in absolute, Flannery followed.

She peeked behind the wooden box, dropping pieces of meat, and saw two orange-striped kittens and one calico. Flannery reached, and the mama cat arched her bony back, took a swipe at her hand, nabbing it with a long, blood-tracked scratch, before running away.

Flannery lifted out one of the kittens, then stole one of Honey Bee's full whiskey bottles from a dusty, cluttered shelf and soaked herself good in the grief, wetting the tiny, mewing kitten with her tears, cuddling the small creature close to her trembling body.

Uncle Mary found Flannery and pulled her thirteen-year-old self out of the barn that evening and lit her tail with a switch all the way back to her porch.

Uncle Mary said, "Lord A'mighty, child, you've disgraced our dearly departed Honey Bee. You don't gulp to a man's life, you sip nice and neat with a prayerful toast or two for honor. And only when you're grow'd up." He switched her legs again. Once more. "And *only* for your papa. Ya hear me, child?" Uncle Mary carried Flannery into the house, dumped her onto the settee, and called to Mama.

That was all it took for Jean Butler to pack her grief, beg ol' Uncle Mary to take on and buy the Butler whiskey business.

Flannery cried buckets for her dear Honey Bee to come back, pleading for another chance with the whiskey. Mama wouldn't budge, but did let her keep Honey Bee's old recipe books. And that was all.

Uncle Mary placed a weathered hand on Flannery's shoulder and told her, "It will be waiting for you when you're good an' grow'd up, girl. Stay off the witch's teat, and we'll partner up in the end, and no charge to you."

But that was all lost now, dead in the water. Age claimed Uncle Mary eight months later. The following week a businessman from Nashville bought the Butler distillery, the stills, the ferryboat, and moved it all downriver.

# CHAPTER 10

*Patsy*
*June, 1952*

Hollis fell to his knees and slumped over in the dirt. He was out cold, the last light of day taking him prisoner, wrapping his backside with thick ropes of golden-green.

Patsy dropped the rock and ran to Danny. He sat crutching himself against the tree, moaning, wisps of whiskey breath in each cry. "The sonofabitch ruined our p-prom," Danny said.

"Danny, shh . . . Oh, Danny, look at you. Where does it hurt? Show me where."

Danny rolled his head, struggling to speak. "Here. Up here." He held his hand high on his left arm, trying to stand. "Damn bullet got my arm. I think it shattered something, some bone too. Patsy, it hurts. All over."

"Dear God," she barely breathed.

Danny touched his crooked nose. "Bastard b-broke this too," he said drunkenly. "Get me to a doctor, Patsy."

"The hospital? The one off the Palisades—?" she asked, trying to pull him upright.

Danny grunted, "Yeah, County Hospital." Danny limped over to the automobile, using Patsy as a crutch, and folded himself into the backseat. Empty liquor bottles scattered onto the floorboard. Danny looked up at her. "What he s-said? What he said, is it true, Patsy?"

"Shh, Danny, I told you, you'd be the first," she answered and shut the back door. "Just look at you. We need to hurry now."

"I—I just want the truth."

"Hush, I said. Just hush now." Jumping into the driver's seat, she was relieved to see Hollis had left the keys. She pushed Hollis's flask out of the way, shoving it over to the passenger side, and examined the dash, knobs, and the gearshift column.

Patsy had been driving, some here, a little there, on two-lane road spurts when Mama thought she and Flannery needed another lesson, or had an errand to run in town. Lately in Mama's small old '40s Ford Coupe with the hard-to-work clutch. And only a handful of times driving in the Palisades when Honey Bee began sneaking her lessons. She'd just turned thirteen, though that was their secret they'd left snagged to the pine boughs up there.

And sometimes when she and Danny rode home with Hollis after school, he'd pull over and let them take turns practicing for a stretch of mile or so in the Henry family's Mercury with its new and fancy automatic, the automobile Sheriff Henry had turned over to his sons.

Patsy looked past her knees and downward, making sure a clutch hadn't suddenly appeared. She poked her shoe around for the pedals, kicking a bottle under the seat, pumping the foot feed and brake, testing. Then she pulled out the knob for the headlights, though a smudge of daylight remained.

Scooting up close to the big, skinny steering wheel, she draped her left arm over it and turned the key with her right hand. The engine gave a tiny growl and went quiet. She tried again and only got clicks with the engine cranking but not catching. "Damn." She pressed her head to the wheel, tried once more, furiously pumping the gas.

"Flooded it," Danny said hoarsely. "Oh, damn . . . This hurts like hell, Patsy. Like a—oh damn, hurts like a sonofabitch!" He hollered out in pain, then quieted a moment. "G-give it a sec. Try again," he said, drowsily this time.

She peered over the dash out the window and saw Hollis spread out by the elm. His hand twitched a couple of times and stilled. For a second, the sun looked like it had lit him on fire, a wave of heat rippling up from his body.

Slowly, Patsy counted to five and then held her breath and tried to turn over the engine again. It didn't catch.

Danny groaned.

Patsy's neck itched, burned from the anxious rash eating at her skin. Her armpits were soaked, the lovely yellow prom dress sticking to her like filled-up flypaper. She scratched her neck, plucked at the fabric pasted under her arms, and again stroked the fires eating at her flesh. *My pearls,* she almost cried out again. She'd have to sweet-talk Flannery into helping her find them before Mama found them missing.

Danny thrashed in the backseat.

Glancing over her shoulder, she saw his grim, pale face, a bloody hand pressed to his sleeve, his busted nose, swelling and bloodier still. Droplets of drying blood freckling his cheekbones.

"Hang on," she said.

"Did you let him do it, Patsy?" Danny whispered. "Let Hollis have what you promised me?"

"Don't be silly," she gasped. "I want *you.* Only you. I saved myself just like I promised I would. You believe me, don't you, Danny?"

Turning back to the wheel, Patsy leaned in even closer. Someone was there, someone in a long blue dress, not twenty feet from the hood. Patsy rubbed her eyes. A woman stood over Hollis, her back to the automobile.

"Help! Oh, Danny, look," Patsy said, throwing an arm over the bench seat. "There's someone here. Do you see her? Do you see the lady? . . . I can't tell who it is. Maybe it's Farmer Parsons's wife from across the field?" She honked the horn and rolled down the window. "Over here. Help us. *Please help.*" Patsy squinted to get a better look.

Danny coughed. "J-Jo," he wheezed out. "Joet—"

"What?" Alarmed, Patsy turned back to the windshield. "Joetta? No," she said, dropping her head down to the big, round dials on the dash, pinning her eyes to the fuel gauge. Shaking, Patsy fumbled for the ignition, turned the key far enough to light up the dials, and watched the gas needle rise slowly. *Half full.*

Patsy turned the key, again got nothing, and then dared to glance back out to the elm. No one was there but a knocked-out Hollis.

She exhaled. "Joetta's ghost is just a tale. You know that." Fear chewed at Patsy, stealing her courage. She rubbed briskly at the panicky stink rising from her chest, fanned herself. *Nerves.* That's all, she thought, and Danny was letting his fever talk.

"I'm cold," he whined, more bothered than before.

Quickly she cranked the window shut.

Danny cried out again, startling Patsy into turning the key once more. This time the engine roared, and she shifted the gear into reverse and backed out, lurching the heavy Mercury away from Ebenezer.

"Hold on." Patsy steered onto Palisades Road toward County Hospital on the other side of the cliffs. "It's okay, Danny; we'll be there in no time. They'll fix you right up."

"Ho—Hollis has been a-acting"—Danny's throat seized, and he hacked once—"pretty cozy with you . . . and if you gave it up to him, Patsy, if you . . . with him, and if you're lying to me 'bout all this, Patsy—"

"Hollis is the liar!" she yelled. "And you're still skunk drunk."

"Patsy?"

"Stop it. You hurting like this is making you mean. *Mean.* Just like Hollis. Just shut up now. Please, Danny. Shut up. We have to get you to a doctor."

"Patsy—"

"I have to keep it on the road here or else." Stretching her body upward, Patsy leaned in to the wheel. The Mercury's big nose was hard to see past. She glanced into her rearview; the shaved trunk dipped heavy and low, awkwardly. It was like driving a big bathtub up and down and around a bumpy roller-coaster.

Gripping the steering wheel, she fought to keep the Mercury on the narrow road, careening too close to one drop-off shoulder and then veering across to the other. The tires sprayed small bites of limestone into the wheel wells, pruned patches of wild rye and mountain lover out from under the low, fishtailing frame.

Danny mumbled something that she couldn't understand, then fell silent.

"You okay, Danny? Danny? Danny, wake up!" Patsy begged.

# CHAPTER 11

*Flannery*
*1972*

Flannery said a silent prayer for her sister's safety, slipped back into the car, and sat for a few minutes, the rocky Palisades cradling her hope, giving her the courage to face whatever was down there.

Out of the corner of her eye, she saw it resting at the end of the rail among the empty beer bottles, scattered cigarette butts, and pieces of broken glass, poking up from the concrete in a spindly thatch of determined grass. The white plastic egg someone had tossed, lying there like a chicken had indeed crossed the road to roost. She laughed at that, a short mad laugh, before marshalling it safely back inside her.

Here she was, going for possibly dreadful news, but thinking about shopping. It was still hard for Flannery to believe you could buy cheap nylons in an ugly fake egg. That women had been scooping them up as soon as the company began selling them last year.

Not Flannery, nuh-uh. She preferred her stockings neatly folded, silky, pressed and packed in slick, fancy cardboard sleeves, and even better, when she could find them, in small, thin linen boxes embossed with a fancy golden script, like the ones that filled two of her dresser drawers in the city.

Flannery jerked her hand down and pulled up the hem of

her jeans. She'd been in such a rush to leave, she feared she'd forgotten to wear them. Relief washed over her as she rubbed a finger over the hosiery. They were a reminder, her armor, and she never risked leaving the house without them, ever since that final evening at Chubby Ray's.

*Chubby Ray's.* Flannery knocked the name onto the steering wheel. It was still there. *Pull up a stool at the all-American Chubby Ray's. Refresh with cold, two-dip milkshakes, luscious sundaes . . . Chubby's, America's home to the tasty hot-rod hotdogs and Chevrolet cheeseburgers and fun treats. Fun, fun,* she recalled the old advertisement she knew by heart.

Though Chubby Ray himself had long passed, and the drugstore and soda joint belonged to his son, Junior, it was still a decent business. A popular spot dishing up the same fifties fun, the only entertainment in Glass Ferry, serving kids like it had when Flannery worked there, like it had, from what folks said, when it opened way back in the late '30s as a diner first. *Fun.*

But Flannery's last night at the soda fountain had been anything but. She'd been out of sorts when she arrived to work her sister's shift. Late. Yet, Flannery felt smug leaving Patsy in the dirt like that, having swiped her pearls without her twin seeing. Patsy deserved it, her sister in the lemon layers of princess tulle, while there Flannery was, stuck in the ugly uniform Chubby made them all wear. The ruined nylons in the dirt. Their jeers. That just flew all over her. Twenty years later it still did.

That spring night in '52, Flannery hotfooted it most of the way to Chubby Ray's, not slowing till she reached the screen door around back of the old red-rose brick building. Breathless, she'd squeezed past Chubby's son, Junior, standing in the back grill room, looking over the kitchen.

She grabbed a ticket book and pen to take orders from the crowd beginning to pour through the front door.

"What are you doing here, Junior?" Flannery asked, smoothing down her skirts, pulling out her soda-jerk cap and bobby pins. Remembering the pearls, she patted her left pocket. She blew a sigh and quickly pinned the hat onto her head.

"It's prom. Pop thought you weren't showing," Chubby's twenty-four-year-old son said, dipping his curly red hair toward the big clock hanging on the wall. "Called me in."

"Oh, that late, huh?" Flannery grimaced, looking down at her own wristwatch. "Real sorry, Junior. I have it now; you can get on back home to Tonya and the baby."

Flannery knew Junior worked the day shift, coming in every day in the long, fat hours of morning darkness. He hated having to work during the evenings, fussed about being away from his new baby. Chubby Ray always took extra pains to make sure his son wouldn't have to.

"If I'd known it was the fair and faithful Flan, I would've stayed put," Junior teased, a spray of freckles playing on his face.

She smiled some. She'd become friends with the young family, babysitting their littlest whenever they called on her. "Well, I'm working Patsy's shift. Guess Chubby got mixed up."

Junior raised a bushy brow. "If I recall, you worked the Cupid's dance for her—"

"I need the extra money, is all," she said hurriedly. "Where's Chubby?"

"Stepped next door to the hardware. And, Flan, extra jack ain't gonna get it." Junior thumped the old wooden worktable with a fist, looked down at her legs. "Gonna need a lot more than pay if Pop catches you working naked-leg like that," he warned kindly.

Behind them, Chute chuckled over the grill, his ink-black face glowing from the heat of the flames, his arms laddered with pinkish-white scars from spitting grease and stove burns.

"You see that?" Junior smiled. "Even ol' Chute knows— knows to wear his bow tie."

"Better listen, Flan," Chute said. "Bossman'll go off like one of them atomic bombs they have in that new uranium plant over there in McCraken County. *Boom boom*," Chute murmured over the rows of cooking burgers, piles of onions, stopping long enough to turn up the volume on the radio perched on the shelf above him. Quietly, he hummed along to the Andrew Sisters' "Rum and Cola-Cola."

Junior adjusted his own tie.

Chubby Ray had a strict dress code for soda jerks, all his employees. The boys' pants had to be creased; shirts, a crisp white, collared, with a red bow tie. A girl's uniform, no shorter than one finger above the knee with a long stretch of hosiery covering the legs.

Flannery peeked out the kitchen door, looking to see if Patsy had shown up. Music streamed from the jukebox as Frankie Laine rolled out a snappy "Mule Train" into the ribbony clouds of cigarette smoke and Emeraude perfume.

Girls in long showy dresses hung on to the arms of spiffy-looking country boys doused in Mennen and Old Spice; the fellers wore white and dark jackets, sported colorful pocket kerchiefs and lapel boutonnieres. Full of that once-a-year fever, a hark to a lifetime remembrance they piled around the juke-box and over at the polished chrome-plated counter with its five swivel stools, chatting, smoking, eyeing one another and every-one else's fancy duds.

Two of the four red vinyl booths had already filled with the revelers. Again, Flannery looked around for Patsy, but didn't see her or the Henry boys. For a second, concern set in, but just as quick, relief. Relief at not having to wait on her, and draw knowing eyes to her own pathetic, dateless predicament. She hoped they wouldn't stop for sodas, instead would go straight to the dance.

Picking up a tray of water glasses, she told Junior, "It's get-ting packed out there. First break, I'll go grab a box of hosiery in the drugstore. Promise. Right now I better get those booths."

"Flan, you grab 'em; I'll stab them." Chute pierced a pickle with a fork, dropped it onto a plate beside a greasy burger, chuckling.

Flannery stopped at the first booth and gave the couples each a glass of water, then took their order of malts and sodas.

At the second booth, Violet Perry and another girl, Bess, sat pretty and poised with their dates. They quieted when Flannery delivered their glasses.

"What would you like?" Flannery handed out the water, lifted the pen and *Guest Check* booklet out of her apron pocket.

"Oh, it's you, Flannery," Violet said, pulling up her gaze, flicking at the satin sleeves of her powdery-pink prom dress, inspecting her wristlet of tiny rosebuds.

Flannery braved a cautious smile at the pastor's daughter.

Violet picked up her cigarette from the ashtray, and with her other hand tapped the table with a long, painted nail. "It's a shame you're working tonight. *Shame.*" She poked the pity to her friends, who batted it around the table. "Shame, Patsy hung you out to dry again." She pursed her pouty pink lips, took a drag off her cigarette, and stubbed it out in the little four-welled glass ashtray, wagging her head, stamping out a string of "tsk-tsks" with it.

Flannery felt her cheeks burn. She pressed the serving tray to her chest, wishing she could cover her face with it and disappear. "Um, shake, or soda, or . . . ?" she mumbled.

The boys called out for lime rickeys and a banana boat and fries. Bess ordered a Cherry Crush cola.

"What about you?" Flannery poked her chin Violet's way.

"Hmm, lemme see." Violet pressed a finger to her rouge-colored cheek. "I suppose I'll have a strawberry sundae."

"One or two scoops?" Flannery asked.

"Well, two . . . Who wouldn't want two scoops of fun?" She lifted her answer to the table.

The boys bobbed their heads stupidly. Choked laughter rumbled under their clenched bow ties.

Bess grinned slyly and said, "Why, if Patsy was working, she'd know it was *two.*"

Violet pulled a glass to her mouth, sniggering between sips. She set it down, smacked her lips, and said, "Looks like her sister *is* having two delicious scoops this evening. Where's your twin and those Henry boys, that devilish duo?"

From behind, Chubby Ray called, "Flannery, grab another bucket of vanilla from the freezer."

Flannery stabbed Violet with a glare and turned, bumping into the shy, but cute Wendell Black, the soda jerk she'd hoped to get Miss Little to approve.

"*Flannery*," Violet and her gang sang out laughingly, "you forgot to empty our ashtray."

Flannery tried to sidestep around Wendell. Awkward, the soda jerk danced in front of her a second, reaching out for her arms. "I'll get it, Flan," he finally said, slipping past her.

"Flat-tire-Flan couldn't catch a beau even if he landed on her," Violet cackled, loud enough for everyone to hear.

Bess chimed, "Can you believe Miss Able Grable got two— *two dates to escort her?* She got—" Secret giggles fell into the boys' horsey laughter.

Shaking with anger, Flannery pinned the tickets onto the order wheel and hurried back to the walk-in freezer for the ice cream, slipping inside. On the floor lay a broken milk bottle. She kicked at the mess someone had left, slamming the door behind her, the light lost with its click.

Darkness took hold, and she closed her eyes and locked fingers against her eyelids. A tiny catch of tears rubbed at her throat. "Don't cry, don't cry," she begged, pressing her palms down, squeezing. "Don't," she commanded. "Not on prom night. Not here. Not now."

A trickle of disobedience slipped out onto her cheek. Another and two more, until her burning eyes were soaked in them, cheeks stinging from the raw, frigid air of the fan.

For a minute or so she let her sorrow empty into the coldness until a bump on the steel panel jolted her.

Chubby Ray swung open the door.

Blinded, Flannery squinted and fumbled for her apron to dab her eyes.

"Where's my ice cream—" Chubby Ray pulled Flannery from the freezer. "What's this? Look at this broken glass." He pointed to the floor, then jabbed a finger toward her legs. "Where are your stockings, Flannery Butler?"

Over by the grill, Chute turned up the radio even louder.

"Where are they?" Chubby pressed.

"Someone dropped a milk bottle, and I was—"

"Get your stockings on now," Chubby Ray snapped.

"I can't. They tore on my way to work."

"You know the rules."

"Yes, sir. But I ripped them—"

Chubby Ray held up a shushing hand. "I've tried. Tried for the sake of my old pal Honey Bee and tried to help out your poor ma. But I can't keep letting you girls off the hook, can I?"

After Honey Bee died, Chubby Ray hired the twins to help the Butler women get on their feet to pay the bills. Honey Bee'd left them a small savings, and Mama got a nice check from the sale of the distillery. But things broke, stuff needed fixing, and the sheriff's property tax bills got higher, eating away at Mama's pocketbook.

Mama went to work as a seamstress. The three of them working like that put food on the table, bought coal for the old furnace, and kept up the fine house Honey Bee'd left them.

"Chubby, I can get a pair if—"

"You can't," he said sternly. "Your sister missed two days last week and didn't work her shift the weekend before that. You didn't show up for her then, and now you've shown up late and not in full uniform. And on one of our busiest nights. It's a bad example for the others."

"I'll go get new nylons right now." Flannery pointed to the far wall, indicating where the outside archway led into the drugstore. "I promise it won't take but a minute. Promise, Chubby."

"You're costing me more time than you're worth."

"I can work an extra shift to make up for it—you won't have to pay me."

"You can go home, Flannery."

"Oh." She wrung her hands. "Uh, I'll just clean this mess up."

Chubby Ray sighed. "Junior will see to it."

"Sorry about the time. It won't happen again, sir. I, I just . . ." The broken plea got lost in a whimper.

"Leave." He turned away.

*What would she tell Mama?* "Y-you mean—"

Wendell pushed open the kitchen door, saw the disturbance, and then thought better and turned to leave.

"You, Wendell," Chubby Ray called him back. "Get a hot water bucket to the spill in there, and hurry. It's freezing up fast." Chubby jerked his head to the freezer.

Wendell grabbed the mop and bucket in the corner near Flannery, sneaking worried glances her way.

Flannery locked eyes with him long enough to see her disgrace in his, a pitiable concern rising.

For one blazing second she prayed to God to light a match to the world, ending her Hell.

"Go home, Flannery," Chubby Ray said quietly.

"Home," she whispered, unbelieving, not wanting to accept she was being fired. *She'd gotten Patsy fired too.*

"*Home.*" Chubby Ray stabbed the finality with a tight nod toward the back door.

Wendell pushed the mop around, ducking low as he swished it past her.

A tear sprang from her eye, dropped toward her shoe, missed, and puddled on the floor. Flannery wanted to beg Chubby. To push, to ask, "For good? Forever?" but she didn't dare. Didn't dare risk calling out the damning disgrace that would have her leaving a bigger mess for Wendell to mop up.

# CHAPTER 12

*Patsy*
*June, 1952*

Danny finally stirred, then slipped in and out of his drowsy state, startling Patsy each time with curses and loud moans. Patsy wasn't sure whether it was the liquor or the wound causing his outbursts.

"You'll be fine," she tried again to quiet him, "but I'm going to be in a mess of trouble when Mama sees me."

Danny didn't respond.

Patsy chanced a glance to the backseat. "Did you hear me? Big trouble, losing those pearls." It scared her a little. Usually Patsy escaped blame and found a way to pin it on Flannery. She didn't see how that was possible tonight. "Danny?"

"Trouble," he whispered, "if-if you and Hollis—"

"Please hush about him. As soon as they patch you, we'll leave here and be together."

"*God*"—he stirred loudly—"this d-damn shoulder. Hurts like hell, gawdammit."

Patsy took one hand off the wheel to rub her sweaty brow. "They'll fix your arm just fine, Danny." *She had to get him well so they could get away and get hitched.*

"Hurry, Patsy. The pain's getting worse."

"Hospital Curve's just up ahead," she said, tilting further into the steering column, the night coming fast now. The Mercury's headlights were weak, and Patsy squinted and squirmed, struggling to see through the shadowy canopy of trees and rocks hugging the uphill side of the road.

Danny whimpered some.

"Soon as we take it, we'll be out of the Palisades and then—" It was more like a prayer than a declaration. "They'll fix you up." Patsy pressed down on the gas pedal, goosed it a bit more. She had to get him there faster, now.

# CHAPTER 13

*Flannery*
*1972*

"Lord, please don't let it be my sister. Don't let my hope become a lie," Flannery prayed again, pressing down on the gas. She tipped her head toward the car window, letting the breeze cool her brow, gulping the fresh air into her panicky lungs.

Guiding the car toward the others parked in the grassy lot beside the boat dock, Flannery tucked in the Chevy's wheels and her amen between an old pickup and a Blue-Bess Ice Cream truck.

She sat there a minute and watched the group of officials and bystanders gathered on the boat dock. Beyond, she saw the swirling bubblegum light of a large tow truck poking up from the crowd.

Once again, Flannery prayed for the car to be empty, even someone else down there in that murky water. Let her sister and Danny be alive far away from Glass Ferry, the two runaway lovers living a secret and better life with their kids. Living a good fairy tale like the ones in the books she read to her young students.

She knew Danny and Patsy wouldn't be the first teenagers to run off and never return. After all, that's what Hollis had convinced Flannery of long ago, and what most townsfolk reckoned and nearly believed.

As if summoned by her thoughts, Sheriff Hollis Henry appeared, parting the crowd, strolling toward her car, his widebrim, Smokey-the-Bear uniform hat shielding his face from the early afternoon son.

Flannery cringed, remembering that awful evening with him in 1952.

Flannery had left through the kitchen door of Chubby Ray's, slinking out into the night air, the stain of blame and greasy onions trailing her. The mess she'd made, crowding her.

She stood there in the back of the business, looking up at the nearly full moon, wondering how to tell Mama and Patsy, what to tell them. The laughter of merry prom-goers floated out from inside, whirled around her.

Ol' Chute slipped out behind her carrying a bag of rotting trash, and stuffed it into the can beside her. He looked at her a little sadly, then pulled out the homemade cigarette he'd rolled and had tucked behind his ear, lit it, and offered her a puff.

Flannery had smoked cigarettes once in a while, in the school parking lot where the principal allowed it, even snuck a puff in the bathrooms, and shared a drag behind football bleachers and a few other places kids smoked to be daring, but she'd never done it with an adult.

She needed Honey Bee's strong whiskey. Still she accepted Chute's cigarette.

As if reading her thoughts, Chute pulled out a pint of whiskey tucked in his britches next to his hip.

He took a big swill and offered the bottle to her. "Here now, Flannery. I can't have Honey Bee's girl all teary. Have yourself a nip of your daddy's fine batch I done saved for these creaky ol' bones."

Honey Bee had been crazy about Chute's steak sandwiches. Chute would make the tasty treat only for her daddy whenever Honey Bee had the hankering. Chute cooked the peppered steak in his cast iron skillet with a glaze of mashed cherries and whiskey and sautéed onions. Then he'd top off the juicy meat with a thick mixture he'd concocted out of garlic, bourbon, and fresh cheese from a neighbor's goat. Sometimes adding a pinch of wild onion and pressed dandelion leaves to the finish, if the season called.

Mama could always tell when Chute fed Honey Bee. He'd pick lightly at his supper, feign a lost appetite, then toss his serving when Mama wasn't looking.

Honey Bee never forgot the treat. He always thanked Chute with a wild turkey he'd shoot for Chute's family at Thanksgiving, and a bottle or two of Kentucky River Witch every Christmas.

Flannery looked longingly at the bourbon a second, thinking.

Chute took another drink, and she pushed his smoke back to him.

He waved it away and lightly patted her shoulder before stealing back into the kitchen, leaving his condolence with her.

She took one more drag, stamped it out with her dirty shoe, and headed toward home, wallowing, worrying how to explain she'd gotten fired.

Following the mile-long row of old plank-board fencing in Paintlick Field, Flannery made her way under a moonlit sky onto Ebenezer Road.

Flannery was so caught up in her own misery, naked-legged, and growing more miserable by the minute, she stumbled over Hollis's crumpled body as she passed under the elm. She nearly screamed as her foot tripped over his.

"Hollis?" she cried out, and then squatted to get a closer look, wondering if he was passed out drunk, or what. When she glimpsed the dried blood on his head and face, she realized it was something more.

"Wake up, Hollis, wake up." She shook his shoulder harder now, rocking him, his fat head rolling back and forth.

Hollis stirred some, grunted, and slowly came to. He raised his head, the moonlight washing cuts of light across his face.

Flannery moved closer and saw the blood in his matted hair. "What happened to you?" She leaned in further. "What the devil happened here, Hollis Henry? Where's my sister? Where's your brother?" She looked back over her shoulder.

Hollis pulled himself up to sit, propped his back against the tree, moaning, touching, then rubbing his head.

"Where's Patsy?" she demanded, still glancing around, growing alarmed. "Hollis"—she shook his arm—"where is she? Where's my sister? Is she okay? Where's Danny?"

Hollis slowly pulled up his leg, rested an arm on his knee. "Fight. Had a fight with Danny. Then Patsy—" Hollis winced.

"What about Patsy?" Flannery smelled the booze on his soured breath. "What did you do to her?" She spotted the nylons she had thrown onto the dirt earlier. Her face warmed, and she snatched them up and stuffed them into her apron pocket.

"*I* didn't do a damn thing. Danny landed a punch, and that bitch twin of yours must've got me from behind." Hollis looked around slowly as if trying to remember how he had gotten there. He nudged his chin at a good-sized rock lying near where she knelt. "Probably with that damn rock."

Flannery followed his eyes and saw the small bite of an old headstone.

"She got in a good lick to my head, same as Danny." Hollis rubbed his glazed eyes, cradled his face, growling.

Flannery leaned over, picked up the rock, weighing it in her hand, pondering Hollis's words. She frowned and tossed the stone away. "What happened here, Hollis? What's going on?"

Hollis shouted, "Your twin is what's going on! She got herself pregnant an' caused all this."

Flannery's eyes grew wide. "What are you talking about, fool? Patsy pregnant? You're not making any sense, Hollis Henry." She studied him, not sure if he was suffering from one of those concussions folks got from bad spills, or if he was too soaked in the stink-drink to think straight.

"*Patsy. Is. Pregnant,*" he spit at her.

Flannery stood up, flared her nostrils. "That's not true." Patsy would never keep something that big from her. Flannery knew she wasn't a floozy, same as her. Accusing her sister of something like that, why, it was the same as accusing Flannery.

"Sure as hell is," Hollis said, trying to stand.

"Nuh-uh. I'd know if it were so—"

"You don't know a damn thing, peaches. She was coming on to me, and here Danny accused *me* of trying to steal her when he caught her trying to cuddle up with me here." Hollis jerked out his arm. "Right here under this damn tree."

"I don't believe it. She loves Danny."

"Believe what you want, but she wasn't acting it. She thought she could tease. Humph, the tramp done got herself knocked up with Danny's baby." Hollis pulled himself up, bent a little from the pain. "My head."

"Your brain's broke, Hollis Henry."

"Oh, my head does hurt like the devil. Shit . . . Hurts . . . But I swear it, Flannery. I swear on my ma." Hollis raised his hand to his heart. "Swear Patsy told us she was having his baby. And then those two said they were going to take off, split for good, run away together. They're probably shacked up a hundred miles from here by now—what time is it?" Hollis looked around like he was trying to remember something.

"After eight." Flannery thought about Chubby griping about Patsy missing work two days last week. Her sister had claimed a stomach ailment as her excuse. And for the missed days a few times before that, and always the stomach sickness, with Patsy insisting it was *the female jitters.* Patsy had thrown up just yesterday morning, calling it early prom nerves.

Flannery and Mama both knew about Patsy's spells, about how she'd always been frailer than most her age. But this? *Pregnant?* None of it made sense.

Flannery burned, felt the smarting lick of Mama's embarrassment, the disgrace that would come down on the Butler name.

Hollis said, "I tried to stop them, swear, but then Danny socked me in the jaw when I . . . uh, wouldn't give him my keys. And Patsy snuck up behind me and—" Hollis pushed a lock of hair away from his eyes, interrupting himself. "Hey, Flannery. What the hell are you doing back this way anyway?"

"Chubby let me off when Junior showed up." She brushed off the question with a quick half-truth. "A baby? Are you sure?"

Hollis studied her closely.

"Guess your daddy's gonna need to hear about it," she said quietly, looking down Ebenezer Road, frowning. "The whole stinkin' town'll hear about it too." She cocked her head toward him. "Everyone fifty miles wide, even."

"Dad probably doesn't need to know *everything*." Hollis lightly rubbed his hurt jaw, touched his head. "We can maybe skip *that* part, the part about the baby."

"We don't even know if it's true," she snapped.

"Maybe we don't," he said as if they were scheming together for some greater good. "But if those two don't come back from the prom, do you want to risk letting everyone gossip about it? Side-talking 'bout big sister like that? The bastard that may or may not be coming?" Hollis poked a finger at her. "Want your mama fretting over that, too?"

She flinched. It would break Mama's heart.

"Hey, peaches." He touched her elbow. "Here's a good idea. If they don't come 'round to their senses, if they don't come back in time, I'll tell Dad those stupid kids stole the Mercury and lit out on their own when I stopped for a whizz. That those lovesick pups were running away to get hitched. That I tripped and fell trying to chase 'em to stop them. 'S'all." He pointed to his sore head. "Or maybe I'll tell the old folks, lil' brother got ahold of a rock and socked me when I tried to talk some sense into them both."

Flannery turned it over in her mind, taking a match to his words, wary of his plan hatched from liquored lips. "Danny sure has been asking for trouble lately." She shot a blaming eye at Hollis. "Used to be a real nice fellow, and he'd hit the books pretty hard. But lately—" Flannery said.

"Pft," Hollis said. "A man don't need those kind of lesson books as long as he knows the 'portant ones. Those good ones like my very favorite, *Under the Bleachers* by Seymour Hiney," Hollis chortled.

Flannery rolled her eyes. "You should know, Hollis Henry. Took you a while to learn 'em. Two years 'a whiles' stuck in Mrs. William's first grade like that."

"Damn straight."

Flannery hoped Danny wouldn't turn out like Hollis, but feared the younger brother already had. She'd have to have a good talk with Patsy one of these days.

Hollis squeezed her arm. "C'mon, peaches. No one will ever know—will ever need to know about all this—as long as you don't tell. No one will know about the baby, about Patsy coming on to me like that. Just say so, that you'll stick with me."

Flannery jerked away from his touch.

"I say good riddance." Hollis straightened and flicked the dirt off his shirt. "They deserve each other." Making a show, he swept the front of his britches, patting at his privates.

Disgusted, Flannery turned away.

"Say the word, sweet peaches," he rambled closer to her ear, "and my daddy, my family and me, you, and *your* family"—he stabbed his finger at her—"will be spared. Spared from the scandal of your sister's shameful, hussy ways."

"Don't you talk about my sister like that." Still, the words pricked at Flannery; humiliation grabbed hold and gnawed deeper. She knew the Henrys were one of the most respectable families around. Proud. She also knew about how Sheriff Jack Henry hoped to pass his job to his oldest son after he got in some higher learning at the university. Sheriff Henry'd told Hollis it was a smart world growing out there, and lawmen needed to be smarter than the lawbreakers.

Flannery knew her own daddy had liked the easygoing sheriff and had held him close over the years—"Keeping the lawman's pockets full, his liquor cabinet stocked, and his eyes turned when Honey Bee'd had his private whiskey dealings," she'd overheard Mama fuss when she thought her girls were out of earshot.

"Look, say the word for us, and for the sake of our families' good names. What this would do to our dear mamas," Hollis added with a plea. "Let 'em come back or leave forever, or whatever. I'll give you my word as a gentleman, a Henry, that I'll never tell. She'll never be disgraced."

*Mama. What would Mama's canasta club say?* Flannery wondered. Jean Butler played cards with Mrs. Henry and the other good and godly women of Glass Ferry. They'd kick her out, the same as they did Mrs. Wilson when her fourteen-year-old girl got pregnant.

"C'mon, peaches. You wanna see Patsy end up like Peggy Ann? Huh?"

Flannery wrinkled her brow.

"Look how Peggy Ann went from valedictorian to being kicked out of school, and now she can't even get herself a carhop job over at Pap's Pig Stand. Nobody'll want anything to do with Patsy or you or anyone else in your family."

Pap's Pig Stand was a newfangled restaurant over in the next county, where you could drive your automobile into a parking lot, and a waitress would skedaddle out, take your order, and deliver it all back to your car.

Both families would be shunned, shamed if the other towns-women even suspected a pregnancy out of wedlock. It was going to be bad enough when Mama found out Chubby'd canned her and Patsy, both, tonight. But whether her sister came home later, or didn't, Flannery wouldn't have to be the one to spill the beans about the baby, and nobody'd be the wiser. Nobody would be shamed.

She snuck a glimpse at Hollis. It felt like he was holding something back, not telling her everything. "Are you sure 'bout all this, Hollis? Sure about them leaving—"

"What do you think? Listen, Danny boy told me he busted his piggy bank a while back, cleaned out his shitty savings account so he could do some serious courtin'. Said he wanted to take Patsy to Joyland, buy her footlongs and root beer and ride the fun rides, maybe even sneak into their dance hall and see Woody Herman."

Flannery had been to the old amusement park up in Lexington. Everybody had. But like most teens, she couldn't wait to have a first dance at the Joy Club inside the park.

Quite the dreamy date the Joy Club was, and Patsy couldn't wait to go dancing there one day. Talked about it all the time. Flannery did too. Likely, Patsy was on her way there now, Flannery sort of hoped, though not without a tinge of jealousy burrowing inside.

"Hell, those two are likely riding the fun rides 'bout now." Hollis bumped Flannery's arm and sneered, pulling her back. "Who knows how their date'll turn out, after all. Or where it'll end. But, Flannery"—he dropped to barely a whisper—"we'll have to be ready for them in case they do come home tonight toting tall tales about who knows what."

No matter what happened, the end result would be the same. It would break Mama's heart. Flannery resigned herself to that.

"Okay. Good riddance," she mumbled under her breath. And then louder and to the star-packed sky for a lucky wish or two, *"Good riddance!"* She tilted her head up to the heavens, searching for a shooting star to punch her testimony.

"Yessir." Hollis yawned, stood wobble-legged. "Riddance!"

Flannery and Hollis stayed there on a moonlit Ebenezer Road, agreeing a few more times to save their own necks, promising to bury Patsy's ugly shame right then and there. If those two came back after prom or whatever, Hollis assured Flannery he'd make sure that, in no uncertain terms, Patsy and Danny would bear the blame for their wrongdoings.

"Can't believe those two bushwhacked me. They stole the automobile." He patted his waist, hitched up his belt underneath the shirt, and Flannery saw a pistol. Everyone knew Hollis loved guns same as his sheriff daddy.

He bent over to tie his shoe. Flannery caught another glimpse of the gun, and it reminded her of one of Honey Bee's.

"Punks," Hollis said, rising, patting his hair.

"They've turned into regular Bonnie and Clydes, is what they've done," Flannery muttered sarcastically, a worry needling her skin.

Hollis cackled. "Dumbass Danny couldn't hit a two-foot dick off a three-legged donkey. Even if it up an' pissed on him." He raised a leering brow at her. "And everybody knows it takes a real man to handle a gun and a woman."

Flannery glared back at him in the fattening silence until an owl from a nearby tree cut the quiet.

"Shit." Hollis tucked his stretched lips over his sucking teeth. "I got to go check and see if they left it. If my Mercury's in the school lot now," he muttered. "Damn fools. Could've at least tossed out my flask after they clobbered me. I need me a drink. Need me one, bad." He lumbered off.

Flannery kicked at the rock her sister had used to brain Hollis. She was tired of cleaning up after her princess sister, angry at another mess Patsy had left her.

Stuffing her hands into her apron pockets, Flannery tucked in her chin and turned toward home, thinking about what Hollis told her. *When Patsy showed up, she'd get an earful.* Flannery glanced back once. Wondered where the hell Hollis had disappeared to, but then, out of the corner of her eye she glimpsed a breezy shadow wafting across a stream of moonlight, spilling out from behind the elm. "Hollis?" she said quietly, then again a breath louder, "Hollis. Hollis, is that you?"

When no one answered, she hoped maybe it was Patsy who'd showed back up, tuck-tailed, to make things right. Still she thought it might be Hollis playing a trick, him still lit with the booze like he was.

Without a sound, Flannery made her way back to the tree. "Hollis Henry, I'm not in the mood for your stupid jokes." She peeked around the wide trunk, hoping to catch him, maybe Patsy and Danny too, come back to make things right all on their own.

Circling the ancient hardwood, Flannery stopped and touched its deep gray furrows, looking up for squirrel or woodchuck. *Nothing.*

Goosebumps pricked her arms. She hugged herself tight. Flannery wanted to be home. Home and in her safe, warm bed. Forget about Patsy, Chubby, Danny, Hollis, and everyone who'd damned her miserable night. To have a chance to sleep on what would come next.

Stepping back, her shoe hit a stone. The same one Hollis had accused Patsy of using. Flannery stumbled and caught herself. *What is that?* she asked no one in particular, seeing something else.

She squinted at it in the slant of moonlight and then stretched her neck upward, taking in nothing but the breeze-soaked shadows of branches and leaves. Flannery stooped over, her nose almost to the ground, and then spotted it. A copper bullet.

Why hadn't she seen it earlier? She was always good at spotting stuff out of its natural order. She nudged the ground with her shoe, swishing a foot over loose dirt.

Puzzled, she tried to spot a pie plate or bottle used for target practice, though she knew the adjoining landowners didn't allow such with their milk cows and horses pasturing nearby. Flannery cast an eye again for the squirrel or critter or crow, any creature that might've dropped it, dug it up, or such. But she didn't find any sign.

Flannery turned to leave and caught the tiny flash of metal again. Scooping up the bullet, she raised it high, inspecting it closely under the light of the moon. Turning it, she brought it closer to her face, then pulled it away, twisting, turning, studying it some more.

The bullet didn't look old at all, or corroded or discolored. Not like old bullets Honey Bee'd pointed out, or the ones she'd found while target practicing.

The color on this bullet was shiny like a new copper penny, but she could see it had been shot, the nose flattened.

From a distance, a hound barked, and another joined its call. Farther away, another dog howled back an answer across the fields.

Remembering how much her daddy loved hunting and how he'd proudly taught his girls to shoot when they were eight, she jiggled the bullet in her palm, then dropped it into her apron pocket.

The bullet rolled and clinked against Patsy's pearls. It wasn't a lucky penny, but it was shiny enough to maybe do the trick, and Lord knows Flannery could use a some-kind-of shiny trick for tonight's troubles.

Patting her pocketed treasures, she hurried off toward home.

# CHAPTER 14

*Patsy*
*June, 1952*

Patsy wondered how deep Hollis's bullet had dug into Danny. How quickly the doctors could patch him up. She swerved the Mercury, dodging some broken glass, hitting a piece that popped like a gunshot, making her jerk the wheel. She flinched, remembering the gun going off, hitting Danny. All her life she'd hated guns, despite being taught how to use them. And she'd only learned to please Honey Bee, and best Flannery, showing the two she was brave and wasn't as weak as they believed.

At first, Patsy had been afraid to learn to shoot, and bawled when Honey Bee ordered her to follow him down to the river. Mama tried to intervene. "Honey Bee, please, you're frightening the child. She's only eight. Just take Flannery and leave Patsy be. She doesn't have her sister's starch. Please—"

"I aim to frighten her; I aim to put the fear in her," Honey Bee'd growled. "Hell's bells, Mama, you would leave our daughter helpless for the wolves out there? For the likes of those we've seen before—"

*Hush,* Mama's eyes warned.

*Silence,* Honey Bee's eyes nailed back.

A stillness crackled in the sudden quiet before Honey Bee snatched the twins to his side and walked them down to the barn. Even Patsy's easy tears hadn't released her from Honey Bee's lesson.

Carefully, he placed the gun and bullets on an old wooden stand under the eaves and patiently showed his eight-year-old girls how to load one round into the .38, and then unload the weapon safely. "It's big for you, has a big bite, but you'll need it for the bigger ones out there."

*"Point the barrel down, Patsy . . . always when handling . . . That's it, Queenie,"* he'd prompted softly.

When he was through, he made each of the girls repeat the steps over and over, until they could load and unload blindfolded. Then Honey Bee stood behind them and showed them how to properly hold and aim the pistol, placing their small right hands around the grip and resting the gun in their free ones for support.

Again, he had Patsy empty the gun and practice her hold. "Not too tight," he cautioned. "The gun'll shake. Place your pointer finger inside the trigger there, and nab your strongest eye down the barrel's nose to a target. That old chestnut over there. Dry fire. Try it again."

Next, Honey Bee went into the barn and brought out old bottles and placed them over by a sycamore. Then he pulled the girls back about fifteen feet.

Slipping a protective, cupped hand under her hold, Honey Bee told Patsy to squeeze the trigger.

Blackbirds flew up. The bang deafened, the flash surprised, but when Patsy got over the shock, she asked if she could do it again. "Please, Honey Bee," she implored. "I want to keep practicing."

Patsy kept shooting and shooting until she could bravely handle the gun, until Honey Bee brought out more bottles, and stepped back, and raised his hands, and let her try it by herself.

Patsy had a good eye and hit most of her targets.

Flannery was next and hit a few of her bottles, tried again and busted two, but couldn't hit more than her sister.

When they were done, Honey Bee seemed to relax. "My girls will never have to fear the devil," he said with a strange mixture of sadness and relief. "Little Queenie"—he beamed at Patsy—"you are going to be a crack shot, and you"—Honey Bee gently pinched Flannery's cheek—"*you* did your papa proud."

Honey Bee was so pleased, especially with Patsy, that he'd pulled out his Boker knife, and let her carve *C S* into the black barrel. "As fine a *crack shot* as I've ever seen," Honey Bee said, and ran a finger over Patsy's crude stamp she'd scratched out.

Then he carried his prissy, brave girl piggyback all the way up to the house, boasting of Patsy's skills to Mama and demanding sweets for his daughters. "Natural marksmen, if I ever saw," he said to Mama, then showed Patsy another gun, Jesse James's Robin Hood No. 2, told her it would be hers one day, and took the girls back down after supper to practice on it.

Shortly before departing the earth, Honey Bee passed outlaw Jesse James's gun and hand-carved bone dice to Patsy, the heirlooms his own daddy had handed down to him.

Both Patsy and Flannery and everyone from around here knew the story. In the 1860s Jesse James and his brother Frank tried to rob a bank in Brandenburg, Kentucky. Jesse was shot and ran into the woods, while Frank retreated back to his home in Missouri. Honey Bee's grandparents found Jesse and took the wounded outlaw in, nursing him. It was a small, modest farmhouse, so Jesse had to sleep with the Butlers' five-year-old son.

One morning the house awoke to find Jesse gone, and a note tucked to the pillow. Next to the note lay his small gentleman's gun, a Robin Hood No. 2 pistol, and a set of the outlaw's bone dice he'd left for the little boy. Jesse liked to romanticize that he was Robin Hood No. 2, wanted to be known as only taking from the rich and giving to the poor.

Jesse wrote in the letter that the Butler child had slept with him and thanked the boy and his family for the tender nursing and fine hospitality.

But Patsy didn't like scarred things, old stuff. Especially the nicked gentleman's gun. It reminded her of the dead, of things that made people dead, of who Jesse might've killed with it. And even though she knew how to shoot and had even enjoyed besting Flannery with her daddy's shiny snub nose, she'd halfheartedly shot the outlaw's pistol, then tucked the old revolver back inside Honey Bee's walnut secretary in the parlor.

"A surefire crack shot," Honey Bee'd marveled over Patsy's deft shooting. With time and Honey Bee's practices, the girls earned his title.

# CHAPTER 15

*Flannery*
*1972*

The sun blinded Flannery as she stepped out of her car. Squinting, she watched Sheriff Hollis Henry standing on the banks, one elbow resting on his holster, talking to another official. Hollis had an outstretched palm pinned to the Kentucky River.

Beyond, a small ferryboat idled past, skimming the still waters, pulling her to a different day on the river—a dangerous one she and Honey Bee had met with long ago on her daddy's old *River Witch* boat, back when Hollis's daddy, Jack Henry, had been wearing the badge.

Hollis standing there like that, hand stuck out, was as if yesteryear had given itself a mirror and reflected it all back into the future.

The wind kicked up, dragging a cloud of angels' share over the crowd gathering below and waiting for the river's latest secret.

Another Kentucky River secret, not too unlike Flannery and Honey Bee's most guarded they'd left in the muddy waters back then.

Flannery was pretty sure Honey Bee'd murdered one of the moonshiner thieves with his old .38, and maybe he had. Because no one ever spoke of it again. Honey Bee had wanted to kill him, taking straight aim at the whiskey pirate on that fine day coming downriver, back in the fall of '47.

That morning Honey Bee had awakened eleven-year-old Flannery just as the moon slipped under its morning wrap. "C'mon, Flannery girl. The river is calling us," he had whispered and shook her, careful not to disturb Patsy.

The sun burst through the fog, announcing the day as they drove the ferryboat up the hushed river. A sheen of fire lay in a wide path on the water.

The Palisades jutted out of darkness, its crags in russets and golds of rock elm and yellow buckeye trees that snugged lace-like into limestone terraces on the early November day.

Peregrine falcons wheeled and soared in the cool morning air. A pair of blue heron skimmed the Kentucky waters for breakfast while Honey Bee and Flannery sipped at the silence. Their creaking boat chugged past the tulip- and poplar-lined banks. Overhead, migrating geese called out their greeting, hurrying on in V formation.

On the other side of the river up ahead, out of the corner of her eye Flannery watched as strange men pushed their small boat off the bank. Lately, she and Honey Bee had seen the pair of dirty-looking boatmen on the wooden flatboat on their trips upriver.

"Look at those boys on that ol' Kentucky boat up to no good and likely dumber than a broom handle," Honey Bee had remarked several times, always passing a testing hand to the small of his back where he'd hitched his snub nose, and keeping a sharp eye tucked their way.

The old boat reminded Flannery of one of Mama's brown shoe boxes, the ones in the cellar on a shelf where she kept all her old letters. Flannery watched as the muscled oarsmen pushed off the muddy bottom, paddling the boat into deeper water.

Honey Bee was always right. On the return trip back downriver, the men stole out of a cove, sneaking their wooden boat alongside Honey Bee's. Then one of the men clambered up the rope near the ferryboat's stern and hopped over the rail and onto their deck. The boat groaned softly from his weight, water slapped at the wooden sides, like it wanted to push him away.

He called out friendly-like, "Hey, Cappy," to Honey Bee. "Fine fishing weather." He rubbed his balded chest, tugged at his wet britches. "My brother and me wondered if you might have some spare bait aboard?" He pointed down over the rail to the other man waiting in the flat-bottomed boat. "We've been trying to catch this grandpappy catfish, and that ol' Lucifer cat's been slipping us every time. Lost two lines to the bastard. Can you spare a 'tucky brother a little somethin'?"

The man smelled dangerous like sour water, dark like trouble that's just blown in its rot. Flannery knew he had the nastiness a lot like their next-door neighbors the Butler family had problems with. But this man's meanness was more sharp and unlocked on the face.

"Get into the wheelhouse," Honey Bee ordered Flannery.

Looking back over her shoulder, she hurried into the cabin, shut the wooden door, and peeked out through its circle window left open to air the cabin.

The man's leer followed her.

Honey Bee just stood there, resting a curled hand on his hipbone, not saying a word.

The man lifted a long hunting knife from a cow-leather sheaf hooked onto his belt, scratched at his scraggly beard, and eyed his surroundings. "Done used up all my chicken livers on that damn cat." He sly-eyed Flannery again.

"Don't think there's gonna be any fishing today," Honey Bee said, and pulled his shoulders back, rooted his sturdy legs to a ready parting.

"Know'd what I think?" The man worked a twisted grin on his mouth. "I think you been scaring our fish away, Cappy. Yup, you and your big fancy boat here been hurting me and my lil' brother's livelihood."

Honey Bee pinched his lips together.

"But, hell. I'm a forgiving man." The man pushed words through brown teeth. "And"—he tipped his blade slightly—"I bet you're a givin' one. Maybe you got something under them benches for me an' Brother's hurtings? Wet our thirst with that good likker you tote, huh?" the man said sneakily, and leaned over and swept a dirty hand along the locked wooden bench that hid Honey Bee's whiskey.

Honey Bee stood quietly, then said again, "Ain't no fishing here."

"Seems you owe us for our hurting. So maybe I should take it all." The man jutted his knife toward Flannery. "Me and Brother could start there first, hook our sinkers into that piece of tail for a satisfying bite."

Honey Bee whipped out his pistol, and a shot rang out. The man screamed, then crumpled to the deck, wriggling, gripping his bloody kneecap that Honey Bee had blown out.

"You fish for trouble and try 'n' rob respectable folk, you'll get a fat tick's worth of hurting in your flesh," Honey Bee snarled, and kicked the man's leg and then booted the big knife off the deck into the water.

Then as easy as plucking a weed from a field, Honey Bee picked the man up under the arms and tossed him overboard, the smack of water, its dirty spray lifting, pulling up a stink into the air.

Flannery fled the wheelhouse and rushed to her daddy's side.

Honey Bee and Flannery leaned slightly over the rail, watching the other man curse and scramble below, pull his screaming, gurgling brother out of the water.

Quietly, Honey Bee said, "Yessir, there's a paddle for every ass. And sometimes you're gonna get stuck picking the paddle for an ornery one. *Lord,*" he breathed, "don't you know those ol' boys have some hard ones coming their way."

Shaken, Flannery stood in the small pond of the man's blood and bites of scattered flesh, gaping at her daddy who was still lit full with a deadliness that leaked from his eyes.

Honey Bee crooked his head to her and tapped his watch. "In as little as eight minutes your life can change, and the time thief can come collectin'. You fight for it, child. You don't let him pinch one tender second from you." Her daddy set his jaw tight.

Honey Bee grabbed the mop in the corner and turned to her. "Not a word to Mama. To anyone. Ever. On these minutes that *didn't* happen and are given to you. *Understand?*"

She didn't really understand all he said, but readily nodded in obedience and knowing to his warning eyes.

# CHAPTER 16

*Patsy*
*June, 1952*

Patsy's eyes lit on the deer standing in the middle of the road. For a second she forgot she was driving Hollis's automatic, and her feet panicked and searched the pedals before finally finding the brake, jostling Danny in the backseat.

He moaned.

"A deer is all, Danny. It's okay. I'll have you there soon. Hospital Curve's just up ahead." Treacherous not because it was the last curve out of the Palisades, or the closest to County Hospital, but because it was the coil that had landed lots of folks in that hospital. And more than a few in the morgue. Last fall, Beverly Auler, one of Glass Ferry High's seniors, was killed when she crashed her automobile into the cliff rocks. A few months back, another boy, Ian Robin, who everyone called "Iam Rotten" because of his dares, broke his back when he raced around the curl of the mountain and pushed the nose of his daddy's truck into rock.

Patsy looked back and saw the deer hadn't moved, its head frozen and feet still locked in the wispy tail of her ghosted headlights. She relaxed a second and sent a prayer up to Honey Bee for that.

When Patsy turned thirteen, Honey Bee began sneaking in

more difficult driving lessons for her, taking her on narrower back roads and over into the Palisades.

Honey Bee had her ride off the edge of the road, between the asphalt and the tall, grassy gullies, kissing the ditch with the tires, then taught her to ride that a bit, steering slowly back onto the road—rather than jerking the wheel and sending the automobile flipping, toppling down embankments, steep cliffs, or swerving into oncoming traffic headed their way.

Frightened, Patsy'd cried, and more than once stopped dead in the road, frozen until Honey Bee would pull out a fresh hand-kerchief from his pocket and dab her tears. Then he'd change sides to take her driver's seat and show her how to do it safely.

A few minutes later, they'd switch back. Honey Bee made Patsy do this over and over until his daughter felt certain she could recover from whatever obstacle she might happen upon while driving. "Drive better than any man three-counties-wide, and get yourself out of a tight spot lickety-split," he'd said.

Patsy had busted up the sides of Honey Bee's old Ford pretty good, dented and scraped the paint off the fenders and doors.

Honey Bee had been sick with his sugar illness then, but he never fussed during the lessons, just bided his time, praising her until they were both smiling and had claimed miles of twisty Kentucky roads. Him always saying when they were through, "Let's not fret Mama with our lessons. Not a word, Queenie."

Mama never said much when Honey Bee returned home with the automobile more busted than when he'd left, only, "Hmm. Don't you know, dear husband, I do believe you need to go see Doctor Silverman in the city about spectacles. That, or someone needs more driving lessons," she'd lightly hint, circling the Ford, flicking her dish towel at a fresh scrape or ding.

*Mama.* Patsy squirmed behind the Mercury's steering column. The hospital would call her and Danny's parents, of course, and Patsy flinched at the thought of seeing the sheriff, even more, Mama's worried eyes.

Stretching up to the rearview mirror, Patsy glimpsed her face, touched her bottom lip swelling from Hollis's slap, lighting a quick hand on her bare neck and then back to the wheel again. Concern settled in her brow at what explanation she'd give Mama about the injury, and worse, losing her grandmother's pearls, the whole prom disaster.

"So hot," Danny gasped from the backseat.

Patsy glanced back at Danny. She could see his chin tilted upward, his face glowing with a dampness.

"Hot. So damn hot, Patsy. Gotta get this noose off." Tugging at his bow tie, he clawed and cursed until he ripped it off his neck and tossed it up front.

She snapped her eyes back to the road. He looked feverish now, when just minutes ago he'd complained of being too cold. "Almost there," she said quickly.

"Did y-you an' him? Are you really preg—?" Danny asked low.

"*No.*" She kept her sight locked ahead.

"You swear it, Patsy? You swear on your dear kin's graves?"

"I love you, Danny. *You.* I can't wait for us to get away. I swear it!"

"People's been talking."

"People talked about you and Violet." She tossed back the blame, trying to keep her eyes on the road.

"Where, Patsy? Where'd he take you that day?"

"What did the nodding Violet say to you? Promise to give you? Her stuck to you like a drunk tick, whispering in your ear like that?"

"Where, Patsy?"

"You know Hollis took me straight home! I told you all that when you came over that night, and the next night after, and every night since then. Promised, same as you did when I asked you about Violet—"

"Dammit, Patsy, y-you're lying to me. I called at five thirty, and you still weren't home. Again at six."

"And I *told you* I was in the barn looking for a box of stuff I promised to find for Mama," she lied. "Now please hush with all that nonsense, Danny! I gotta pay attention here."

That much was true. Patsy and Hollis had argued a little

more on Ebenezer until she had run home, sneaking inside. She'd found supper warming in the oven and a note from Mama saying she'd gone out. Flannery wasn't home either; she'd stopped by Chubby Ray's with a few of the girls from baton club.

Not wanting to risk being seen in her state, Patsy disappeared into the barn, but only to hide out long enough till she was sure the liquor was good and gone from her. Long enough till she'd drained herself of the disgrace of what Hollis had done to her. She'd heard the whispers from a few girls about a home remedy that'd get rid of any baby that might've seeded. Frantic, Patsy searched and found the cure—an old jar full of her daddy's turpentine—and swigged it some, until she retched again and again.

"Patsy?" Danny said.

Patsy dropped a hand to her belly, pressed on her girdle beneath the layers of fabric, knowing. *It hadn't worked for her.* She and Danny needed to get married quickly. She couldn't risk waiting any longer. *The baby was born early,* was what she'd tell others. She'd heard the tales of how to spot the so-called early babies. "Look at its nails," old women gossiped. "Won't find nary a long nail on a true early." But she'd hide its hands in tiny mitts so they couldn't tell the baby had fingernails, had come to full-term, couldn't gossip that the corn had been planted before the fence planks were put up.

"Damn that sonofa—" A pain struck Danny, and he yelped. "Damn him trying to squeeze in on my girl—"

"Danny! *Please.* I'll have you there in a few minutes."

"I—I'll never be no use to anybody with a gimp shoulder. My nose. Oh, shit, my nose, too."

"They'll dig that bullet out of you, straighten your nose, and you'll be just fine, you'll see."

She snugged the automobile tight into dangerous Hospital Curve, fighting the play in the big steering wheel.

# CHAPTER 17

*Flannery*
*1972*

River breezes dipped into another sunny day; the tang of fish and muddy water filled the dank air. The warm weather brought out folks who'd heard about the old vehicle the fisherman had discovered.

Hollis broke away from the banks of the Kentucky and plodded toward Flannery.

He hadn't changed much since '52, just a little wider in the belt and a little fatter in the jaws, and even more naked, thicker in the stretch of neck he lacked.

"Is Jean here?" he asked, slightly bending over to look in the car windows.

"Mama's taken a spell. I've come for news on the car down there. Heard it was a Mercury," Flannery said straight out, trying to glimpse over his shoulder.

Hollis tucked his hands into his pockets, glanced down at the ground, answering her question.

She grimaced. "I prayed it wasn't."

After a minute, he said, "It's our old Mercury. Sure never dreamed I'd see it again. Never like this, anyway."

Flannery sucked in a breath.

"The fisherman who found it said he's been going to this same hole for damn near two decades. Said he could've reached over his canoe, dipped his arm into the water, and touched it all along in the low water these past months. He went to put his boat in this morning, and there it was, the red trunk poking up from the shallow Kentucky. This drought finally told us the truth."

Hollis stepped forward, touched her shoulder. "Could be it's empty, Flannery. Hell, could be anything. We won't know till they get it out and comb the inside. State police wrecker's winching it up now."

Flannery raised her head to the cliffs. It was highly unlikely the car had just driven itself off, floated downstream without leaving a trace of paperwork, and a whole lot more likely someone inside had lost control. She knew that Hollis's words were empty of hope.

"*Danny*," she whispered. "He must've wrecked it."

Hollis's face paled a little. He looked like he was turning his brother's name over, maybe even thinking about the last time he'd seen him, the last time he'd run into Flannery on Ebenezer. "You can wait at home—"

"I'm staying," she said, her eyes threatening to tear.

"You don't want to see this. Shit, we've pulled a lot of bad stuff from this river lately, and more than a few bodies. Better off waiting at home with your mama."

"I promised my mama I would bring her home. And if Patsy's down there"—Flannery pointed to the Kentucky—"I don't intend to waste another second just waiting and pining. I aim to take back news, and if the situation warrants, prepare for a burial this very afternoon."

It was almost a relief saying it. *Burial*. Relief she wouldn't have to go through another fake birthday.

"Let's not jump to conclusions," Hollis said, but Flannery knew he was thinking the same thing.

"Mama'll want to have a proper one, give her a nice service." Flannery tasted each word as it traveled from the heart to the tongue. "We'll need to have a funeral as soon as the officials give us the . . ." For a minute she couldn't imagine what the officials *would* be giving them. What remnants of young lives, what mottled human remains they might find in that crusted, old Mercury? Still there needed to be a ceremonial good-bye of sorts. An ending to wishing, the yearly birthday celebrations. The madness. Mama's and hers.

The whole town knew about the sham. The parties, the waiting. The disappointment and depression that followed Mama for weeks after, until she'd shake it off and start talking about the next year's celebration.

"Dad will want Danny buried in the Catholic cemetery," Hollis said. "If the kids are down there together, you and Jean might want to think about leaving them together that way. Be less talk knowing our families are together on this."

A deputy with a different county badge interrupted. "Excuse me, sir. Brought you a coffee." He handed the sheriff a Styrofoam cup.

"Thanks, Howland." Hollis took a small sip.

The deputy sipped from his own cup. "Sorry about all this, sir. I was hoping it weren't the Henrys' car. Thinking how terrible—"

Hollis nodded. "Thanks for the coffee. How's Ginny feeling? I know she had a headache when she left last night."

"Right as rain. Sure was a good get-together you threw yesterday, sir," the deputy piped, his voice picking up a notch as if he was relieved Hollis'd changed the subject. "Thanks for inviting us. Ginny's still talking about your vittles. All the fine things you do for the school kids."

Flannery raised a brow.

Hollis mumbled a thanks through the steam of his coffee.

The deputy told Hollis, "Mayor Conner said it was your best barbeque yet. One of your biggest. Said it was real generous of you to do all that, donate your home and all that food to raise monies for the high school like that. Yessir, thinking of them kids so they can have themselves a proper band and nice decorations for their big prom dance. Ain't right you have this in your lap, now." He squeezed Hollis's shoulder and slipped off.

Hollis smiled at Flannery, looked a little embarrassed, and

said, "I try to make sure the students have themselves a nice shindig at the end of the year."

"That's real nice, Hollis," Flannery said, meaning it.

"Just something I always wished for Patsy and Danny. Louise and I decided a while back, we'd make it happen for Glass Ferry's kids—have us a barbeque to raise the funds. They can have themselves a real band instead of a jukebox." He cleared his throat. "Flannery, Dad'll want those two buried—"

"Mama will want her on Butler Hill," Flannery said firmly.

Hollis shook his head and walked away.

Flannery lagged behind him, slipping past the small crowd of onlookers and over to the sycamore trees near the Kentucky's banks.

Hollis stopped to talk to a couple of state troopers, all the while keeping an eye on Flannery and the Mercury.

"Hell, are you kidding?" Hollis laughed weakly at something one of the troopers said.

The trooper said, "Yup, I missed my pool buddy this weekend. Gravey's Bar just wasn't the same without you, Hollis."

"Likely to be missing me a while if Louise has her way," Hollis told him, and snatched a more direct peek at Flannery.

Flannery turned away and pretended she wasn't listening, but snuck glances at the two, perked an ear to pluck their conversation.

"Your wife's still bent about the last time?" the trooper asked Hollis.

"That woman can light a meanness *anytime*." Hollis sighed loudly. "I was cleaning up the picnic tables after the barbeque, carrying in the dishes for her. Soon as I hit the door, here she came a'harping. I tried to get her out of my way, but she stumbled and twisted her ankle. Hell, all I wanted, Billy, was to get out of my clothes and pop me a cold one. But, damn, that beer cost me a week's salary what with the doctor bill." Hollis shook his head.

"Sorry, buddy," the trooper said.

Flannery gasped and moved a step away. She forced her attention back to the river. Bracing herself against a tree, she watched the tow truck driver try to secure the winch to the back of the Mercury. The man disappeared under the murky waters several times, attempting to attach the cable to the car's frame or axle or onto something that might work. After the third try, he got it hooked and pulled the lever on the winch, and the metal cable popped and tightened.

The old Mercury looked like a giant catfish poking up like that, still half-stuck, mud-soaked in debris and strangling algae.

The tow truck operator turned off the winch and restarted it again, but the old catfish wouldn't budge. The nose of the half-sunken Mercury clung to the muddy floor of the Kentucky, slowly pulling, sliding the wrecker back toward the water, the heavy engine weighing it down. Finally, the man took the smaller winch on the front bumper of the wrecker and wrapped its cable securely around the nearest big tree.

As the Mercury was pulled up and out onto the gravel boat ramp, dirty water and mud sloshed out from underneath, poured out of cracks. Sediment, muck, and other debris that was hard to pinpoint, oozed out of its metal cavities.

Flannery edged closer. She didn't notice Hollis had slipped up beside her. He gave a low whistle and said, "To think all that's been right under our noses all along."

Flannery strained for a better look, but couldn't see inside, what with every window, every door and opportunity coated in thick, foul-smelling sludge.

The big tow truck pulled the vehicle up the ramp and onto a small, grassy knoll. A group of law officials surrounded it. A trooper stepped forward and pushed the small crowd of advancing watchers back, behind some imaginary line, urging folks to keep clear, go on home, threatening to ticket anyone who disobeyed.

Soon the coroner and his men arrived.

The tow truck operator slowly began wiping down the doors, handles, windows, and windshield with rags and long squeegees.

Hollis started to walk over and join the other men, but Flannery touched his uniform sleeve, tugged. "I want to see when they open it."

He wrinkled his brow. "You can't mean—?"

"I've been waiting twenty years, and I mean every word. Take me over there with you. I have every right to see. To see the last place I know she was. The last place you said she was."

Hollis looked like he didn't have the energy or time to argue with her and nodded. "It's gonna be bad, and it's gonna get busy. Stay out of our way," he warned. "Us big dogs don't play much," he said in a stiff voice, again reminding her of that night in '52.

Flannery crawled into bed on prom night, telling a string of half-truths, pretending to Mama she had the cramps and that Chubby'd told her to leave.

Mama had come home a little after nine, surprised to find Flannery in her nightgown, lying in bed, cuddling the water bottle to her stomach.

At once, Mama got the slippery elm lozenges out of the medicine cabinet and handed the tin to Flannery.

"Thanks, Mama," Flannery said, taking out a lozenge and popping it into her mouth. She couldn't stand to look at Mama with all the fuss she was making over her, all the untruths threatening to bubble up any minute, breaking open their story. Patsy's and Danny's, and hers and Hollis's. It was so painful, she'd gotten herself a real whopping tummy ache for real.

"Let me go get you some more hot water in that, baby girl." Mama lifted the rubber bottle off Flannery's stomach.

"It's okay." Flannery tried to pull it back. "I know you want to get into your gown."

Mama waved away her protests. "We'll just make you some tea, too."

Flannery knew it wouldn't do any good to refuse.

Mama brought her some tea and the water bottle, then pulled the quilt up over her, tucking her in, telling her to sip some and get rested up.

When Mama finally abandoned her fussing with a good-night

kiss and left, Flannery leaned over and flicked on the nightstand lamp.

She waited a second, listening, before getting out of bed. Then she dug the pearls out of her apron. Inspecting them, Flannery wondered what she should tell Mama, if anything, and when. *No.* No, Flannery decided; she'd surprise Patsy and pull them out in front of her in the morning, leaving Patsy to explain why she went off with those two drunken fools in the first place, tore her sister's nylons, and stole Hollis's automobile. Teasing the boys. All that for *fornicating.*

*I'd know.* Surely I'd know, Flannery thought. Though she didn't know how, Flannery had always known things about Patsy before her sister shared them with her, just like Patsy knew things before Flannery told her.

There was her sister's first kiss. Patsy'd come home, giggling, and dragged Flannery up to their room. Flushed, Patsy whispered, "Guess what, tadpole? Guess!"

Flannery saw the secret in her twin's eyes and burst, "You've been kissed! What was it like? Who—"

Patsy laughed and grabbed her twin's hands and pressed a long, hard kiss onto Flannery's lips.

Shocked, Flannery's eyes widened, and Patsy nodded her head and sighed. "It was the dreamiest."

"Damn you, Hollis," Flannery said. *It'd be just like you to carry tall tales. Lying through your teeth.* Still, Flannery wondered about him being knocked out like that. Hollis had been so sure. What could've happened so horrible to make Patsy and Danny hurt him like that?

"You better get home and explain yourself, Patsy Butler," she said under her breath, "before Hollis gets his tongue to wagging—and I strike some choice ones off of mine."

Mama would blame Patsy for everything, for getting them fired, for the whole cursed night.

Flannery slipped the pearls back into her apron pocket alongside the lucky bullet, rubbing the shiny copper for extra measure. Looking over her shoulder, cocking an ear for Mama's footsteps in the hall, Flannery quietly pulled out her bottom dresser drawer and sat it on the floor. Carefully, she folded up her apron with the pearls and bullet inside and placed it against the back wall of the cubby, then slipped everything back inside its shelving, hiding her secrets.

*Maybe she'd even make Patsy wait a few days. See her squirm some. Patsy would never find the pearls until Flannery was good and ready to let her.*

Flannery tucked herself back into bed, keeping an eye on the dresser drawer, switching her gaze to the little bedside clock every few minutes. Soon she grew groggy and closed her lids.

It felt like she had been asleep only a short while when her mama woke her. "Get up, Flannery. Your sister's not home from prom," Mama said. "Baby girl." She shook Flannery's arm.

Flannery rubbed her sleepy eyes. Then, remembering everything, she pulled herself up onto her elbows.

"Patsy hasn't come home yet. Do you know where she could be?" Mama asked.

Flannery looked to the clock, reached over to the nightstand between the beds, and picked it up. "She's only an hour late, Mama." Flannery plopped back down, groaned. "It's only one fifteen."

Outside, gravel crunched and popped. A flash of lights slashed through the darkened bedroom, spilling across the walls and furniture. Then came the slam of an automobile door. And one more.

Mama switched on the lamp.

"There she is," Flannery said, burrowing her head back into the pillow.

Mama hurried over to the window and parted the sheers.

"Flannery, it's Sheriff Henry," Mama whispered over her shoulder. "Whatever could he want at this hour?"

Flannery bolted up from the bed and looked out the window with Mama.

Then Mama flew out of the room.

Scrambling into her robe, Flannery followed after her, peering over Mama's shoulder as she opened the door for Sheriff and Hollis. Hollis peeked around his daddy's shoulder, looking like he wished he could be anywhere but there, hands poked deep into his pockets, head hanging.

"Jean." Sheriff took off his hat. Mama stepped aside, motioning for him to enter.

"Jack, what brings you out at this hour?" Mama asked nervously, tightening the sash on her robe. "Is Martha okay?" She asked after the sheriff's wife.

Sheriff raised a hand. "Martha's fine, and thank you for the nice apple crisp you gave her to bring home from canasta tonight." He patted his belly in appreciation. "I'm here about Patsy."

"Patsy? My Patsy?" Mama looked at the sheriff and then to Flannery.

Flannery shrugged.

Sheriff pulled Hollis up to his side. "Yes. I'm sorry to say the kids were drinking."

"Drinking? Patsy wouldn't." Mama's eyes widened. "Jack, you can't mean—"

"Yes, ma'am, it appears they were. They got into a scrap with Hollis here and took off in the Mercury. Haven't been seen since."

"Oh. *Oh my.*" Mama pressed a hand to her chest.

"I've been looking some, but they're tucked tight outta sight so far," Sheriff said.

"I need to sit," Mama said.

Flannery grabbed Mama gently by the elbow. "Let's go into the kitchen and have a seat, Mama," she said, guiding her there, sneaking glances over her shoulder to Hollis.

The Henry men followed the Butler women. Flannery set Mama onto a chair and poured two glasses of water. One for Mama, one for herself. She didn't think to ask the sheriff if he wanted one.

Mama, always gracious, never forgetting her hospitality, above all, caught it and questioned Flannery's manners with her knowing eyes.

"Oh." Flannery raised her glass to the men, offering to get them a drink.

Sherriff and Hollis wagged their heads no.

Sheriff Henry started in. "Hollis went looking for them at the prom, but the teachers said they never showed up. He waited around most of the night." The sheriff looked at Flannery. "Did you see them down at Chubby's?"

Flannery couldn't speak, only shake her head and quickly gulp down her water.

"Flannery came home early," Mama piped.

"Yes. Yessir, I sure did," Flannery sputtered, and only that.

Hollis stepped forward and told Flannery's mama, "They clobbered me good."

Flannery hid her faked surprise behind the lip of the glass, chugging down more water.

Then Hollis looked at her and said what they had planned. "Took a whizz, and they off and split on me. Can barely remember it. Nothing." He rubbed his head.

Mama said, "Poor dear. Does it hurt?"

"Well, my ma put some Mercurochrome on it. Burned like the devil," Hollis said, a pity-poor-me dragging his bottom lip.

"I don't mean to frighten you, Jean." The sheriff laid a hand on her shoulder. "Most likely those two will come around once they've had their fun."

"*Fun,*" Mama turned the word over a worried tongue.

Sheriff gently cleared his throat. "When they, um . . . when they see the trouble they've caused."

"What in the world?" Mama said. "Trouble, those two?"

Mama had turned into a mockingbird, lost for words, shocked by the distastefulness of the choices her daughter, her good Patsy, had made that evening. "Inebriated, stealing automobiles, fighting," Mama said in a high voice, and pulled herself up from the table. "Jack, do you think they are in danger? Some sort of bigger trouble?"

Hollis hung his head, couldn't look at Flannery's mama.

"No, no," the sheriff assured her. "Danny and Patsy are smart kids. Good kids. You know how kids like to goof off at this age. They'll probably show up here any minute, wearing hang-dog looks and giving heartfelt apologies."

Mama stared hard at the door like the "minute" might happen any second now. "Whatever has gotten into those two?"

"If they don't come home shortly, I'll have my deputy go looking at first light. Don't you worry, Jean. I'll let you know." Sheriff pulled his hat back on and righted the brim, then made his way back to the foyer. "Let's keep the drinking amongst ourselves, Jean. Hmm? No sense lighting fast tongues."

All Mama could do was nod and follow the sheriff.

Hollis stayed behind, snatched Flannery close to his side, and whispered, "You're not telling, right?"

Flannery said, "You done told too much. Thought you were going to say you fell."

"My ma saw the cut. And it all spilled out before I could help it. You're gonna keep quiet, right?" Hollis gripped her shoulder, squeezing too tight. "Nobody wants to hear about a baby out of wedlock."

Flannery bumped him off. "Says only you! Mama's pretty worried. We should tell them what we know. I think we need to come clean, Hollis—"

"You saw your mama. If you care about her, you'll keep your trap zipped." He put his hand back on her shoulder.

"I—I don't know." Flannery jerked away and whispered, "I don't feel a bit right about all this. I think we should tell—"

Hollis caught her wrist. "You don't side with me, I'll get Danny to say Patsy's bastard belongs to a greaser who used to work with me—the punk who got picked up for stealing the distillery's tools. All on you. Nothing to do with me or Danny boy. *My family.*"

"Hollis," Sheriff called from the foyer, "say good night to Flannery. We've taken enough of the ladies' time."

"Shut up," Flannery hissed.

"Us big dogs don't play." Hollis released her from his vise grip. "And if you know what's good for you—"

"Let's get going, son," Sheriff Henry called out. "Good night, Jean. Try to get some rest. I'm sure they'll be home shortly. I'll be in touch."

Mama slipped into the rocker on the porch, watching and

waiting. "Lord, Lord," Mama said, and prayed. "Please let my baby be okay."

"Mama, come inside." Flannery pushed open the screen door and peeked out. "You know a watched pot won't boil, remember?"

"Yes, but a mother has to keep her baby's hand from its fire, too," Mama replied, keeping a sharp eye toward Ebenezer Road.

# CHAPTER 18

*Patsy*
*June, 1952*

Patsy pulled inside the curve, gripping the wheel so tight she could feel her nails pricking fatty flesh, burning a fire into her sweating palms. The tires slammed into something that made the front end shake and wobble like the fat Roly Poly clown toy Honey Bee'd given her when she was a baby.

Danny stirred and awakened the argument. "You better not have been h-helping *Hollis* s-s-slap his Sammy," he spit.

"Stop, Danny, just stop it." She fought to straighten the Mercury, flexed her hold on the big wheel. "Stop being ornery. Stop with the lies! You promised not to talk about him anymore when I promised not to ask about Violet—"

"You've been sick with the s-stomach ailments a lot . . . a whole lot lately," Danny slurred, coughing.

"My female spells is all. Hollis is a liar. A dirty, rotten, filthy liar. Look what he did to you, Danny. Look—"

"Don't you be l-lying to me," Danny said, struggling, pulling himself up to her back. He reached out and gave a slight tug to her hair.

"Danny, don't." She threw back her arm, then latched back onto the steering wheel.

"Hey, hand me that whiskey, baby." He hung heavy over her shoulder, groping for the flask lying on the seat beside her with his good arm. "Busted shoulder hurts like the dickens, Patsy."

"Be still." She batted him away. "We're almost there."

"Just one pull; it hurts." Danny couldn't reach the flask, and weak, he slumped back in pain, knocking Patsy's shoulder and head.

Patsy flinched and ducked, losing her tight grip. She pounded the brakes, pumping hard. The steering wheel shimmied in her slipping hands.

A startling image of a proud Honey Bee draping his protective arms over her shoulders, helping her sight in the snub nose, flickered before it waned, then Hollis's gun with the scratched-in initials.

Patsy's last thoughts rose up from her tightened throat and screaming lungs. Those of her hunger for Danny and a new life, hate of Hollis and his unborn baby . . . of lost pearls, proms, princes, and princesses . . . of the cold loneliness that would come from missing Mama and Flannery, and the coming chill.

She realized how damning her eight-minute-early arrival into the world had actually been—and thought to pray, call out her sins before the river claimed them.

"*Dear God,*" Patsy urged.

"*Oh-o—*" Danny breathed.

The automobile skidded, hit rock and skinned trees, somersaulting, tumbling down toward the night-blackened waters of the cold Kentucky.

"*Oh, Fatherrr—*" Danny hung his sobering prayer into the rot of dying air, the screams of squealing tires and hissing brakes.

"*God—*" Patsy cried out. Her head batted against the door, off the roof. Hard blows rocked her shoulders, her skull, bruising, crushing bones. Shards of metal and glass flew at her eyes and neck, blinding, burning, stabbing everywhere before God could collect her paralyzed prayer.

# CHAPTER 19

For twenty long years that murky river had been the Mercury's watery grave. Layers of silt mudded the protective coffin. Algae clung to the dented-in roof, draped over its sides and onto all the windows.

Despite being less than twenty feet away, Flannery couldn't see anything inside the mud-stuffed car.

Hollis had gone off for coffee and brought her back a cup. Grateful and needing a break, she sat down on the grass and drank it.

He cleared his throat as if to speak, and then hesitated like he wanted to chat for the sake of being polite, nothing more, though Flannery knew he wanted to say lots more. "How's the city?" he finally piped.

"Fine," Flannery said. "How's your family? Louise?"

Two weeks after they'd last met on Ebenezer, Hollis graduated high school and moved to Lexington. He started his first year of college (and his last) at the University of Kentucky, and met up with some college girl right from the start. But the girlfriend ditched him three months in, and talk from Hollis's roommate was that it happened after Hollis smacked her around.

He was one of those, Flannery knew. Just like her own ex-husband. The type of man who thought he had to display his manliness in order to be one. Always talking with closed hands on a woman to make himself feel bigger. Though, Hollis had most in Glass Ferry fooled.

Flannery had heard the talk, the high points, or rather lower ones, on her yearly trips home. Hollis and his roommate, another Glass Ferry boy, Cook Garner, had been drinking heavily in their dorm when Hollis's girlfriend, Jane, snuck into the boys' building. But not to see Hollis; to visit another boy.

Lap-legged drunk, Hollis spied them and took a tire iron to the boy, sending him to the city hospital. Hollis roughed up Jane too. And when Jane's daddy found out, he whipped Hollis's butt and demanded the dean kick Hollis out of school.

Soon after, Hollis had slipped into a howling despair and spent the next year freeloading off college pals, boozing it up, and fighting in bars tucked off gravel lanes, gambling in seedy juke joints out on country crossroads until his daddy put his foot down and snapped him back home.

A short time later in another county, Hollis met a girl at the Truth of God's Point Pentecostal tent revival that an old chum dragged him to. Hollis married her within four months, then had himself three babies before you could sweep the snow off as many springs.

"Louise is a'growing meaner by the minute." Hollis laughed, answering Flannery. "Ready to drop our fourth any day now. How's the teaching job?"

One of Mama's old canasta-playing friends, Alice Locke, interrupted and gave Hollis and Flannery each a plate lunch from her home. Two more townswomen pushed beyond the troopers and offered Hollis freshly baked cookies. "Sheriff Henry," one said, "you must be exhausted. Here you worked so hard feeding the town yesterday, now having to suffer this." She flicked an arm to the water. "Poor dear." She passed him the plate.

Hollis took a cookie, hiding a grateful smile behind a bite. "Mm. Thank you, Mrs. Winter and Mrs. Knightly. It's delicious, and you do mighty wonders for the sad soul."

Flannery declined the sweets.

The women disappeared back into the growing crowd.

Flannery's stomach had been lit from the nerves, her insides so twisted she could barely keep the coffee down. Still she did her best to take a tiny nibble of the meatloaf, gravy-covered potatoes, and butter beans before tossing it all into a bush. She stole away to the onlookers long enough to return the plate and thank Mrs. Locke again for her generosity and the tasty meal.

Gilly's Tow Truck Service worked hours on the car, trading their squeegees for brooms to clear off the thick coating. A spiderweb of cracks blanketed the windshield.

The state police and the sheriff's department and the coroner loitered around the old 1950 vehicle, watching it all, sneaking glances Flannery's way.

From a distance, an official-looking person, maybe a man from the local newspaper, Flannery guessed, took pictures of the Mercury, of Hollis, of her, and a lot of the folks behind them.

Then a lawman stepped forward and tried the partly caved-in door on the driver's side.

Flannery held her breath. The door wouldn't budge. The man jerked on the big metal handle again, then circled around to the other side and tried that door's handle without any luck.

The tow truck worker called out for a crowbar, and someone fetched one. Together those two worked on freeing the door, prying it loose until at last the Mercury creaked open, splashing out more river water and spilling muck and foul-smelling, slurry sediments onto the grass.

Flannery saw it on top of the grass, sticking out of a pile of mud. A scream cartwheeled in her throat, whisked off her tongue into a scratchy cry she didn't recognize.

Hollis must've seen it too. When she took a step toward it, he latched on to her arm and snatched her back.

Flannery slipped free and darted over to the Mercury. A state trooper caught her arm, and she broke his grip and dropped to the muddy ground, screaming wildly.

She plucked up one of her sister's leather Mary Janes and swiped away the gunk. The pretty organza bow Mama had made and fastened to Patsy's prom shoe was clumped in dirt, the inside packed full of more mud.

Flannery pulled herself up to her knees, slowly stood, and peered into the opened door.

The Mercury was cramped with mud, stacked thick and almost up past the steering wheel. Two necks of broken whiskey bottles poked up from the muck like headstones. Patsy's other shoe lay on the dash beside a billfold and a long, human bone.

Slowly Flannery looked to the rear. Someone from behind grabbed her and tried to pull her back. Flannery clung to the door frame, her eyes locked to the backseat.

A man yelled, "Get this woman outta here!"

Someone else hollered, "Secure this vehicle."

And another screamed, "Don't touch anything! Dammit, don't—"

But it was too late. Flannery's eyes touched everything, burning the memory into her, cutting through the stitches of sanity, branding her with a grief that balled up in her hot-white fists. A scream turned sideways and tightened in her windpipe.

Her wet eyes soaked it all up, every drop of mud, every speck of dirt, every inch of grime and what it tentacled—old bottles, Danny's leather belt, one of his black dress shoes with the odd penny plastered to its sole, Hollis's metal flask, and the parcel of two cracked and muddy skulls, resting in the back dash, wedged against the sloping window, locked eternally in a grotesque lover's kiss.

# CHAPTER 20

Flannery clung to Patsy's mud-filled prom shoe, its heel snapped and missing, as the men surrounded the car and carefully extracted the remains held within. Hollis tried to take it from Flannery, but she held on tight, and growled like a mean dog.

Around her the coroner's people sealed bone, bottles, and belts. Everything they could find and even things that couldn't be named were carefully wrapped in plastic and tucked into boxes labeled *Evidence*.

Flannery knew she looked like a crazy woman standing there gaping. For a short while the men didn't bother her and left her to soak in that madness, so full of the brokenness, they weren't sure how to approach. They moved around her, a mixture of fear, curiosity, and pity in their stolen glances.

Flannery thought about the bones scattered in the car. Patsy's painful death. *It's okay, Patsy. Don't cry, don't cry, sister; I'll do it for both of us now.* Flannery did, feeling like someone was tearing at her flesh, plucking the very bones off her body, snapping them in twos and threes.

After a while Flannery had spent her tears. Touching her swollen face, she swiped the mud off. Her clothes were filthy from the grime and the scattered mud around the car.

For years she had thought of, fought against, the nagging possibility that her sister, her *one and the same* might be dead, each time sweeping away those thoughts with more hopeful ones, imagining a happy family for Patsy somewhere else. Somewhere far away with the man she loved and who loved her back. But always the anger perked. The pent-up fury surfaced for Patsy leaving them like this, leaving Flannery here to fix Mama's broken heart and her own, leaving them all this time wondering.

Those angry thoughts would come and go over the years, leaving Flannery spent, weighted down for weeks, where she wouldn't talk to anyone unless she had to, answer her door or phone, or so much as stop to chat with her coworkers at school.

She looked around for Hollis.

A man came over and tried to pry the shoe from her, and she doubled over, clutching it firmly to her chest. "No, you can't have it. You can't have this one last piece of her."

The exasperated young man went off to get Mr. Flagg, the old coroner. Hurrying over to the gentleman wearing a dark suit, he pointed back to Flannery.

Another coroner's assistant hollered for Mr. Flagg to come quick. The assistant whistled and passed a large bone to the coroner, flicking muck and dirt off his vinyl gloves. "May have us a murder instead of a drowning, Roy."

Roy Flagg flexed his gloved hands and took it from the assistant, turning it over carefully and inspecting.

"See the bullet hole and bone shatter? Right there on the upper part of the humerus," the young assistant eagerly pointed out, announced excitedly.

"We're going to have to rake inside there, comb this whole area." The coroner frowned, looking around. "Secure this area. Only my two assistants, no one else."

"Murder?" Flannery walked up to the men. "Wh . . . what do you mean?" she asked, confused, throwing an arm up to the treetops as if the cliffs would right what she'd just heard. "It was a crash."

"Ma'am, you shouldn't be down here, and you should give me that." The coroner placed a hand on Flannery's shoulder, and she flinched and hugged the dirty pump closer to her shirt.

"It's not yours," she said. "And I'm taking it home. Taking part of Patsy home. Home to Mama."

"Miss," the old gentleman said softly and spoke slowly, "I'm

Roy Flagg, the county coroner from the coroner's office. I remember your daddy, Honey Bee. Sure miss him. Now don't you
look just like him, sweetheart."

Flannery's shoulders slumped some, and she let down her
guard a bit, feeding a tear into his soft words.

"Yessir, just like Honey Bee. What ya got there, sweetheart?
A shoe?" Mr. Flagg asked.

"It's Patsy's. But, what's this about murd—"

"May I examine it?"

Flannery shook her head and tucked it behind her back.
"Wh-whose limb is that, Mr. Flagg?"

"Right now, all I can tell you is that it looks like a male's.
Now please, miss. I can't speak about anything else right now.
I need to pack *everything* here and take it to the state medical
examiner to be tested. You'll need to step back, sweetheart, so I
can help you here, help put the deceased to rest."

"So you don't think it was an accident? Is that what you
mean—"

"We'll know in time. Now I need to do my job and collect
everything." He cocked his head to one of the troopers waiting
nearby. "The law says for me to collect everything here." He
talked to her like one would a young child. "Won't you help
me?"

Flannery eyed the two troopers standing around, realizing
they and the others could easily take the shoe from her. Behind
them, Hollis made his way over, an anger set in his brows, his
walk.

She held the shoe up to Mr. Flagg and he took it, but not before she'd sneaked and snatched off the little flower Mama had
made for it.

*I have to keep it.* She needed to hold on to something, to
some piece of Patsy, no matter how small. Hold something that
said this was all real. Take a part of Patsy back home, a missing
part of herself. Flannery closed a fist over the muddy clump of
tattered threads, moving her hand behind her back.

Mr. Flagg handed the shoe over to his assistant and dismissed
him.

"I'm sorry for your loss, young lady. And your mother's, of course," the coroner told her. "We'll take good care of this, and get everything back to you as soon as we can." Turning to Hollis, he added, "Mighty sorry, son. I'm glad Martha isn't alive to see this."

Hollis hung his head at the mention of his mama who had died a decade ago.

"I'll be in touch," Mr. Flagg said to him. "Please give my condolences to your father." The coroner lightly patted Hollis's shoulder before heading back into the small crowd of officials.

When the coroner was far enough away, Hollis took Flannery's arm. "Why don't you go home and let these boys do their job."

"They said something about murder, Hollis. *Murder.*"

"What? What are you talking about?" Hollis peered over his shoulder to the Mercury.

"How could that be?" she asked.

"I don't know. But it sure as shit wasn't no murder, peaches. Now you need to go home to Jean. I can have my deputy drive you."

"I can make it okay," Flannery said, suddenly thinking about her mama. *Mama. How would she tell her; what would she say?* It would be rough telling her Patsy would never have another birthday, take all Mama's hope like that. Flannery felt the horror rise up.

Hollis saw it too. "Maybe I should see you home. I can talk to Jean with you—"

Flannery stiffened, remembering the last talk that had taken place, the night of the prom. "I'll be okay. When do you think they'll hand over the remains?"

Hollis grimaced. "Soon as they sift through the bones. They'll need to photograph, identify, and sort them."

A trooper came up behind them and tapped Hollis on the shoulder. "Can I talk with you a sec, Sheriff?"

Hollis moved away, and Flannery sneaked closer to the assistants who were working their way around the car. She watched quietly, listening to them describe items they'd sealed into plastic.

Minutes later, one of the coroner's assistants piped up. "Found something, Roy."

Flannery turned to the voice and stepped up even closer, cat-like, toward the man, stretching sideways to steal a peek, listen in.

The assistant held up Patsy's other prom heel in one hand and a bullet in the other. "Bingo," he said, placing the muddy shoe to the side. "Damn. Would you look at that, Roy," he marveled, unaware of Flannery. "The river sure keeps a strange grave. Found it crammed inside this mud-caked shoe." He wagged the bullet and then dropped it into a plastic bag with bits of other small debris, jiggling the sack before passing it to the coroner. "Those two had trouble on their tails, sure enough."

Flannery heard the bullet's tiny clatter in the sudden quieting; the sound pulsed loudly in her memory. Hollis's voice on old Ebenezer Road back then, her fevered lucky wishes, and the clapping of pearls against the shiny bit of hard luck she'd pocketed it with that night.

# CHAPTER 21

Feeling faint, Flannery dropped her head and reached out an arm. Hollis rushed over and grabbed it. Carefully, she straightened with his help, unsure of her footing.

"I better see you home right now," Hollis said, his face rinsing of color.

"No," she said, struggling to pull herself out of the haze. "I can see myself home—"

"Don't worry. I'll have my deputy drive your car out to Jean's tonight. I'll follow him and make sure he gets it back safe to you."

Reluctantly, Flannery handed him her keys.

They drove in silence back through the Palisades. Flannery stared out at a whir of passing mountain rock and scraggly trees.

After a bit, Hollis said, "That bullet could've come from anywhere, you know? We don't want to alarm folks. We have to stick to what we told back then. For our families' sake."

Flannery shook her head. "We need to tell them what you know. Should've told them everything back then on prom night. Everything."

Hollis tightened his grip on the steering wheel. "Flannery, think how it would crush our families, your mama hearing about your sister's . . . well, your sister's indecency like that."

"It's indecent *not* to tell," she huffed.

"Not to tell everyone what? That we're burying the town tramp?"

"How dare you."

"You don't know what you're saying, Flannery. To drag up old hard feelings like that. I'd have to tell everything. I've got a wife and kids to think about. A good, decent job here."

"This isn't about your decency. You have to tell now. Someone was shot, and someone else did the shooting."

"It's likely Danny did it playing around."

"We can't be sure someone didn't aim to hurt them. You don't get shot in the arm playing around. I think someone did this."

"Can't think of a soul who would wanna hurt those two."

"I didn't see him toting a gun that night. Only you. Where did he get the gun to play around with, Hollis? Huh?"

"Dammit, Flannery! He had himself an old .22. Shit, you know my family." He cut a worried eye to her. "Us Henry boys have always had guns. We grew up carrying guns around with our teddy bears before most babes can suck a month off their pacifiers." Hollis shifted uncomfortably in his seat, glanced out the car window.

"You're the sheriff. You need to go right back there and tell about prom night. About the fight. About the drinking. You—"

"Quit harping on me, dammit!" Hollis stuck up a hot hand and banged it on the steering wheel, making Flannery sink back into the seat.

"You need to listen to me on this one, peaches," he snapped, slamming his fist down on the dash twice, "and shut your big flap. Shut it."

Instinctively, Flannery raised a hand to shield her face, shrinking back against the door.

Her ex-husband behaving like that and worse, countless times, surfaced like a striking rattler. It didn't matter that she had long since left him. It didn't take much to rise the fear. She had struggled mightily to shed that history. But no matter how much she tried, something as harmless as the unexpected slam of the door from a burst of wind or a dropped dish or the pop of a bottle cap brought it screaming back, the terror, the overriding fear of what would come next. It'd been many years, but it felt as raw as yesterday.

"H-Hollis," she tried to breathe.

"Shut up about old history," Hollis ordered with a final thump to the dash. "That's nothing but school-yard shit, and ain't half of it true."

The summer of '52 came and lingered in Glass Ferry with no word of the missing teens, and nary a peep from Patsy.

Flannery longed for any sense of normalcy, for school even, looking forward to September. She and Mama barely slept, keeping at least one ear cocked for the telephone to ring, a window to open, or a door to shut. Hoping.

During the day, Mama kept the curtains drawn tight. She wouldn't let any of her canasta-club ladies come visit, telling Flannery to send them away when they tried. Keeping her teen daughter inside, refusing to let her walk to town or see anyone herself.

If Flannery argued to go out, Mama would cry, scaring Flannery into silence. When the twins' birthday rolled around, Mama surprised Flannery and pulled back the drapes. Then Mama baked Patsy a strawberry cake, the first one.

Flannery had been so relieved to see Mama up and moving, lit up like that, she'd passed on Mama's offer to make a birthday pie for her own celebration.

Mama was sure the birthday cake would summon Patsy home. And soon the house was festive with their chatter. "Go bring up my music," Mama said, sending Flannery down to the cellar for the old records she'd stored after Honey Bee's death.

Flannery scampered downstairs. She remembered how scared Patsy was of the dark cellar. How her sister would cry if she had to go down there alone. How Honey Bee'd used busted tombstones for the cellar floor because concrete was so expensive. He'd collected and hosed off the crumbly gravestones to "keep you from carrying the dirt upstairs to Mama's nice rugs."

Honey Bee and Uncle Mary had gone over to Pleasant Hill to see the folks called the Shakers. The religious group sold pieces of spent and busted tombstones, the ones that were old and broken, erecting new ones for their dearly departeds. Honey Bee covered the entire cellar floor with the Shaker gravestones.

But in order to turn on the light down here, you had to stand on Polly Meachum's headstone, the pitted slab rugged under the dangling bulb at the bottom of the stairs.

Patsy'd claimed her legs pricked with a rash, darn near buckled, every time she yanked on the light chain. That the young girl, Polly, was reaching up to snatch her away to the dead. Patsy mused Polly'd surely died of boredom, same as the rest of those boring deceased folk in Pleasant Hill, Kentucky, after Honey Bee had come home talking about the ways of the peculiar folks.

Honey Bee and Uncle Mary told Mama that the Shakers didn't believe in getting hitched. They thought God was both a man and a woman, so all folks were made the same as Him. "All of us are brothers and sisters," the Shakers proclaimed to Honey Bee and Uncle Mary that day, and they'd insisted it would be a sin to marry your relations like that. Have babies with your kin.

Honey Bee'd said the Shakers were simple folks, smart farmers, but for all their religion, and it was indeed mighty, they sure knew how to put a fever in their feet and kick up a heel or two.

"Saw 'em grab the Hallelujah in their bones and shimmy like the devil with its tail caught under Heaven's porch rocker," Uncle Mary'd said. "Shakers they be."

At the bottom of the cellar steps, Flannery reached a hand down and scratched furiously at her itching leg, snagging her nylons. Sighing, she yanked on the light, eager to get Mama's records. She thought about the Shakers' simple life, and how Patsy liked to make fun of them.

Flannery knew her sister didn't want simple, didn't want to be a farm wife, Patsy wanted a smart businessman, tall, red dance heels, fun friends, and a fancy Sears Modern home in a pretty place that didn't stink of bourbon. Flannery worried that Patsy might never come home.

"Flannery," Mama called from the top of the steps, "don't forget Jelly Roll Morton."

"Found it," Flannery said, spotting it atop the stack of albums on the shelf. Honey Bee had picked up a lot of records in his business travels downriver.

Happy for Mama's changed mood, Flannery toted the records

up from the cellar for the birthday celebration and plopped them on Honey Bee's old cellarette in the parlor. She cranked up the Victor record player in there and put on all of Mama's favorite music. Spun Cab Calloway tunes for her, played Joe Turner's "Low Down Dirty Shame Blues," and watched Mama light her itchy soles with some fancy footwork when Slim Gaillard's "Palm Springs Jump" swept through the room.

It was the very best birthday present Flannery could've had, seeing her Mama living and the life lit in her feet like that. The first of many of the false celebrations.

And a week later when the cake still sat on the counter, Patsy's sixteen white-striped candles cemented in the pink icing, Mama's mood changed, the curtains were drawn again, and Flannery pleaded with Mama to call the doctor. "Mama, I heard the doctor can fix all kinds of ailments, and he has medicine—"

"Will his pills bring Patsy home?" Mama said, saddened, tamping the discussion.

Sylvia Jenkin came over three times that summer and probably snooped a lot more that Flannery didn't know about. Twice with her husband, Davey. Mama looked at Flannery and pulled her into the dark hall, tapping a hushing finger to her mouth as the neighbors knocked on the front door. In a moment, Mr. and Mrs. Jenkin went back to the kitchen door.

Flannery poked her head around the corner. Slinking up to the windows, the Jenkins cupped their hands to the glass, peering inside.

Mr. and Mrs. Jenkin were troublesome neighbors, "busybodies," Mama and Honey Bee told the girls long ago. Meddlesome folks who worried and wormed their way into other people's affairs, pretending to be helpful. Until no one was looking. Always doling out advice with a Bible in one hand and a gun-cocked finger in another, the Jenkins had a need to feel almighty.

Childless, the Jenkins would yell at the twins if they wandered onto their property, chase Flannery and Patsy off, or scold Mama if the girls' laughter carried too high a pitch. Once the neighbors sent a note to the girls' teacher, complaining about their tomboyish ways after they'd climbed the chinaberry tree down the road.

Honey Bee was sure the difficult neighbors had poisoned his beloved cattle dog after the old pooch dug a hole in their flower bed to escape the heat on a summer day.

"There's a name for those kind of folks," Honey Bee'd said, "a name good folks don't say but they all know, and it comes from the most disgraceful part of a foul person."

Then Honey Bee would mutter under his breath, "Liddle dirty diddle-dicks," until Mama had to shush him, run him out of the room with a snapping dish towel she always had stuck in her apron pocket, taking halfhearted licks to his tucked hip and head.

With Patsy gone, Mama wandered the old house endlessly like a ghost looking for its haunt, calling the bones of their dwelling awake with her restless pacing throughout the nights, her breaths of despair filling wall-to-wall, rinsing the corners and crevices with her tears.

Flannery knew the house itself was miserable. It shifted differently, popped and screeched, wriggling its bones from the weight of all that sadness. Flannery begged Mama to have the ladies over so the two of them could bake cookies and forget about Patsy, just for a while. Asked to go to town so she could see some kids from school since they lived too far out for classmates to come calling.

"Come on, Mama. A little company. *Please*," Flannery whittled. "Or, let's dress up in those pretty little circle dresses you made last fall. Put on our gloves and go to town. We can take a ride to Lexington and see the window dressings downtown. Maybe a trip to Joyland—"

"I'm too tired, Flannery." Mama brushed the thoughts aside. "And it's stingy to think of yourself when your sister could be in trouble out there."

Flannery hadn't been to Joyland since Honey Bee'd passed. She thought of holding Honey Bee's strong, leathery hands, strolling amongst the booths, seeing the rides and all the happy folks with the smells of summer lit in cotton candy, hot dogs, onions, and sweaty excitement.

He'd taken the whole family many times, mostly on the last day of the season when the park would give away a shiny new automobile to one lucky visitor.

Patsy and Flannery had ridden the carousel with the big, sparkling gold and blue horses. Flannery loved the carousel. On the hottest days, the horse and saddle felt cool on her skin. And always later the girls would dare each other to ride the big wooden Wildcat roller coaster.

They'd go off together on the Pretzel canal ride favored by the older kids, eagerly climbing inside the metal cart that promised a mysterious trip into a cool, dark tunnel. In the channel they were spooked by the sudden and loud, creaky noises, panicked by loudly clanging cymbals, and unnerved by the film of thin, creepy hanging threads, until the cart glided around the last bend for an abrupt but terrifying glimpse of a wooden cutout of a bucking billy goat. Flannery always had to beg Patsy to ride it with her. She just couldn't do it alone even though Patsy was sure to suffer nightmares for a week or more after.

Nothing changed over the years, but going to Joyland always seemed like her very first visit. And nothing beat the pool either. During the summers the twins had taken some free swimming lessons offered by the park. Though Flannery had learned to swim in the river, it was still a blast to dip into the big Joyland pool whose signs boasted that swimming in it was like "swimming in drinking water."

At night, Joyland brought in famous singers like Duke Ellington and Benny Goodman to their dance hall. For a fifty-cent admission adults could have themselves a big shindig.

One summer, a townswoman, widow Nester Parrish, joined the Butler family at the park. After a full day packed with swimming and rides, Mama and Honey Bee went dancing that night inside the Joy Club, leaving the twins in Nester's care.

Flannery and Patsy got to see the amusement park all lit up, and when Nester wasn't looking, the girls peeked inside the dance hall and saw Count Basie playing to a packed dance floor full of twisting, hopping, jitterbugging adults.

The girls had caught the fever too, all riled up, shimmying and dancing together under the twinkling Ferris wheel lights, giggling and singing until Nester threatened to turn the little heathens over her lap and whoop them a good one.

Thinking about the old days like that made Flannery press Mama again.

"Mama, come on, let's go back to Joyland. *Please,*" Flannery said, digging in harder. "It's too sad waiting around like this. Joyland's a short drive. A fun day away. Summer is nearly gone. It'll be fun, and if Patsy comes home—"

"*Flannery Bee.*" Mama warned the discussion was wearing her.

"We could have your ladies over and chat some?" Flannery pushed harder. "Please, Mama. I'll make some Benedictine sandwiches and mix the punch for your card game. You can fix your deviled eggs, and oh, some of your orange pound cake would be nice. *Please.*"

Mama wouldn't budge and dug deeper into her despair.

It nearly drove Flannery crazy, and at times she was sure she'd done went and caught it. Sometimes Flannery slipped outside and ran down to the barn. Inside, Flannery would kick and cry her pent-up howls, soak the worm-worn rafters and dirt floor with her helplessness, cursing Patsy for the nightmare she'd left Mama and Flannery to live with.

"Patsy," she'd cry, "how could you do this to us, how could you? Damn you! Damn you to Hell for leaving me. Come home now!"

And in a while Flannery would plead and beg God, "Bring her home, Lord, bring Patsy back to us. Keep her safe and lead her home."

Then splintering her pleas, Flannery'd bargain. "I promise to be the best sister. Promise to take care of her and treat her like the queenie she is if You'll only just return her to us. Just *please, please* give me back my sister, and I'll never be jealous or angry with her or You again. Please, God, please."

One day, Mrs. Henry stopped by. Flannery rushed out to the porch to greet the sheriff's wife before Mama could snatch her daughter back inside. It didn't look like Mrs. Henry was faring any better than Mama. Or herself. She had a dish in her unsteady hands. "I brought you and Jean some of my chicken corn casserole."

"Mama's resting," Flannery told her, dying to know if she had any news.

Mrs. Henry handed Flannery the dish and pushed back the flowery scarf covering her head, letting it hang off her shoulders. Flannery could tell Danny's mama had been "resting" too. The worry over her missing son had kept her confined to the house, left her with dark bags under her eyes. Mrs. Henry stood there balling up the side of her pretty, blue-blossomed dress. She looked frailer than the last time Flannery had seen her at Spanks Grocery a few weeks before.

"Thank you, ma'am," Flannery said. "Uh, is there any word about my sister? Danny?"

Mrs. Henry shook her head. "No, I thought I could ask the same?"

"No, ma'am. Nothing."

"Flannery, I've been thinking. Is there anything Patsy might've said that night about leaving Glass Ferry? Hinted where she might've gone?"

The question struck a nerve. Flannery and Hollis hadn't rehearsed that one. It made lots of sense for Patsy to have hinted, to have packed something if she and Danny had planned to run away. It'd be best to take the easy way out. "I don't recall Patsy saying anything about leaving, ma'am."

"Are you sure they didn't mention where they were headed to?" Mrs. Henry looked at Flannery, her soft brown eyes desperate. "Anybody say—"

"Nuh-uh. I . . . Uh, no, ma'am." Flannery felt the lie bloom on her cheeks. "I've been here, helping Mama."

"Have ya heard anything? Any kids talking? Anything? A letter from her?"

For a second, Flannery wanted to tell. Tell Mrs. Henry everything she and Hollis hadn't. "Nothing, like I told Sheriff. Maybe Hollis knows some of Danny's friends who might know more?"

"Hollis has left for the university. He hasn't called much. His father is still looking for the missing automobile—and no one's seen it."

For the first time ever, Flannery thought about leaving too, thought about going to school in the city. Getting herself a higher education to snag one of those fine secretarial jobs like the ones the teachers raved about. Leave this old town. Maybe go to work at the Stagg distillery downriver. Flannery'd heard the talk, how the company was getting bigger, and liked hiring educated folks and smart females for their secretaries. Who knew, maybe she could open a liquor store and saloon, get herself a bartending license like Abraham Lincoln had done over in Illinois. After all, if a president could do that, it surely was a smart thing to do.

"We haven't heard a word, Mrs. Henry. Sorry, ma'am."

Mrs. Henry grimaced. "How is Jean?"

Flannery looked over her shoulder to the door. The sheriff's wife grabbed hold of Flannery's hesitation. "Maybe I'll send the doctor out," Mrs. Henry said. "I'm sure he'd like to see how she's doing. Might have some tonic for her ailings."

"Yes, ma'am, that'd be real nice. Mama's been a little peaked. Well, I . . . I better get this food inside and check on her." Flannery patted the casserole lid. "Smells real good. Thank you. We'll return the dish soon."

The doctor came by, but he didn't seem concerned with Mama's withering state. He told Flannery the *rest* would do her good, then left pills to help with her female nerves too. The doc peered over his thick glasses, studied Flannery, and said, "If yours act up some, you can take half a pill with your meals, same as her. Mighty fine for the female hysterics." Then he wrote the instructions on the bottle and left.

Many times Flannery fell asleep on Patsy's bed, hoping she would awaken to find her sister across from her. That Patsy would again be able to raise a fuss, telling her to get her lazy bones into her own bed. And Flannery would yell back at her twin for leaving, but then they'd make up, and everyone, especially Mama, would be happy.

Each morning Flannery awoke to silence, rousing to a startled hopelessness, her heart knocking her fully awake, her thin gown soaked in panicked sweat. Hollow, she'd beat the pillow and mattress with her fist, damning Patsy for abandoning her, screaming inside herself for her sister to come home. When Flannery wore out her bruising knuckles, she grabbed her baton out of the closet.

One morning in late August, Flannery stood breathless over the bed, slamming the short metal rod against the feather pillow, again and again, tearing the ticking, whacking until she couldn't lift the baton another inch. Couldn't drag another ugly fit across those silent sheets one more day.

She watched the feathers sail into the charged air for a good while, fearing she'd gone mad. Flannery thought about her sister crying in school for her when they were young. Clung to the one thing she could always count on Patsy for. Clawed to keep it. If she could hold on to that till Patsy came home, it would keep the insanity away.

Who would care for Mama if they toted Flannery away, locked her in an asylum like the one way out off State Road 80? Mama was already as good as there in her folly; Flannery knew folks were speculating, talking. How else would Mrs. Henry know to send the doctor around if they weren't?

Flannery tried to fill her mind with sensible, calm things to keep her sanity, but soon it would all slip and she'd push her angry face into the pillow, or bark wretched sobs into a pile of bed linens, fearing Mama or anyone else would see she had caught the madness.

School started in September, and Flannery was more than ready to escape the house and Mama. Excited to push through her senior year, yet scared she would be doing it without her twin.

She had not done a single thing alone, Flannery realized, and with that thought her stomach grew queasy, and she had to run to the bathroom.

Flannery had barely slept the night before her first day back, up several times emptying her nervous stomach. She dreamed Patsy had come dragging in. Same ol' Patsy, but in a new pink dress, all darling and dazzling, wearing her pearls and carrying schoolbooks. And Mama'd never said a word. Not one in her dream. Just sent Patsy off to school with a big piece of strawberry cake. The dream roused Flannery from her sleep, and it had felt so real she jumped up and checked the drawer where she'd stashed the pearls.

But it was only that, a dream. Flannery walked alone on the first day of school.

A carload of boys slowed just enough to toss out a jar and a curse. "*Bootlegging floozy.*"

"If you're gonna drink 'shine, Luke Spears, at least make it better than that nasty cat piss your daddy sells," Flannery yelled at them, booting the empty Mason jar of hooch out of her way.

Spears stuck his arm out of the window and raised his middle finger.

Flannery and Patsy were used to the kids' teasing about moonshine, getting railed upon despite Honey Bee's good reputation, his business license, and the hills being full of bad bootleggers like the Spearses. It wasn't a big deal except to the kids whose parents had found other jobs, who thought they were better off finding a different trade that might make them richer: mechanic, shop owner, preacher, or such.

Most everybody in Glass Ferry had kin who were, or who had been in the whiskey business. It was a way of life here, food on the table, a roof over heads, a means of survival. And it had been that way for her parents in the '20s and '30s and their parents and those ancestors who'd started before them with the old, squatty turnip-pot stills.

Mama'd enjoyed the money from it until Honey Bee got sick and before the sheriff began taking more food from their table with his higher protection fees. *The taxes.*

Even Violet Perry's preacher daddy was the son of a moonshiner, but he'd snuck and bought the best spirits off Honey Bee instead of from his kinfolk.

Some kids had lost relatives who'd been killed in moonshining raids. And more than a few teachers had husbands working at the legal distilleries downriver, and even more kin lighting illegal stills tucked way up in the hills—with one family going so far as to dig a room-sized cavern into the grounds of their family cemetery, then covering it with borrowed tombstones to hide their operation down there from the government agents.

"There's a lot worse things a man could become in this dark, bloody Kentucky land," Honey Bee'd said. "Kentucky without its whiskey men, its stills, would be like New York City without business suits and buildings."

But everyone knew being a floozy—a mother having a baby out of wedlock—was the very worst a girl could become around here.

Flannery wished she had fixed the flat tire on her bicycle before school started. She picked up her pace and hurried down the road.

"Heard tell Patsy ran way." The kids in the school lot pushed and poked for answers. "Heard she ran off to marry Danny," they whispered. "Heard why, too." They looked over their shoulders for teachers, snuck hands to their bellies and poked them and then one another for amusement.

Violet Perry perched on the rail leading into the school building. She wore a tight new sweater she'd pinched her falsies into despite the hot September day. Her friend Bess leaned in beside her. Violet pointed her finger and said under her breath, but loud enough for Flannery to hear, "Imagine we won't be seeing Patsy again until that bread in the oven is good an' done."

Bess smirked. "Maybe a tad longer. Loaves from *two* bakers might need to bake extra long."

"Don't you know it," another girl squeezed in and smarted. "What with two bakers there's no telling how many are in that twin's oven."

"Humph, twins, have you ever?" someone else squeaked. "My mama said it ain't natural for a woman to have a litter like that. Them's circus freaks."

"Dumb bootleggers," Violet muttered.

"Like your kin," Flannery said low.

Violet glared.

"She'll come back a'toting," the girls pecked. "Toting a double stack of diapers."

"Ew," one girl said. "My daddy hadn't never seen twins 'fore the Butlers and says it's bad luck for folks and only fit for beasts to birth more than one at a time."

Flannery hated how they were the only twins around, the only ones that folks from around here had ever seen, despite Mama insisting it was doubly good.

"My girls have what others don't," Mama had told them. "An extra life inside them, another branch, reaching, sheltering the other, like God's angels protecting this old earth when He's busy. Look after each other, girls." She'd hugged and reminded them when they worried about their peculiarity.

Flannery and Patsy'd been relieved last winter when they heard about a set of boys born two counties over on New Year's Day. "1952's newest babies are, of all things, twins!" the radio announced.

Flannery growled at the girls' bad-mouthing Patsy like that and pushed past them, biting down on her tongue.

"Flannery Butler," the girls called after her, "where's Patsy *Baker?*" Their laughter trailed.

Inside, Flannery headed to her classroom. A few girls from baton practice huddled together in the hall. They shot Flannery nervous smiles, but never called her over.

Wendell Black spotted her and raised a shy hand. Flannery stopped and tossed one back. For a second it looked like he might come over and talk to her. Then her freshman teacher, Mrs. Goebal, called, motioning Flannery to her side. "You look lost. Looks like you lost your other half, Miss Butler. Did Patsy join the circus with that clown Danny?" She chortled low with another teacher locked beside her in a classroom doorway.

The gossip punched to the bone. At that, Flannery drew back her shoulders, screwed her face, and lit a look that meant to do a'cuttin'. Slipped the teacher the meanest eye she could muster for trashing her sister's good name.

Mrs. Goebal dropped her jaw and pressed a hand to her chest. "Well, I never," she exclaimed, patting. "*Heathens*." She snatched Flannery's sleeve. "I should paddle you."

But something in the hardness trapped in Flannery's eyes made the woman release her.

When Flannery got home from school that afternoon, she found Mama on the porch, upset, clutching something wrapped in cloth.

"What is it?" Flannery said warily, grabbing the wooden porch rail. "What you got in there, Mama?" She lumbered up the steps with her schoolbooks and set them on the rail.

"Those awful kids," Mama said. "They came speeding down the drive, and one of them jumped out and threw this on the porch. I was resting, but I came running when I heard them whooping it up out here. I saw the two Scott boys and the Franklin girl in that old green pickup of the Scotts."

"Bess Franklin," Flannery said.

"Yes, that's her. Violet Perry's friend. See what they left? Look, Flannery. *Look* . . ." Mama worked up a wail and shoved the lumpy package in her daughter's face.

Flannery peeled back a dirty blanket and saw the small baby dolls, their bald, rubber heads marked in thick, tomato-red paint that read *PATSY'S BASTARDS.*

# CHAPTER 22

"Nothing but school-yard shit then and nothing that needs attention now," Hollis repeated, thumping the dash again.

"It was more than that," Flannery whispered. "That's your brother and my sister in your car."

"It's over, dammit. I'm not going to be hurt anymore," Hollis said, pressing down on the gas, eager to drop her off.

"We're all hurting." Flannery tried to reason with him.

All those hurtings eventually drove Flannery away. In her senior year at Glass Ferry, she'd kept her nose in the books, earning good grades and the principal's favor.

Before the ink dried on her high school diploma in '53, Flannery fled Glass Ferry for the city and the University of Louisville.

Mama'd cried and begged Flannery to stay. And if the principal hadn't intervened on Flannery's behalf, she surely would've been stuck. In the end the principal called Mama and insisted that Flannery should have the higher learning so Glass Ferry could get themselves a new teacher. Mama sold some of Honey Bee's things to pay for that learning, and soon Flannery left.

Getting miles away from Glass Ferry and her mama's sadness, from those rumors and half-truths of small-town living, helped some.

In Louisville, Flannery kept her eyes peeled for a glimpse of her missing sister. But it wasn't long till she forgot, hardly bothered, and only then if a familiar sound or sight jolted her into remembering to be on the lookout for Patsy. She pretended to be an only child to those she met. And soon she believed it. *Isn't that what Patsy was doing, probably at this very second?* Flannery always rationalized.

A sound sleep still was difficult to get. Class work in Latin and geography seemed easy enough, but Flannery still missed more than a few lessons. It was hard to memorize all the Latin grammar rules, rivers, mountains, and country capitals when she couldn't fall asleep sometimes until near morning.

But the one class she'd roll out of bed for in her sophomore year, be on time for no matter what, was better than all the rest. His name was Mark Hamilton, a visiting lecturer for one of her sociology courses. He talked soft and slow like Honey Bee, reminded her of him and the other kind but strong menfolk back home. "I'm in ministry training across town at the Southern Baptist Theological Seminary." His words slid all over her. "From Alabama now, but as the son of missionaries who struck out early in cotton and other goods, I've been all over," he'd said at the start of that first class. A dreamy Ashley Wilkes-looking fellow, everyone thought.

He invited questions after class. She found one, though the second she asked, it was lost to his boyish smile, his big green peepers. And when he looked at her like no one else had, she felt alive. His eyes roamed appreciatively, more boldly and unapologetically than those of others had, and for once she knew she looked like Betty Grable, her flat tires aired nicely.

They'd stood there for a few sparking seconds, taking each other in, when he grabbed his jacket and said, "Let's go get coffee, and I'll give you a better answer."

"Let me powder my nose," she practically sang. Inside the bathroom, Flannery freshened her makeup and at the last minute reached under her sweater and rolled up her skirt. She gave the waistband another tuck, looked at her legs. Just another inch, enough that she hoped he'd notice.

Shifting her weight, she popped out a knee and inspected. Her nylons had been cleaned just last night with the Lux Flakes that Betty Grable advertised on their box, washed gently with the tiny diamond soap flakes. Flannery smoothed down her skirt and smiled.

Coffee turned into lunch, a lazy stroll around the campus, and then a fine steak dinner at a restaurant called Hasenour's, the fancy kind of place she'd read about in books.

Inside the darkened restaurant foyer, Flannery looked beyond to the black leather booths tucked along ruby-red walls against a backdrop of tall, gleaming mirrors that circled a large room in a dizzying display.

Flannery touched the pearl button at the top of her pale yellow sweater, nervously tugged.

Mark whispered something to the maître d', and, without hesitation, the man led the couple into the big dining room.

Crystal goblets and silver sat atop red linen-draped tables. The tinkling of fine dishware and soft chatter of folks floated across the room.

This was not the darkened cellar of the Seelbach. The expensive cigar, aged bourbon-soaked, whispery room that Thomas had treated her to. Appreciatively, Flannery took in her surroundings. Fancy-dressed people were served by men who were all gussied up like dandies. This was something bigger, a clip of what could be better for folks who were better. She was impressed and a little scared.

Quickly, they were seated at a center table. Two groomed waitstaff wearing tuxedoes and white gloves served them water, bowing slightly to Mark, uttering clipped sentences and putting on city airs.

Mark ordered a martini for himself and an iced tea for Flannery, then picked out dishes she couldn't pronounce, quickly dismissing the two hovering waiters.

Flannery and Mark talked a lot during the meal, and mostly about him.

She fell for the slow, smooth-talker, marrying him at the end of her sophomore year. Then: "Stay put here where you belong, honey doll," Mark insisted. "You don't need higher learning to be a good wife. My dear mama, rest her saintly soul, took care of her man, never once neglecting her duties, never once needed the book learning for *that*. I'll take care of you. I sure don't want my lovely bride dirtying her lily-white hands working for others." Mark sweetened and topped it pretty and draped it over like a warm quilt on a chilly day, adding Scripture from Ephesians, "Wives, submit yourselves unto your own husbands, as unto the Lord."

It wasn't long before Flannery dropped out of college to fully undertake her wifely duties. And by the time she found out about her husband's cheating ways, she was ballooned with pregnancy, with twins at that, their second year of marriage not even tallied and toasted.

Many times, Flannery smelled the perfume on him, waited for him until supper grew cold, telephoning his office at the seminary to no answer.

The first time she called him out for cheating, he looked at her like she was daft.

The second time she accused him, he yelled at her and called her stupid for reading trashy books and silly women's magazines that put sinful notions in her head. The third time, he smacked her, though lightly, then more forcefully as time pushed on.

She had dismissed it while they were dating. The quick anger. The insults that he softened with an "only teasing ya, honey doll" innocence.

He had struck her the first time on their seventh date, accusing her of flirting with another guy after she'd dropped her books and the student helped her pick them up.

Mark Hamilton had hit Flannery hard enough that she tasted blood. Immediately he begged her forgiveness, blaming his actions on too much work, his pencil-pushing professors for overworking him, the long-winded sermons he had to go around and preach.

The next morning after that first incident, Mark showed up on her doorstep. "Forgive me, honey doll," he'd begged. "Let me make it up to you." He lifted a forlorn smile. "Please, Flannery. I promise that ol' devil has scatted off my shoulder for good."

He drove her to a flower shop. Inside, he waved a fat wallet at the shop owner.

"Pick your apology," he said to Flannery, loud enough for everyone to hear. "Grant me your forgiveness."

Embarrassed, Flannery grabbed the nearest flowers, a posy of daisies.

"*Those?* Not those little ol' weeds." Mark shook his head and snapped his fingers at the owner. "Wrap every damn bloom in this shop, every bud, every leaf, and send them over immediately." He pulled a pen out of his jacket and wrote an address on a slip of paper for delivery.

"Send enough for my next twenty transgressions," Mark said. "Hell, for the next hundred years. I intend to marry this girl." He bowed to Flannery.

Flannery had been shocked. And when all the girls in her dorm oohed and aahed and told her how lucky she was, she believed them, nearly bursting from the conviction when the flowers overflowed her dorm room and out into the hall. The girls giggled and called him a darling, a knight in shining armor. "A real dreamboat, the perfect catch," they declared, toting off vase after flower vase to their own rooms.

The flower shop trip played in Flannery's mind many times over the years, and she never brought another flower into her house. Just the smell sent her reeling, had her choking, leaving her skin crawling.

During their first two months of marriage, he'd shoved her a few times, knocked her out of his way when something upset him. *Something* could be any little thing that ticked him off, with the scary *somethings* always on the verge of boiling over into something much bigger.

By the end of their first year together, Mark had grown bolder. When she forgot to put the mayonnaise on the dinner table, he jerked the tablecloth off, sending dishes, food, everything crashing to the floor and a plate flying at her face, blackening her eye.

Soon her minor transgressions started adding up, and, by 1955, when she became pregnant, Mark sermoned her punishment, preaching she was ungodly, a sinner, and a blemish on his eternal soul.

By her sixth month of pregnancy, he began watching how much she ate, taunting her with names. *"Pig face, fat ass,"* he'd needled her, until her stomach soured and she was shamed from the table.

Flannery's mama would call to chat, but it seemed to irritate Mark, and soon, he'd answer most all the telephone calls, telling her mother that Flannery needed her rest.

A day shy of her seventh month, Flannery stood in the kitchen preparing his dinner. Uncomfortable, tired from having to serve him another late supper because he'd been at church with yet another professor, Flannery waddled over to her chair with a platter and took her seat across from Mark.

She passed him the fried chops, but he wouldn't take one. Instead, he stared down at his empty dinner plate, his jaw twitching.

Flannery fearfully wadded her napkin in her lap, her chest tightening, heart thundering as she tried to figure out how she had wronged him this time.

Her eyes scanned the table, the condiments, dishes, glasses, and came to rest on the silverware.

He gripped a fork above his plate, and she saw his knuckles whiten.

Flannery felt the terror bead up on her forehead, heat her neck. Instantly, she realized her mistake and reached over to correct the place setting for him, but it was too late.

"How many times do I have to say it? To the left. *Left!*" Mark stabbed her hand with his fork. "Again, you've set the silverware on the wrong side of the plates," he barked into her screech.

A few days later, Mark said he was going to a professor's church sermon at the Southern Word Baptist Church. He didn't come home until the morning paper hit the stoop, drunk, smelling of woman and wearing his tomcatting on a telling collar.

When Flannery heard the car door slam, she jumped up from their bed, gave a quick brush to her hair, and hurried into her robe and satin, high-heeled house shoes. Mark had bought her the red slippers trimmed in feathers for Christmas. Winking, he'd told her, "wear 'em always, in the bedroom for me, like one of those beautiful burlesque dolls on a matchbook cover."

Flannery stood at the top of the steps watching him slip through the front door. Her eyes pulled to his clothes as she wrapped her robe closer, tightened the belt over her bloomed belly. She glowered at him when he mounted the stairs, flicking at his lipstick-stained shirt as he moved past her. "Don't think you're going to leave *that* for me to clean," she snapped.

"Watch your mouth, fat ass," he growled over his shoulder.

"You can just take yourself back to where you got that and have your whore wash it."

He wheeled around and wrapped his hands around her neck, squeezing.

Clawing at the air, she nabbed his chin with a nail.

He jerked himself out of his fit, surprised. "I'm sorry," he said, and released her with a small push. "You make me do this—"

But Flannery stumbled, and her arms flew out from her sides.

A putty of fright piled into Mark's stretching grimace, and he yelled and grabbed for her.

Flannery reached wildly back for him, then brushed the banister, missing both, tumbling down the stairs, her screams caught in her bruised windpipe.

She awoke to the smell of disinfectants coating the floors of Saint Anthony Hospital. The cold glare of fluorescent lighting bounced off pale-green walls, shot up from polished floors, circling nearby voices.

Flannery squinted and looked around, tried to pull herself up, but her bones were too busted and sore. She wanted to call out, but her jaw froze halfway and lit a fire inside her ears, spreading to her head.

They had put her in a six-bed ward with other mothers. That was almost the worst part of it all. Then Mark strolled into the room with her delivery doctor, the distinguished Dr. Vickers from over at the university. Her husband was telling the good doctor how careless and godless she'd been with the pregnancy.

"My wife," Mark said to the doctor standing at the end of her hospital bed, "refused to take care of herself. Tripped because she insisted on wearing those damn high-heel slippers even though her feet couldn't fit into them anymore. Took up with the devil with some vodka nipping too." Mark looked pitifully down and clasped his hands in prayer.

*Vodka,* she thought, muddled. *No.* There was no place for vodka in Kentucky. But Mark kept a flask of it, sipped from it quite a bit. She'd seen him take up the habit lately, doing it at first light, even. Flannery couldn't stand the smell of the cough-syrupy liquor, the nose of the sickly bitter tang she found on Mark's breath that he claimed could never be detected.

Honey Bee'd always said that a Kentuckian, a gentleman, would never rendezvous with vodka, never light the Southern tongue with potato juice.

*Honey Bee,* she mouthed, aching for his strong, protective arms.

Flannery moved her feet, wiggled her toes, trying to feel. Lifting her head slightly, she looked to see if she had on the slippers. Weak, unable to, she collapsed back into the pillow.

"Shameless," Mark said to the doctor.

Flannery tried to find her voice to deny it all, but could only manage raspy squeaks.

"You know how it is, lad," Dr. Vickers groused quietly. "Some of these hens aren't made to sit on the soft nest." The old doctor squeezed Mark's shoulder and then looked over his spectacles down at the bed and chided Flannery. "Mrs. Hamilton," he gruffed, "as your doctor I must say it is a woman's duty to take care of her husband and children. A good wife must first be a godly woman—must care for the vessel that carries the child. Even the wildest creature knows this," he preached to her failures.

Flannery turned her face away from the man, trying to bury it and her shame into the thin, lumpy hospital pillow. But the very worst was when she finally saw the babies, their babies.

Two women rested in iron beds across from her, their eyes filling with horror and pointed blame, shooting daggers her way. Cradled in their arms lay content, sleeping newborns.

Flannery lifted a wanting arm, wishing she could for one second, hold the babes, cradle them to her breast.

One of the mothers covered her baby's head with her hand, shielding the infant from Flannery's disgrace, as if it might infect her newborn.

"Mrs. Hamilton"—the doctor tapped her shoulder—"did you hear me? . . . Twins, a boy and a girl . . ."

A boy *and* a girl? Flannery slowly cut her eyes back up at the doctor who hovered close above her face. "Patricia and Peter," she said, faintly calling the names she and Mark had decided on long ago when they'd gone over all the birth possibilities. A girl would be named after her sister, and a boy for Mark's dad. "Where are they, my Patricia and my Peter? Where are my babies?" she asked unbelieving into his foggy cloud of speech. Flannery turned her head back to the mothers across from her.

The doctor mumbled something about the babies, something fleeting about her "body not being suitable for carrying babies anymore . . . lost . . . something had been torn, gone missing inside."

She moved her hand down to her stomach, felt the flatness under the bandages, a fiery pain rippling, a loss that stabbed its finality deeper. "*Missing?*"

"No children for you . . ." his words muddled. "The Cesarean section . . . Your husband signed consent . . . *Sterilized*," he lit more forcefully, and his spittle landed on her cheek. "For your own good."

Flannery tried to speak, lift herself up, but her tongue thickened, her head felt too swimmy. "*What do you mean? What . . .* s-sterilized?" The cold question lay lodged in her throat.

The doctor's face blurred as he leaned sideways and whispered to her husband. "You did the right thing. My sympathies to you, Mr. Hamilton. I'm sorry for your losses."

"My babies. My poor, poor babies. Gone to my Heavenly Lord too soon." Mark shook his head. "Gone to be with my saintly mother."

But Flannery couldn't hear them anymore. Her own thunderous screams, the pounding of her fists against the bedrails roared up hot into her ears.

Mark and the doctor placed her in a locked ward for a month. Kept her long enough that when the nurse came in with the medicine tray, Flannery's hands took on a mind of their own and trembled as if they spoke for her, reaching out in silence.

Flannery spent most days sitting in a chair beside her hospital bed in the dark, dingy room waiting for her medicine. She loved the yellow ones better than the white ones that they'd given her the week before. The only thing that really stuck out from it all was the pills. The yellow ones made her float high, high, higher until she was up in Heaven with her babies.

One day the nurse took two Valiums from the tiny paper container filled with pills and handed them to her. Flannery didn't wait for the water.

Lifting Flannery's right arm, the old nurse inspected it. "Mrs. Hamilton, are you poking yourself again? *You are.* What did I tell you? If you keep this up, you're gonna be here till the '60s, forever."

Flannery shook her head no, and then nodded a yes. She didn't want to tell the nurse she needed to forget. She needed to forget for a while how everything was gone. But when she felt the pain, she had hope, a safe province to retreat to without fear of Mark taking it away. Absently, Flannery rubbed the wound.

"Where is it?" The nurse fumbled around Flannery's lap until she found the pencil that had made the marks.

She ripped it from the pocket of Flannery's gown. The flimsy covering was brushed aside, exposing another puncture wound on Flannery's leg.

"Good night!" the nurse said with an equal measure of wonder and disgust. "You're a crazy one all right. And already up to three pills, and still, this . . ." She smacked the side of Flannery's leg several times, left it red and smarting, then wagged a nicotine-stained finger in her face. "He'll have you on the blue ones if you don't stop doing this kind of thing to yourself."

"I like yellow," Flannery said softly.

"You're a bother." The nurse shook her head. "Batty," she muttered, then gave Flannery another pill. "This should keep you outta my hair for a while."

Yes, the yellow ones. Like floating on a yellow river, Flannery thought. *Yellow is my favorite color.* Better than the white ones. Yellow. Yellow. Yellow. Flannery wanted to clap out the word in a cheer. Instead she greedily swallowed the pill and pulled the baggy hospital gown back over her knees. Leaning back into the chair, she closed her eyes, dismissing the nurse. In a while everything was sweet from her peak of Yellow.

They held her in the psych ward three more weeks. She was sure Mark would've left her there forever if Mama hadn't found him out. By the time Mama rescued her, Flannery had left her lapping, sunny Yellow river for Blue. Bigger Bluer skies.

# CHAPTER 23

Flannery hated that Hollis could make her feel weak and scared, take her back into her old fears so easily. She had needed years to regain some control, to feel any wanting for a life after Mark and the babies. She glared hard at Hollis, pushing up the muster to light back.

"It's not right to leave it all like this. Something bad had to have happened to them," she said stonily, rolling down the car window for air.

Hollis gripped the steering wheel and cut his eyes at her. "Lot of things in this world ain't right. And I'm going to *right* this my way, peaches. I aim to give my brother a fine burial, and, if you're smart, you'll give your sister a decent one too. Let it rest now."

"Folks need to know," she pushed. "Everything you know and didn't say."

"Shut it down, Flannery. Zip it."

"W-we have to tell. You have to tell what you know. I have to tell what I know. It's a sin—"

"It's my church now. *Mine*."

"Hollis, you gotta tell—"

"Shit. They're dead, Flannery. Nothing's gonna change that. We can't help them now. We have to deal with the facts as they stand. I'm not about to go putting my life, my family's reputation—and yours—on any line because of what *they* did."

"What? What could they've done?"

"You don't even want to know about the shit Patsy buried in the dirt on Ebenezer. But I'm going to tell you anyway, and maybe it'll shut you up once and for all. Her shamelessness is right out there under the elm. Buried her panties under that elm, she did. Your sainted sister? Played both me and Danny good. Do you hear me, peaches? Hear what I'm trying to tell you? If you're smart, you'll leave it be. For God's sake, girl, just leave it alone!" Hollis yelled at the windshield, spit flying from his mouth.

Flannery cowered, stunned into silence, her eyes filling.

In a second Hollis reached over her knees, hit the glove box with his fist, popping it open. "Get yourself a tissue, and get yourself together for your mama's sake."

Flannery grabbed one from the crushed box inside and saw one of Hollis's guns poking from beneath, a barrel of a snub nose.

Quickly he leaned back over and slammed the glove box shut. Stomping down on the gas pedal, he barreled toward the Butler house. When he didn't pull into the drive all the way, and stopped at the mailbox, Flannery reached shakily for the door handle and looked back over her shoulder, wanting him to make it all right, wanting to say something more, not let it all just lie there.

He turned his head away. "I loved her, too. Never stopped."

Flannery flung open the door.

"Just didn't know quite how to back then," he whispered, and cut on the radio and sped away.

Mama was dozing on the porch with her sewing basket at her feet and several tins of loose buttons stacked beside it.

"I'm home." Flannery gently tapped Mama's shoulder.

Mama startled. "Flannery . . . I thought I'd try and sit on the porch. I feel useless waiting in the bed. Was that Sheriff Henry?" Mama asked, pulling herself up from her rocker. She peered around Flannery's shoulder. Mama cupped a hand over her eyes, stretched her neck toward the trail of smoke the sheriff's car had left.

Hollis hadn't bothered to come in, and Flannery didn't fault him for it. She didn't know what she should tell her mama, what to spill about today or what she and Hollis had left out long ago.

"Where's your automobile?" Mama asked. "What happened to your clothes? What did you find out, Flannery?"

Flannery kicked off her muddy shoes. "Come on inside, Mama. It's been a long day, and gonna get longer." Flannery held open the screen door for her. "Let me get out of my wet hose, clean up, and we can have some tea and talk."

"But what about your automobile? And the one in the river—?"

"Let's go in. I felt a little weak, and Hollis offered to drive me. His deputy will drive my car out here later."

"Tell me. What's going on, baby girl? Did they find them?" Mama rushed nervously.

"Please give me a minute; let me get out of these filthy clothes, and I'll tell you everything," she promised, borrowing time.

"But—"

"One minute." She hurried past before Mama could see her wet eyes and could fill her own. Flannery peeled off the jeans and her nylons beneath them, tossed the dirty clothes onto her twin's bed. Nothing had been changed in the room since the day Patsy left. Mama'd bought new pillows and sheets, but kept the old coverlets and matching drapes. It was as if time had stopped, held its musty breath for her return.

Flannery slipped into clean stockings, a fresh shirt and pants.

Mama did little more than dust the old maple furniture. Flannery ran a finger along the lip of the dresser, then dropped to her knees in front of it and pulled out the bottom drawer. It was exactly where she'd left it and exactly how she'd left it, though Chubby's apron was rust-spotted and yellowed some.

Flannery had lied to Mama back then about so many things, too many things that couldn't be righted easily now. When after a few days Patsy still hadn't come home from her prom date, Flannery'd needled Mama into letting her "quit" Chubby's, telling her she'd find babysitting jobs. Wrecked with worry, Mama agreed to keep her younger daughter around home more.

Flannery never told Mama about Chubby firing her. As far as Flannery knew, Chubby never had the heart to tell either.

Shaking, Flannery dug out the necklace and bullet, rolling them in her hand, clinking, clapping the loose pearls against the cold, copper bullet. She wanted to give the heirloom piece back to Mama. It would be a small consolation, maybe a balm for the bad news coming. But if she gave the pearls back now, Flannery would have to tell everything—both her secrets and Patsy's. The way Patsy lit out with the drunk Henry boys that night. Hollis's argument and the heinous acts he'd claimed her sister did. And the pregnancy Hollis accused her of having. That is, if Hollis didn't spark the words first and twist them uglier.

Flannery inspected the bullet, its shiny copper jacket, the pushed-in nose. The sound of clanking rose up and stole her breath, grounding today's memory of the assistant tossing the other bullet. The one dredged up with the Mercury.

Flannery was sure Hollis knew more than what he'd told back then, that he was hiding something, maybe a lot of bad somethings. She'd have to figure a way to find out what he was hiding and if it was true what he'd said about Patsy.

Until then, how was she going to explain today to Mama?

Mama's heart was going to break now, no matter what Flannery told her. The unanswered questions, more doubts that would soon leave her mama more heartbroken, and worse, shamed. Flannery was ripped from moment to moment. *How much and what to tell her?* She was sure Hollis would say anything to save his own neck.

One truth welled up. Flannery couldn't have the town thinking her sister was a whore.

Flannery looked down at her watch and made up her mind: She'd tell Mama as little as she could get by with. *Grab those fleeting seconds,* like Honey Bee'd taught her long ago, *fight for 'em,* before the time thief snatched them up as his own.

Flannery pressed the pearls to her mouth. She tried to think through the jumble of what ifs and what fors.

Mama called for her. Flannery rolled everything up in the apron and put it back in the drawer. She'd break it to Mama bit by bit. Later Flannery would have to find a way to make Hollis tell her everything. She stuffed the only piece of Patsy she had left, the stolen shoe ribbon, into her jeans pocket.

Flannery walked into the kitchen and found Mama by the radio, her hand frozen in the air above its knob. Mama's face was weighted, the flowery duster she wore drooping, a sleeve slipping off her slumped shoulder.

"The radio just told folks," Mama whispered incredulously to Flannery. "Just told us they found them . . . Glass Ferry's missing teens. Danny Henry and our Patsy. It can't be true."

"I'm afraid it is, Mama." Flannery went to her side. "It's them."

Flannery dug out the piece of fabric that Mama had long ago tacked to her daughter's shoe. "I'm sorry. It was the Henrys' old Mercury down there. And our Patsy."

"*Patsy.*" Mama held up a shaky finger and trailed it lightly over the bow. Tears leaked from Mama's eyes. "Dear Lord, my Patsy girl. I'm going to have to bury her. Bury a child again," Mama cried, collapsing into Flannery's arms, rocking her daughter with sobs until they both crumpled and slowly sank into a tangled heap on the kitchen floor.

On the bright yellow counter above them, Patsy's strawberry birthday cake sagged under the weight of the afternoon hours, its thick, pink icing cemented, the berries shriveling in the dead air of Mama's earlier festivity, a soured decay rising into the rot of heartbreak and despair.

A burst of wind pushed through the screen door, rippling curtains, smacking at the bones of the old house and its weeping mistresses.

# CHAPTER 24

Sometime during the night while the Butler women slept, Hollis and his deputy returned Flannery's car.

The next afternoon, Flannery lit out on foot to Ebenezer with a shovel in hand while Mama tried to rest back at the house.

Flannery knew she would have to see what was buried there with her own eyes to believe what Hollis had told her about Patsy.

She dug under the elm for an hour with no luck, the roots bigger, thicker, and spread out more than twenty years back. Knee-walking around to the next spot, scratching in the dirt in another, looking over her shoulder all the while doing it. She moved to the back of the tree and stood. As she cut the dirt with the shovel, the metal hit something hard. Flannery dug around it and unearthed an old distillery bottle, tossing it over her shoulder, shaking her head at all the holes she'd made when she saw it snugged next to a root.

Flannery tugged and pulled up some elastic and tattered bits of a thick nylon fabric. She poked the shallow grave with a stick and brought up another tiny piece of material with a faded imprint of pink polka dots, then pulled out another bigger section attached to dirty, limp elastic. Scratched at the fanning threads.

For a moment she tried to believe it could be anyone's from anywhere. From a bird's nest, a passing stranger, or a dog?

When she was little, a farmer's collie had gone around stealing folks' shoes and boots from their porches and would carry 'em all back to its master's steps. The farmer could never break the dog from doing that and spent many mornings trying to find out whose shoe was whose. Most times, understanding folks just stopped by the farmer's home to collect them quietly from his porch. Then someone, robbed of his working boots and time, up and shot the old collie.

It was no use. This was a different type of dog who'd done this. "Her shamelessness is right out there under the elm," Hollis had told her. "Do you hear me, peaches? Hear what I'm trying to tell you?"

Flannery knew these underwear belonged to Patsy, identical to the matching ones Mama had bought Flannery long ago, the twins both begging for them in the fancy department store. She remembered how mad Patsy got because Mama had purchased the same pair for Flannery.

Hollis had been there, watched her sister take them off. Likely even had a hand in getting them off.

He had to be part of it. A big part of something, something ugly that he knew a lot more about and was hiding.

"*Tramp,*" he'd called her sister. Hollis's words lit Flannery's skin like someone had poured turpentine all over her and struck a match. She raised her head, belling the winds with her cries. With a heavy heart, she stuffed the pieces of Patsy's panties back into the dirt, and slowly, unrelentingly, a cold revenge began to nest deep, padding her bones, and for a horrifying second it took her breath. The urge to avenge her sister struck hard, held fast.

Almost a week had passed since Patsy had been found in the Kentucky, and her mama still wouldn't toss this birthday cake into the trash.

They both knew it would be the last cake, the final birthday for Patsy. Flannery didn't have the heart to fight her mama for it, though she did manage to battle the fruit flies for the strawberries, picking them off and dumping them when Mama wasn't looking.

Mama mostly sat slumped at the kitchen table, staring out into nothing and nowhere.

"How about I fix us a sandwich?" Flannery offered one afternoon.

Mama didn't say anything. Flannery pulled out the skillet. "I'll make us a peppery egg sandwich just the way you like it." She set out plates, placing one in front of Mama, and topped them with slabs of bread.

Flannery fried an egg sunny-side up just the way Mama liked hers, then slid it onto the plate and passed her the ketchup. Mama always poured it on her eggs. Flannery liked mustard on hers, same as Honey Bee, and she set the jar of French's beside her own plate.

"Go ahead and try to eat, Mama. Don't wait for me." Flannery went back over to the stove and cracked another egg into the skillet.

Flannery winced when she saw the double yolk. She let it cook a few seconds and stabbed at it with the spatula, flipping the egg over. Then she carried it in the skillet over to her plate.

Mama pulled herself back from where her mind had wandered and stared at Flannery's open-faced egg sandwich. "Oh, look. Look, Flannery. There's still hope," Mama whispered.

"Mama, please." Flannery shook her head and put the skillet back on the stove.

"But it's right there, baby girl. We're gonna have twins again."

"It's just an egg sandwich. Don't."

"Oh, Lord, Flannery, Gramma Lettie would turn in her grave if she heard you talk like that. Double yolk always means a birth coming—twins a'comin'."

"*Mama.*"

"I've had double yolks only twice in my life, and look at my babies. You, Patsy, and—" A gloom passed over Mama's face, and she cut herself off with a soft "God bless."

Flannery wrung her hands in her lap. Her brothers were born five years before her and Patsy, and had lived only a short life.

Flannery'd never told Mama she'd carried twins or how she'd lost them. Never told a living soul. Mama knew there'd been a miscarriage, and only that. Knew what Mark had told her mama and others: "I put my wife in the asylum when she wouldn't obey me, couldn't dry herself out from the whiskey."

Any talk of Mark Hamilton, as much as a peep or mention, and Flannery'd light up a shushing hand to the person prying.

"Maybe you'll remarry someday, Flannery. You've been teaching in Louisville a long time now. I thought there would . . . Well, I bet there's lots of good men who—"

"No, Mama." Flannery pinched her lip. She didn't have the strength for that again. Could never take away the hurt soaked inside her. She felt like one of those dogs that had lost its wag. She was sure she'd never trust another marriage.

"Look at the time. I better call Mr. Flagg's office," Mama said, and pushed back her plate.

Mama'd been anxious, calling the coroner every day, hoping for word of the remains. Twice she'd sent her pastor to inquire.

Flannery picked at her own sandwich before tossing it still whole into the garbage.

A few minutes before nine on Friday morning a state trooper pulled up to the Butler house.

Flannery and Mama met him on the porch.

"Mrs. Butler," he said, "I'm Trooper Claymore Green. I'm sorry to call so early, but I wanted to speak directly with you. Ask you a few questions, if I may?" He tipped his uniform hat and nodded toward Flannery. "Mrs. Hamilton." He fumbled with a notebook.

"Come in . . . come on in, Trooper," Mama said, pulling the young man into the house by his arm.

Flannery thought Trooper Green was all but twenty, still wet behind the ears from high school, still full of boy, the smelly lockers, red-eared crushes, passing notes, classroom chalk that sticks till the world grows the boy up into something tougher, machined.

She knew the man from somewhere, but couldn't place it, and wondered if he was kin to one of Mama's friends. Flannery shrugged it off.

Mama made coffee and carried the server into the parlor and

set it on Honey Bee's cellarette he'd built from poplar and yellow pine. The trooper stood, admiring the old wooden case, helping Mama lower the tray, careful not to nick or scratch the liquor cabinet.

The cellarette had been one of Honey Bee's finest projects, a handsome piece of furniture bathed in warm, golden tones, simple but elegant, its only ornament a brass skeleton-key lock, the chest perched regally atop a matching base with tall, tapering square legs. It no longer served as a liquor case; instead, Mama'd stuffed all of Honey Bee's old recipes inside and had given it to Flannery. But Flannery had never gotten around to hauling it back to her apartment.

The three settled onto the green velvet chairs. Trooper Green leaned forward. After a long pause, he said, "Ma'am, uh, Mrs. Butler, I wondered if you can tell me anything about the bullet we found in the car. Might you have any ideas why there would be gunshot on Mr. Henry's body?"

Mama dropped her sugar spoon onto the floor. It tumbled and bounced off the trooper's glossy black uniform shoe.

The trooper grabbed it and set the silverware on the coffee table.

Flannery placed a hand on Mama's shoulder, not sure whether she was steadying herself or Mama.

"What, whatever do you mean?" Mama croaked. "Whatever does he mean?" She looked to Flannery for explanation.

Flannery squeezed Mama's shoulder. "I don't know," Flannery said.

Trooper's face reddened. "I'm sorry," he said to Mama. "I thought you knew. It's been on the news. I thought Mr. Flagg would've told you."

Flannery grimaced.

"No one told me," Mama said, puzzled. "Poor Danny, shot—"

"Appears that way, Mrs. Butler," the trooper said.

"Patsy. Was she hurt? Shot?" Mama swelled up with tears. "Those poor babies hurting like that. Like before. Oh, I feel light-headed."

"Mama." Flannery touched her arm. "What do you mean?"

Mama brushed Flannery's hand off. "I can't think." She rubbed her forehead.

Trooper looked lost, uncomfortable.

Mama took a breath. "What did they do to my girl? Did someone shoot—"

Flannery hugged her. "No, Mama, he's saying it was the Henry boy. Right, Trooper?"

Trooper said, "That's correct."

"Danny Henry was a good boy," Mama said. "Why would anybody shoot such a good boy?"

"We're trying to find out," Trooper said.

"Trooper, I need to lie down." Mama stood.

"Mama, let me help you upstairs." To the trooper, "Excuse me while I take her up to her room. I'll be right back."

"Yes, help me to my room. I'm sorry, Trooper Green. I've not been myself lately. Flannery will see to you," Mama said, fatigued.

Trooper nodded sympathetically, though Flannery could tell he wanted Mama to stay, to ask her more.

Flannery put Mama into bed with a sedative the doctor had left last week.

She came back into the parlor and found Trooper Green still seated, fiddling with his hat, sneaking looks to the mantel where Mama had lined up a long train of framed photographs of Patsy.

Flannery sat across from him. "Trooper Green, are you sure Danny was murdered?"

"We only know he was shot. The state examiner confirmed it. Did Patsy and Danny have any problems? Anyone who would want to harm them?"

"Not that I know of. We didn't talk much then. We'd been growing apart ever since my daddy died. But I don't think there was anyone who would hurt her. Or him."

"Did Patsy act upset that night? Anything unusual?"

"She was excited about going to the prom, that's all."

"And when was the last time you saw her?"

"Uh, well, right here before she left." Flannery hadn't told a soul about her last argument with Patsy on Ebenezer. It would break her mama's heart to know they had behaved badly toward each other, fought like the heathens their old teacher had always accused them of being. Flannery didn't need to share that. She didn't need anyone else knowing their business and casting a shaming eye her way.

"Here with the Henry boys," Flannery added.

"Danny *and* Sheriff Henry?"

"Yes. Patsy and Danny didn't have their licenses yet. When their double date canceled, Danny's daddy had the older brother, uh, Hollis, drive the two to the dance."

"And you say the Henry boys came over and picked up Patsy? You last saw them here?"

"I . . . Well, I had to go to work that night. I left as soon as they got here. Mama had canasta club and left before the boys arrived."

"Okay." He scribbled notes. "So the last time you saw them was here at your house?"

"Yeah, and we all took off about the same time. I walked to Chubby Ray's, and they drove off to the prom."

The trooper made more notes in his pad and then piped, "Did Patsy own a gun?"

"Gun? Patsy? You don't think Patsy—?"

"Ma'am, we're just trying to locate the gun. Did Patsy have a .38? Your family own one? Ever have one?"

"She did inherit an old pistol from my daddy, but she never bothered with it." Flannery went over to the secretary, opened it, and found the old Robin Hood No. 2. "Loaded, Trooper." She pointed to the gun, and he stood and took a minute to study it. "Just a .32. Supposedly, that and some old bone dice were given to the Butler family by Jesse James in the 1800s."

"Sharp five-shooter," the trooper said, picking it up, inspecting the walnut handle, the name on the barrel, before putting it back. "Any other guns?"

"A shotgun in the hall closet, same as most families have. These are the only ones I can recall," Flannery lied, dropping her gaze to her daddy's old wristwatch, tugging at the leather band sweating her skin.

"Other than James's pistol, any others—a .38?"

Hollis had one, and so did Honey Bee, but she reckoned now was not the time to talk about that to a lawman.

"Mrs. Hamilton?" The trooper cocked his head at her. "Ma'am, if there's anything else you can remember, anything you might want to—?"

"No, Trooper, just the old Robin Hood," Flannery said, knowing her own paddle would be just as hard for all her lies.

Her daddy had given his .38 to old Sheriff Jack Henry that fall day in '47 after the run-in with the moonshiners. Sheriff was waiting at the dock when they'd pulled the ferryboat in. Waiting with an outreached hand and his own knowing. "Honey Bee," he'd called out to her daddy.

"Skip the trial, Jack, and let's go straight to the execution," Honey Bee'd said.

"I better keep that fine snub nose for your and everyone else's safety," the sheriff said, and nothing more.

As far as Flannery knew, no one, other than her, Honey Bee, and the old sheriff, ever learned about the pirating fishermen. *Well, maybe Uncle Mary knew. He knew mostly everything and had the eyes of an eagle.*

"Did Patsy or Danny ever drink alcohol?" the trooper asked, taking his seat again.

Flannery hoped he was through with his questioning. Reluctantly, she sat back down and said, "Mama doesn't allow liquor in the house."

"Ma'am"—the trooper tapped his pen on the notebook—"do you know where those two might have gotten a gun? Anybody else who owns a gun like that? We heard Danny only owned a .22. Any ideas?"

She knew a .38 and .22 were worlds apart. Honey Bee'd taught her, same as every Kentucky daddy taught his small sons about guns and bullets, and even skilled the sons they didn't have: their tree-climbing daughters. And, Honey Bee'd even gone after his prissy Patsy, too, demanding she learn to shoot so she could defend her property and her honor from the "dangerous hill men, even madwomen," he'd claimed, who were lurking in these parts, ready to strip her of either. Or both.

Flannery rubbed her sweating palms against her jeans. "I can't be positive about all that back then. It was so long ago." She looked up at the ceiling as if trying to recall. "No, I can't think of anyone who has a gun like that."

"Any friends who might've been mad at both of them? Or maybe one of them?" the trooper pried.

"No, and I know my sister wouldn't have done it, shot him in the arm like that. If Patsy aimed to shoot someone, she'd hit him dead-on in a killing spot like my daddy taught us. She wouldn't have had to waste a second bullet."

The trooper bobbed his head a little proudly, understandingly, like he'd been taught the same.

He stood. "If you can think of anything else, anything at all, please call Post Seven and ask for me." He handed Flannery a card, turned toward the door, and stopped. "Oh, there's one more thing: The examiner needs to make sure each family receives, uh, everything."

"When can we bury her?"

"The coroner is set to release the remains as early as Monday. You can call the funeral home and have them picked up from the examiner's office. Let me just make sure I have everything. Can you tell me exactly what Patsy was wearing that night?" He opened the pad, waiting.

"An ankle-length lemon chiffon dress and cream-colored Mary Janes," Mama called down from the stairs behind them.

"*Mama.*" Flannery whipped around. "You need to relax some before you fall flat on your tail."

Mama waved away Flannery's concern and slowly descended. She rested a shaky hand on the trooper's arm. "She was so beautiful, Trooper, in her grandmother's pearls. Did you find them, Trooper? Did you find my family's pearls?"

Trooper Green flipped back through the pages of his notebook, studying. "No, ma'am," he said, stumped. "None listed here. They combed every inch of the car, and all around in the water where the car rested down by Johnson's boat dock, Mrs. Butler. There were only her shoes and a compact mirror, I'm afraid." He looked through the pages again and checked to be sure. "No, ma'am. Nothing's here."

"But she had on the pearls I gave her." Mama hurried over to an end table in the parlor, and plucked up an old photograph of her mother wearing the pearls. "Here." She shoved the frame into the trooper's face. "They're right here on Mama. Same as they were on Patsy. They have to find them," Mama insisted, looking at Flannery, her old eyes crinkled and filling fast. "I want to hold them and remember my baby just the way she was on her last night with me. Smiling like that, looking dazzling for her dance in her grandmother's pearls. We have to find them, Flannery. You saw them on her, didn't you?"

Flannery could only nod, the truth swollen in her throat.

# CHAPTER 25

To have lost so much and so fast before the old electric daisy clock in the kitchen could strike ten that morning was more than her mama could bear. That her daughter was dead was insufferable; that she could possibly find another part of her, hopeful.

"Take me there," Mama begged after the trooper left. "Flannery, take me to the Kentucky so that I can at least search for them. Have the one last bit of her happiness to remind me how she was the last time I held her. Take me to Johnson's boat dock. I have to find the pearls. For the sake of—"

"No, Mama. You need to try and rest some—"

"I'll rest when I have all of her. I can't have my beautiful baby back, but maybe I can have at least that much. What that wicked Kentucky robbed me of, and is still thieving from me."

Flannery called the doctor to the house. He gave Mama a newer sedative, more powerful, he promised, telling Flannery to make sure they both took it easy.

Flannery went to the hall closet and rummaged through boxes of bullets on the shelf. She found an old carton of .38s pushed toward the back. She looked inside. They were the same size as the one she'd found on Ebenezer back then. And the same kind of bullet that fit into Hollis's old snub nose.

She rattled the box, and a sickening feeling had her reeling, left her weak and reaching for the doorjamb.

Rubbing her brow, she felt an early truth sink in. "I loved

her, too," Hollis said. *Had he been jealous of Danny all along? Loved Patsy more than Danny?* "Never stopped," he admitted.

She tapped the box of bullets, remembering Honey Bee's gun they'd fit into.

Flannery took another kind of inventory—about Hollis, Patsy's buried underwear, and the odd bullet she found prom night—and the more she thought about it all and that day back then, the more she worried that Hollis had done something bad, awful, maybe even as dreadful as shooting his own brother. Those brothers must have fought over Patsy.

More awful, Hollis's snub nose had to be the gun that discharged, the only gun shot—Honey Bee's gun that the old Henry sheriff had taken for hush, the one he'd passed to his son—and the pistol that had, in an unknown way, done Patsy and Danny in.

The older brother had been packing that night. What Hollis had done, she could only surmise. But what he was hiding was big, and they both knew it.

Exhausted, feeling a headache coming on, Flannery shoved the bullets back on the shelf and went up to her room to lie down. A minute later, sleep grabbed hold.

It was nearly three in the afternoon when Flannery awoke. She hadn't slept that soundly since she got here, and she yawned and stretched, feeling somewhat better. Then just as quick plucked through her worries again, letting them scrape at her.

Padding down the hall to check in on Mama in the master bedroom, Flannery had an uneasy feeling, a foreboding. Mama was gone.

Calling out for her, Flannery hurried downstairs to the kitchen. But Mama wasn't anywhere. When Flannery looked outside, she saw that her mama's old Buick was gone too.

"Dammit." She cursed herself for not keeping a better eye on Mama and not hiding the car keys. *Where could she have gone?* Flannery's heart sank as she called up Mama's last words. "Take me to the Kentucky."

Surely she'd just gone to town on errands. Maybe picking up some groceries at Spanks, or something she needed from

Chubby's drugstore. But the doc had promised Flannery, her mama's medicine was newer, powerful. Mama could hurt herself, or someone else, lit like that, driving those twisted roads out there.

Flannery called the sheriff's office. Hollis answered, all business. And she was too, the urgency too great. She asked him to send someone to Johnson's boat dock to look for her mama, then pulled on her sneakers and hurried out the door herself.

Flannery drove to town first. Hurrying into Chubby's, she looked around the drugstore and in the soda fountain area. The place was full of old-timers drinking coffee, chatting at the lunch counter. It got quiet when they saw her. She walked past two boys playing a pinball machine and over to two men seated at the end of the counter, asking if they had seen Mrs. Butler.

"No, ma'am," one fella said. "I hope Jean's okay. Sure sorry about all her troubles. Yours too."

Flannery looked closely at the man and remembered Smitty Donner was the old hardware store owner. "Thank you, Mr. Donner."

Mr. Donner nodded. "Never seen such a mess of trouble. Poor Jean, having her daughter murdered like that."

Flannery winced. "Mr. Donner, Patsy wasn't murdered."

"Well, her beau was, and that's close enough. And folks ain't talked of nothing else since, worrying who might've done it. Lord, there ain't been a murder here"—he scratched his chin, trying to recall—"well, since Leelum Shrivers shot that hobo for stealing his pig near 'bout thirty years ago."

Mr. Donner goosed his jaw and looked around at the counter and tables shrewdly like the murderer might be in the store, sitting at this very counter.

The other folks lined up on stools beside him murmured agreement, shifting their eyes Flannery's way, crackling their red-vinyl seats, stretching for a peek.

"You shouldn't carry tales," Flannery chided Mr. Donner, and shot a scolding eye to the others.

A woman poked her head up, leaned out from the end, and

called, "Oh, hush, Smitty, you know the sheriff done said his brother probably shot himself."

"Yeah," another said. "I remember when Danny got it for squirrel hunting, and his pa always fussed about him shooting up barns. 'Member that, Smitty?"

Mr. Donner grunted over his afternoon coffee.

Flannery sighed. "Mr. Donner, if you see my mama would you tell her I'm looking for her?"

A woman sitting at a table behind Flannery cleared her throat. Flannery turned and saw Mrs. McGregor, her and Patsy's old eighth-grade teacher. "Always knew Patsy had a bit of wildness. Chasing the two Henry boys like that. It don't surprise me one bit." Mrs. McGregor murmured her blame over the lip of her coffee cup and sweetened it with a "bless her heart."

A few teens huddled at another table drinking sodas, whispering, and darting nervous glances Flannery's way.

In the booth across from the teens sat Violet Perry with three small kids. Violet pursed a vinegary red pout at Flannery, then dismissed her and pulled out a tube of lipstick from her purse. Flannery watched Violet sweep her lips, hideously stretch her thin mouth, twisting all catawampus-like with the paint.

Violet hadn't softened her makeup with age. Instead she wore the bright apple-red rouge and lipstick to liven up her long, spent-bloom face. It looked to Flannery like her two scoops of fun had melted long ago.

"Mommy, my straw. Can't get it, Mommy, help," Violet's toddler daughter whined, and shot up from the bench, teetering on her knees, wagging a paper-wrapped straw above her cola.

Scowling, Violet hit her nose with the lipstick and slapped the straw out of her daughter's hand. The girl shrank back into the booth, eyes welling, and turned her face, ducking. Flannery saw the bruises covering the child's neck and jaw. Violet grabbed her daughter's arm and squeezed hard, jerking, leaving behind another angry red mark.

Flannery felt the fire crawl up her neck, the same as on that prom night, the same as when Violet Perry and the others had left their invisible angry marks on her. No different than those her ex-husband had given her many times.

For a minute Flannery wanted to leave her own right across Violet's tight and overripe tomato-red lips. Smear that cheap lipstick right into the dangly grape that hung in the back of her throat and down into her dark, ugly soul. Leave her with what she'd given the child. She was halfway to Violet's booth when a voice stopped her.

"Flan?" Junior Ray creaked opened the kitchen door and called out, marshaling her anger back. "It's Flan." He sidled up next to her, wiping his hands with a dishrag. "Good to see you." Junior smiled a little sadly and kissed her forehead.

"Junior." Flannery turned herself from her flame. "H-How's Tonya and the kids?"

"Fine. Tonya and I were just talking about dropping by with a dish this weekend. I'm sorry, Flan. Really sorry for your and Jean's loss. We always prayed to have those two home. Just not like this."

Grateful for his kindness, Flannery thanked him. She muttered something about finding Mama and quickly excused herself. Standing out on the old broken sidewalk in front of Chubby's, she felt busted. A shop bell rang, and she sucked down fresh air and shook off the helplessness filling her.

After a moment, she looked over at the tiny post office, the washateria, the lot next to Spanks Grocery Store. Her mama's car wasn't anywhere around. Shading her eyes with a hand, Flannery searched on the other side of the post office to the sheriff's small building. She didn't see Mama's car there either, or any official ones parked in front for that matter.

Walking shop to shop, Flannery asked around, though deep down she knew it was a delay. Mama was likely where Flannery thought, and the law would beat her to it. It was all a postponement, a farce, and she was avoiding having to face herself, face what she'd been hiding all these years, and what Mama and others might find.

Flannery turned to the hardware store next to Chubby's and stepped out farther on the sidewalk, peering past the drugstore to Junie Bug's Hair Styling. She walked down to Junie's and glanced in the big window, then on past the barber's to peek into Glass Ferry Dry Goods.

Finally, Flannery got into her car and drove off to Palisades Road. She pulled into the grassy lot at Johnson's boat dock and easily spotted Mama standing in her nightgown, knee-deep in the muddy Kentucky. Onlookers pointed to the old lady and screamed for her to come back.

Flannery opened her car door at the same time a deputy arrived, and they raced to the river.

The deputy yelled out, ordering Mama back onto the bank.

Car doors slammed behind Flannery, and there were more shouts, more warnings. Then the sound of a siren.

Mama looked up and spotted Flannery. "Help me find Patsy's pearls, Flannery. *I can't find them*," she hollered, waving and splashing in the water. Mama ducked under for a few seconds, then bounced up, her gray hair plastered, her cold lips trembling, her old powder-pink gown soaked, clinging to her old. sagging flesh and brittle bones.

The deputy hollered again. "Mrs. Butler. Come back here! Mrs. Butler . . . Get back now."

Mama waded out farther and ducked under the dark brown waters yet again.

"Mama!" Flannery screamed and rushed into the river, fighting the cold, pulling water to get to her.

Someone called out, shouting *"Mrs. Butler!"* and dove into the water, passing Flannery and pulling hard, arm over arm.

Flannery shook her wet head and wiped the water from her eyes. Trooper Green swam toward Mama. He grabbed the old woman's arm, but she wriggled out of his grip and went under again.

The trooper disappeared under the murky waters, and seconds later buoyed back up. Taking in a big breath he went under again, and, after many agonizing seconds, he popped back up with Mama in his grip.

Flannery made her way sloshing back to shore with Trooper Green trailing and her sputtering Mama despondent in his arms.

The trooper stepped aside, and Flannery gathered Mama in her arms. "Mama, I'm so sorry. Mama, are you okay—"

Mama wailed, "Let me go, please. Just let me go find them." Mama stretched her arms for the river. "We have to find them."

"C'mon, Mama, we need to get you home."

"Not without her pearls! I have to—"

"Dammit, Mama. They're gone forever, like her. Patsy's gone. The pearls are gone. For good!" Flannery snapped and flicked her hand down her own soaked clothes, smacking the water off herself.

Mama lowered her head. Flannery immediately regretted the lashing. *What is wrong with me, talking to my dear mama like that, continuing my eternal lie on top of other lies.* "C'mon, Mama," she said more kindly, taking a gentle hold of Mama's arm. "Let's get you dry. Home."

The trooper latched on to Mama's other arm, leading both women to his car. Embarrassed, Flannery whispered to the trooper, "Mama's not well. With all that's happened, she's having a hard time. Thank you, Trooper." Then louder and to Mama, "Thank the trooper. You nearly drowned yourself out there."

"Thank you, Trooper." Mama hung a meek, wet head and mumbled something more about the pearls.

The deputy rushed over. The trooper took him to the side and said, "I have it here; you can go on, Deputy. Everything's fine now. Mrs. Butler is okay."

Trooper Green picked up his discarded uniform shirt, grabbed the shoes he'd thrown onto the hood in a hurry, and said to Flannery, "Glad I was close. I got the call on my way in." He turned to Mama. "Ma'am, you can't be in the river like that. Someone could get hurt." He pointed to an old, crooked fence-post sign the state or someone had planted near the bank long ago. *No Swimming* in bullet-riddled red letters.

"I'm sorry, Trooper," Flannery said. "I'll take her straight home."

Mama's lip quivered as if she understood.

The trooper sighed and swiped at his wet trousers. "It's too dangerous."

"I'm sorry about your uniform," Mama apologized, shivering.

Trooper studied her, still unsure what to do. "The river is too dangerous for a little lady like yourself," he went on. "Unsafe for most men."

"Unsafe," Mama repeated numbly. "But my Honey Bee taught me to swim."

"No. It's too dangerous," he repeated.

Mama bobbed her head. "Y-yessir."

"I'm glad you're okay, Mrs. Butler. And no harm. I live over the ridge." He pointed to the cliffs. "Won't be no trouble to run home and change," he told her, easing up on his lecture, offering a kind smile. "Okay. No more swimming for now. You best get dry, ma'am." The trooper dipped his head to Flannery.

Mama's old friend, Myrtle Taylor, walked up behind them. "I heard there was trouble. I heard the sirens and told my Harry I'd walk straight down to the dock and see. Look at you, Jean. Oh dear," Mrs. Taylor fussed. "Let me help you home, honey. Home and dry, sweet pea."

Flannery released Mama into Mrs. Taylor's steady arms, grateful for the help. "Thank you, Mrs. Taylor. You're a godsend." Flannery balled the hem of her shirt and wrung it; the sopping clothes clung wet, chilling.

Mrs. Taylor helped Mama into her car, easing her into the passenger side. Flannery jumped into her Chevy and pulled out of the lot, with Mrs. Taylor following Flannery close behind in Mama's car.

Inside the house, Mrs. Taylor phoned her husband and told him to pick her up later in the evening, that she would be helping the Butler women, visiting with her old friend Jean.

Flannery mounted the stairs. She changed out of her wet clothes and took a bath, while Mrs. Taylor fussed after Mama.

Flannery soaked up the horror of the afternoon and the close call of almost losing Mama. A hard, undeniable truth crept in.

Something had to be done, and she now knew exactly what that something was. Flannery finished scrubbing and stepped out of the tub.

She dressed and then went to Mama's room. Mrs. Taylor had a blanket wrapped around her dear friend. "I should draw her a hot bath," Mrs. Taylor said. "It'll take off the chill. Wouldn't that be nice, Jean?"

Mama nodded weakly.

Flannery offered to lend a hand, but Mrs. Taylor insisted she would help, for Flannery just to relax, that she'd see to Mama's bath, give her a clean gown, and put her friend to bed. "Heavens, you women have been through enough. It's time to let an old family friend help some." Mrs. Taylor smiled.

"I'll just be downstairs," Flannery told them. "I'll put on a pot of tea."

Flannery pulled out a pair of her old leather boots from her closet and slipped down to the parlor and pulled them on. In the kitchen, she made tea and then dialed the old rotary. "Sheriff Henry, please," Flannery said quietly for the second time that afternoon.

Seconds later Hollis answered the phone. "Sheriff Henry."

"Hollis, it's Flannery—"

"Flannery, I heard. Is Jean okay?"

"She'll be fine."

"Good, the last thing I need is another body in the river."

"She's okay. Mrs. Taylor is here helping me with her now. I need to talk to you right away." Flannery wrapped the phone cord around her hand, gripping the receiver, looking out the window toward the river.

"What about? Look, Flannery, I'm very busy," Hollis said, annoyed.

Flannery looked over her shoulder, then cupped her hand over the receiver. "It's about Patsy and—"

"I already told you. You need to let that go."

"I need the truth."

"Listen—"

"No, you listen—" She squeezed the phone, knocked her boot against the base of the counter.

"Patsy was a whore," he bit out in a hard whisper.

"That's my sister you're talking about, you bastard, and I won't let you—"

"God, woman, give it a rest. Give your mama some peace!"

For a few seconds the phone went silent, and she feared he'd hung up on her. Then he said, "Shit, for the love of all that's holy, leave it be."

Flannery flexed her cramping fingers around the phone and whispered, "I'm telling you, Hollis, if I don't talk to you soon, I'm going to go talking to someone else. Maybe"—she drew a breath—"the state police . . ."

He hissed into the receiver. "Shit, Flannery. I'm in the middle of something." She heard paper rattle, then his sigh. "Okay, I'll swing by tomorrow at lunch."

"No," she said, shaking. "Not tomorrow. Not here. Mama . . . Mama's not well, and she can't be disturbed. I'll meet you now."

"It's too busy and loud here, and I can't get away until after six."

Flannery stretched the cord over to the screen door and looked out toward Ebenezer, then down at Honey Bee's old watch to her fast-ticking eight minutes—Patsy's minutes, all Flannery's stolen minutes, and those robbed from her unborn children.

In Hollis's voice came a ringing of untruths and truths. It all hit her. Flannery knew she wouldn't have left Glass Ferry if Patsy were still here. Wouldn't have cut off her *one and the same* and married that bastard Mark Hamilton. Wouldn't have lost her babies and with them a chance for family, for children of her own.

That all of it was, most surely, Hollis's foul doing. He'd interfered with so many lives. Hers, Patsy's, and Danny's. And Mama's, poor Mama's. His meanness, lust, and false, rotted power had rooted all this. Flannery pulled her anger into a hard fist, slapped it against her thigh, knocked her boot against the door.

"Listen. I sure hate to hear you tearing yourself up over all this old stuff, peaches." Hollis dropped a concern into his voice. "Henrys and Butlers have been like family," Hollis murmured, soft and syrupy, pulling in doubt.

She let the anger in her voice weaken some. "It hurts not knowing, Hollis—"

"I'm feeling it too. Danny was a good brother. Hell, a better kid than me. I'm trying to be a better man now, Flannery."

"I just can't take knowing they were harmed. That my twin might've been hurt like your brother. My poor mama's beside herself just thinking—"

"Hell, I love your mama like my own. Louise checks in with a dish every month, visiting Jean. I lowered her property bills the last ten years to ease her pocketbook. Did Jean tell you that? Tell you I only stamp a due of a measly two dollars on her yearly taxes?"

Her mama hadn't asked her for extra money in a long time, though Flannery sent her a check every month.

"I care, Flannery. Let's just put this behind us. I know your daddy was a forgiving man. Me too—"

The words of the thieving river rats lit fresh, and she shifted, tapping her boot against the floor. The crumbs Hollis fed Mama came from guilty fingers.

"Fight for it," Honey Bee'd said. "Don't let him pinch one tender second from you. . . ."

Flannery slipped out the door, stretching the long curled telephone cord with her. "Meet me on Ebenezer."

A short silence filled the airwaves, then Hollis grumbled, "I can be there at 6:15."

"I'll be waiting."

# CHAPTER 26

Flannery moved under the old elm, the last hours of daylight falling through its branches, dancing across her itchy feet.

In the distance, sleepy cowbells jangled over on Parsons's farm as his cows lumbered home for the evening. Overhead, swallows swooped for supper, and a single cardinal tasseled a lilt onto its crest, racing home to its branch. A wind dropped and set its teeth into tall grasses, combing wild onion and tangling fencerow jasmine honeying the June air.

Flannery trembled a little. She couldn't shake off the earlier chill from the river. And being here in the pull of the leaving hour didn't help matters. Normally, it didn't bother her, but today it exaggerated all uneasy feelings.

She spotted an old gasoline can sitting next to the cemetery's iron gate and frowned. Folks were always dumping stuff out here, the high school kids leaving behind their beer bottles and trash, and once even a ratty couch.

Flannery tried to flick off her bad feelings and nudged her boot at the patch of dandelions and forget-me-nots beside her foot.

She looked over at the scraggly flowers at the crumbly chimney, and hugged herself, remembering the time when she and Patsy had gone picking where they weren't supposed to.

Flannery had talked Patsy into coming along with her to the Deer homestead, to that ol' garden of forbidden fruit her parents warned them about.

They'd found some Easter lilies that had sprung up by the chimney blocks and brought them home to Mama.

Honey Bee asked where the pretty flowers came from, and when he found out, he puffed up in a fit of anger and lit both their little hineys with a switch, fired their backsides up so bad they had to carry pillows around to cushion their bottoms for three whole days.

Mama had been angrier, and that scared the girls most. Mama never showed an ugly side, ever. But on that day, her face took on a hardness, and her eyes flickered dangerously, Flannery remembered as if it happened just last week.

Mama had firmly shaken each of them, saying, "Don't ever do that again." Then she took those flowers straight out into the yard and poured kerosene onto their pretty, sunny heads and set them on fire. After, Mama cried and disappeared into her room for the rest of the day.

Flannery and Patsy cried too. Though they didn't rightly know their entire wrongdoing and were confused. Patsy was so frightened she broke out in hives.

To this day, Flannery still wondered about those Easter lilies and why Honey Bee and Mama had acted that way, why they wouldn't speak about it ever again.

Flannery turned away from those thoughts and those clumps of flowers. Once more, she looked down the road for signs of Hollis. Pulling the cardigan tighter to her chest, glancing at Honey Bee's old wristwatch on her arm and then back down Ebenezer Road and doing it all again.

Several times, Flannery checked her jean pocket, patting. Nearly thirty minutes later than he'd said, he was *stealing her time.*

His crookery riled her, boiled in her blood. She knew Hollis was just as bad as her ex, always thieving time from her, nipping here and there until it was all spent. Flannery growled "robber" into the winds and tapped an angry foot on a thick tree root.

She couldn't be gone too late. Mama might need her. Flannery had told Mrs. Taylor she was going out to stretch her legs while Mama napped, maybe take herself a walk to the barn and along the banks of the river.

"The fresh air'll do you good, sweet pea. Take your time. I'll take care of things in here." Mrs. Taylor had happily shooed Flannery out of the kitchen, saying she would stay and put together a meal for them.

Flannery'd walked toward the barn and then, halfway there, cut through the trees, stealing away toward Ebenezer.

Just when Flannery thought he wouldn't show, and a full hour had been chiseled from her lifetime, Flannery heard his car speeding down Ebenezer, flying gravel biting at the frame and its tires.

Hollis pulled in next to the cemetery gate, started to get out but left the engine running. He stood leaning against the open door with his left foot on the ground and the other propped on the running board.

"You're late," she said, annoyed.

He held up a hand. "Louise is expecting me home for dinner. I've had a rough day. I sure hope you're not going to make it worse with more of your nonsense."

"Depends," she said, walking over to him. "I want to know about the fight you had with Danny and Patsy that night. Why you shot him. Shot him with *my* daddy's gun."

"Dammit, Flannery, that's not true." His jaw hardened.

"Isn't it? You were packing that night."

"You don't know anything."

"I know you owned a .38 just like what they said was used on Danny. The very gun your daddy pinched off my daddy for hush pay."

"He never—"

"I know he did."

Hollis tightened his mouth and sliced his hand through the air. "Your sister caused this mess. Damn well did, and now I'm left to clean it up."

Flannery shook her head and poked a finger at him. "I'm going to the state police and you—"

He grabbed her wrist, pulled her to the door frame. "You

need to stop this now. Stop railing about this old shit. You'll have folks upset and talking—"

"Folks'll know the truth."

"It'd kill mine, for all you care. Ruin my job, ruin my life. Hell"—he grimaced—"nobody needs to be hurt, and nobody, ain't *nobody* needs to know this old, ugly history. Now look, Flannery," he wheedled, "you can have yourself a nice funeral and put Patsy to rest. Me and my dad'll even pay—"

"Pay with Butler money." Flannery gave a short, tight laugh. "All those taxes he slapped on Honey Bee. He got rich off. *Your* family got fat from. I believe the Henrys could pay all of Glass Ferry's funerals while you two are it. I was there when your thieving daddy stole Honey Bee's gun after my daddy tried to protect us from a few river rats who were set on robbing—"

"Watch what you say. My dad's not a thief. Everybody in town knows he's an honorable, respectable retired lawman. And I don't know a damn thing about that old stuff you're try-ing to bring up. But you wanna run 'shine, you're gonna pay. And Honey Bee wanted to run 'shine," Hollis said, shrugging. "Them's the rules. *That's* the truth."

"Honey Bee was a respected businessman with a license, and your daddy—"

Hollis turned and grabbed the car door, dismissing her. "Shut up and go home. You're just trying to damn the whole town along with you and your mama with the likes of stuff nobody needs to know. Get on home, Flannery, or I'll throw you in the pokey for disorderly conduct."

A fear gripped her; memories of her ex having her locked in the insane asylum thumped hot into her eardrums. For a second she almost bolted. A crow cried from its perch on the elm, caw-ing twice, grounding her. She thought about Patsy's fear, what might've driven her sister to bury those garments under the tree like that. Flannery cut a stony eye at Hollis.

"I need to know the whole truth, Hollis," she said quietly, taking a breath.

"It won't do anybody any good. Not now."

"I know what you did to Patsy."

"I cared for her."

She lit her eyes to the old elm.

"Look, Flannery, we were just kids. All of us, dumb kids. Doing dumb stuff."

"I have to do this, make this right. You have to do this. For me and Mama, for everybody."

Hollis gritted his teeth. "It'll surely do your mama in. My dear old dad, too."

"Not knowing will do her in." Flannery pulled out the bullet from her pocket and wagged it. "I found this prom night. Right over there by *your* dirty secrets."

Hollis's eyes widened in disbelief. "Th-that old bullet don't prove a thing. Not a damn thing, peaches."

"Unless this and that bullet in the Mercury match your snub nose. *You* shot him with my daddy's old .38 that *your* daddy pinched from him. You shot Danny, didn't you? It was you. Not Patsy. And I mean to safeguard Patsy's memories. For Mama's sake. My family's."

Flannery could see the truth tightening in Hollis's cold, silent eyes. "I knew it," she said. "The one and only question is, you going to tell? Or am I—"

"Dammit, it was an accident. *Please*, Flannery." Hollis moved out from behind the car door and faced her. "I swear. Danny went for my gun, and it went off. She was trying to pin her bastard on me first, then Danny—"

"I don't believe you—"

"It was an accident. She came on to me. Same as she cheated on Danny—"

"Liar!"

"Look here. Nobody killed anybody. Hell, I can't even remember much of that night. Nothing but getting knocked out by them. Out cold. You saw, same as me. I was lying under the tree over there, coldcocked."

"Then tell them everything. Tell them about Patsy—"

"Tell 'em WHAT?" he roared. "*What?* That she played me?

Tell them I gave her what my little brother couldn't? Right over there." He snapped his arm to the elm. "Tell that the bastard she carried was mine—"

"You . . . you said it was Danny's on prom night. Right here, you swore it."

"I know'd it was mine. Saw the truth on her panties she buried," he said weakly, rubbing his brow, like he suddenly remembered it all. "Shit, Flannery, I would've given the bastard my name—could've made an honest woman outta the moonshiner's daugh—"

"You don't deserve a good woman."

"I have myself one—kids now, and another on the way. Look, Patsy was just an easy piece of tail. Hell, you can't fault a young Kentucky buck for—"

"Patsy would've never been with you. The likes of you. She loved Danny. *Only* Danny. You forced her—"

"You know better than that. Shit." Hollis hissed, and his breath came hot and heavy at her face, a whiskey'd pant riding it. "Know that kind of girl needs a real man."

"You let your whiskey talk too much." Flannery wiggled the bullet again. "And you're a liar, a long-tongued liar."

"Humph. Who're you to be talking to me about drinking? The daughter of an ol' moonshiner who drank himself to death? Hardly. Hell, nobody'd begrudge a hardworking lawman having himself a cocktail or two after duty."

"You mean the dirty, lying dog folks are going to hear about when I tell 'em how you violated my sister. Shot your own brother."

Hollis laughed cruelly. "Nobody'd believe ya. You're a gawdamn blue book."

Flannery felt the punch in the gut.

"That's right." Hollis smiled ugly. "You think nobody knew about you going to the loco house? Was about 1955 or thereabouts, I believe." He twirled a finger in front of her face. "Your dear mama got worried for word. Hadn't heard from you in a month, I recall. Said she couldn't reach you. And then she came a'callin' to her old friends, the Henrys. Asked us to find you. I searched and searched for the sake of your dear mama. I found you all right."

Flannery held up a hand. "Shut up."

"Found you tucked in the Louisville Police Department's blue book, right smack in their list for touched folks. *Cuckoo, cuckoo,*" Hollis sang.

"You won't be singing when they come a'calling for your snub nose. When the law finds out what you did to my sister. Your brother—"

"*You're* gonna keep that fat trap of yours shut." He stabbed a finger at Flannery. " 'Cause she came on to me, and I did no more than oblige and did the whore right here, right here in the dirt." He spit and slammed his fist on his hood. "Had a piece of that right there, peaches. Oh, she cried some, but I gave her a few belts of hooch to heat her up, and she warmed real quick."

"You sorry, no-good bastard, you raped her. Raped my sister! Sent her and her baby off to die! They put rapists in prison. And we both know you'll find out what happens to the likes of those in there."

Hollis's face darkened with rage, and he turned and kicked at the old gas can somebody had left, spilling out a little, tumbling the container near his car door. "Yessiree, folks." He raised his hands and called to the wind. "Yessiree, good folks of Glass Ferry, let me tell *you, and you, and you,* about the whoring Miss Patsy Butler!"

A puff of gasoline fumes licked the air.

"Shut up, you sonofabitch! Liar. You call yourself a lawman—"

Cocking his head sideways, he eyed Flannery. "Oh, wait. Maybe you'd like a little of what she had, some of this lawman. What that ex of yours couldn't give you. No wonder you went cuckoo."

"I said shut up."

"You needing this. Is that it, peaches? All you had to do was ask." Hollis grabbed her hand and slipped it to his crotch.

Flannery jerked back, slapped him hard across the face.

"Had her begging, I did," he whispered low, rubbing his red, smarting cheek. "By the time I was through, Patsy girl was asking for more. Praying for it, peaches. Wonder what Mama will say 'bout *that?*"

Flannery tried to hit him again, but he knocked her arm away and snatched the gun from his holster.

"I *swear*—" Hollis tucked his teeth over tight lips and shook the weapon at her.

"W-what are you going to do? Haul me to jail? Arrest the woman who just lost her sister? Folks'll surely talk and ask why. They'll see who's crazy then. I'll sing—" Flannery stopped when she saw a killing take hold in his eyes.

"I swear you and that bitch ain't gonna take everything I have. Everything I've worked for. I've paid my dues."

"You took—"

"*You!* You think you can smear the Henry name? The bootlegger's family dirtying my good family's name. I won't let you. I won't let you do that."

"I . . . I made one more call, to the state police, before I came." Flannery squeaked out the lie, praying he'd buy it.

Hollis looked down Ebenezer like he believed she had.

Flannery struck out and grabbed for the gun, getting a grip on his hand. Hollis whipped an elbow up and caught her chin.

Fury anchored and brought forth a might she didn't know she had. Flannery's head snapped, and she lunged at him, clawing at his eyes.

Hollis yowled, and pressed a hand to his face, dropping the gun.

Flannery whipped out the Robin Hood pistol tucked inside her boot and stumbled back. "You . . . you sinful son of a bitch." She shifted her eyes between him and the gas can. The gun shook a little in her hands. A glint of late summer sunlight bounced off her wristwatch, slashed across Hollis's eyes. "You'll not steal another second from me," she breathed.

"D-drop it," Hollis said, stooped, cupping his eye, stretching the other arm blindly toward her. "Drop it."

Pointing the pistol at his head, then at the rusted gas can near Hollis's feet and back and forth, and then back on the can, and once more to him, she looked down the barrel, cocked the hammer, shifted, and squeezed the trigger. Then came the muzzle flash. The loud crack. She fired once more and heard a clang as if the car had been hit once, maybe both times. Sparks raised from the gas can.

Hollis screamed.

Flannery staggered backwards.

A strange rush of wind lit the air. *Charged.* The devil stuck his fiery hand up through the hot earth, looking for his sinner.

Flannery scrambled away from the flames that licked out, leapt into the car, onto the grass, exploding, and lighting that time thief on fire.

Hollis turned in tight circles, shrieking.

Flannery screamed too. Then she looked at the outlaw's gun in her hand and quickly slipped it back down into her boot.

The car hissed and popped, burst from the heat. She pushed back, covered her eyes, and cursed into the snapping flames.

"*Here's your paddle,*" she yelled at him for what he'd done and the precious time he'd snatched away from all of them.

Shards of glass and metal shot out of his car. Flames flew, licking, yapping at the ground, hopping in fiery stacks across the grass, pushing Flannery back even more.

Flannery heard crying, weeping, someone else's, maybe her own? She darted her eyes all around and rested them on the elm. A haze of smoke crawled across the trunk's rooted feet, turned upright into a wispy cloud, and disappeared.

Hollis whimpered. When she turned to him, he cried out once again. Weaker this time, then rattling out a calf-sick bawl before quieting.

Flannery watched him twitching in the dirt, engulfed in flames, the last cry caught in his chest.

In the distance, hounds yapped, jarring Flannery out of her unbending. She lifted an ear to the barks, and then dared to peek back at Hollis again. Horrified at what she'd done, what she'd allowed to happen, she covered her face, choked out a sob.

Turning her back against his dead-eyed stare, Flannery lit out for home.

# CHAPTER 27

Reaching the porch, Flannery bent over to catch her breath. She grabbed the banister for support, the wood slipping in her buttery hands.

The screen door creaked opened, and Mrs. Taylor stepped out. Flannery swallowed her surprise and straightened.

"Oh. It's you, sweet pea. I thought I heard a loud noise out here," Mrs. Taylor said, then widened her eyes. "What on earth happened? Look at your—"

"I-I'm fine." Flannery touched her cheek and felt the soreness where Hollis had hit her. "Just stumbled back there a ways." Flannery made a show to dust herself off, grabbed the banister. "Is Mama okay—"

"Yes, she's still napping. I've had dinner ready for a while and I was just waiting on you." Mrs. Taylor looked past her, and Flannery followed her gaze to a plume of smoke rising in the distance. "Look. It's a fire, Flannery," Mrs. Taylor said, pinning a finger to Ebenezer Road.

"Sorry, the time got away from me. I heard something too, Mrs. Taylor. I, uh, I was in the barn. That's why I came running," Flannery lied. "I wonder if one of the farmers is burning something. Maybe someone's tractor caught on fire or . . ." She tried to think of more excuses to give the old woman.

"That doesn't look so good. I should call the fire department," Mrs. Taylor said.

"I better check on Mama." Flannery hurried past her and into the parlor. Trembling, she stuffed Jesse James's pistol back into the secretary drawer and then looked in on Mama, who was still sleeping, out cold from her swim.

Flannery pulled a quilt up over her mama, pushed a fallen lock off her cheek. "You rest, Mama; get better. I won't let anyone hurt us again." Flannery retreated to her own bedroom.

Digging out her old sky-blue Samsonite suitcase from under the bed, Flannery laid it on the mattress. She flipped open the clasp and scattered the small pile of clothes, locking her fingers around the smooth neck of the fifth of whiskey Honey Bee'd given her long ago.

A swallow would help knock down her fear. Or knock her on her tail. But just one long pull could right her nerves. That's all she wanted. Just to steady her nerves. So she could right her mind with calm thinking.

Flannery pressed the cool glass to her forehead. From outside came the long, quivering cry of sirens. A few seconds later, another, and another. One, then one more wailing, piggybacking onto the others.

Rolling the bottle over her cheek, she pressed the glass to her hungering mouth, tapped. "Not for the Devil," she finally whispered, and stuffed it back into the suitcase. She wouldn't open it, not unless it was her daddy's birthday, and then only for a nip to toast him and his goodness. *Certainly not for the likes of Hollis Henry.*

She would never do that again. Wouldn't disgrace herself and her kin, like Uncle Mary had rightfully accused her of back then. It might start her hankering for bigger things that were locked up in white apothecary cabinets kept in bigger places. Couldn't risk the long tooth for those pills again, those stronger, newer medicines, those feeling deadeners. Those bigger things that at one time helped bury her drowning aches and despairs. Those tonics and elixirs in locked, sterile hospital wards.

Flannery teared up remembering what she'd just done, all of it, the bullets, the silences when asked—and called for Honey

Bee to help her, prayed that she'd given Hollis no more of a paddle than he deserved, and then begged for her sister's peace. "Patsy, your secrets are safe. You can sleep in peace now."

She prayed that justice had been met, and that there was nothing more needed telling. Her sister's and her family's reputation would remain unsullied, and Hollis's tale of Danny playing around with a gun would eventually stick. Stick like most tall tales and gossip did in small-town Glass Ferry.

Mrs. Taylor came to her bedroom door and said she'd reheat the dinner and it would be ready shortly, chattering on about the "fire over yonder." Flannery stood in the middle of her room, waiting for the officials to drop by, to come snooping, and told Mrs. Taylor she'd be down shortly. When minutes rolled past and still not a one had called, she started breathing tiny sighs of relief.

Mrs. Taylor served up chicken and dumplings, cornbread, and mustard greens. Mama ate hearty, and Mrs. Taylor said she was relieved to see the color bloom in Jean Butler's cheeks.

Flannery picked at her food, tried to eat, but couldn't stop thinking of how she'd robbed Hollis of his last meal, couldn't stop her hands from shaking.

Mrs. Taylor and Mama chatted about old times, and soon Mama smiled.

Flannery washed the supper dishes, while Mrs. Taylor visited with Mama on the porch.

Myrtle Taylor left just before a storm blew in. It rained hard, coming down in sheets that pelted the panes, whipped at the old two-story, dropped dead branches onto both the roof and Flannery's spirit. She checked on Mama several times, wearing out the floorboards in front of her window, jumping at the slightest sounds.

Parting the curtain, she looked out. Again and again. When the rain settled into a mist, Flannery seized hold of a thimble of hope and magpied it away. The rain was a good thing, she surmised; surely it would hide any footprints left on Ebenezer. Hide what the fire hadn't—and maybe erase her deed completely.

Holding that hope, Flannery fell into bed, tossing and turning most of the night until she climbed back out at four in the morning.

Flannery dug in the drawer for Patsy's pearls, then packed the family heirloom back inside, damning the night she'd found them and all the lies and souls she was stacking up because of them. *For God's sake. What have I done? I only meant to scare Hollis.* She spilled bitterly into her pillow until spent; her head ached, and a fitful sleep took hold again.

In the morning, Flannery served Mama breakfast, keeping their conversation away from their worries. She chatted with Mama about the weather and other meaningless things that wouldn't beg for more, and Mama stuck with it, the meds sedating her old nerves and then sending her off to nap.

Flannery cleaned up the kitchen, made iced tea, and whipped together ham salad for dinner. Turning on the radio, she kept one ear cocked on it, the other bent to the drive for unexpected visitors.

She rested at the counter with a glass of iced tea. The radio announcer interrupted a Marvin Gaye song. "It has been confirmed that Sheriff Hollis Henry of Glass Ferry died last night on the way to County Hospital, Deputy Miles of Glass Ferry's Sheriff's Department said. The sheriff died of injuries sustained in an accident."

Flannery's hands shook, and she set down the glass, pressed a hand over her mouth.

The announcer went on. "Apparently the Glass Ferry sheriff was removing an old gas can, and it blew up due to an unexplained cause, fatally injuring the thirty-nine-year-old father of three, husband to Mrs. Louise Crawford Henry. . . . Deputy Miles said that the department does its best to control litter, picking up everything from old ammunition, lighters, and all kinds of trash kids leave behind. Sheriff Henry was particular about keeping vandals off Ebenezer Road, but the department had seen an increase in offenses now that school was out. . . . The department will now permanently close off the old gravel road with a bull gate that neighboring farmer, Rusty Parsons, offered to have erected."

A puff of static lit the airways.

Flannery leaned into the counter and turned up the dial. ". . . Deputy said many times the good sheriff took it upon himself to pick up the trash. . . . Funeral arrangements are being made by . . ."

Flannery sank down onto the kitchen chair. She wasn't happy or proud that Hollis was gone by her doing, but a deep gratefulness slumped her anxious shoulders.

Mama came into the kitchen. She peered at Flannery's face. "What is it, baby girl?"

"Oh, Mama, more bad news."

The house creaked, gasped like it couldn't take anymore, couldn't choke down one more sorrow.

"Flannery Bee?"

Flannery wiped the reprieve from her damp eyes. "It seems Sheriff Henry had an accident. A horrible accident."

# CHAPTER 28

Flannery and Mama made arrangements to bury Patsy in their family cemetery. But old man Mr. Henry had other thoughts and came out to the Butlers to share them with the women.

The former sheriff suggested the three—Patsy, Danny, and Hollis—share funeral services, even be buried beside one another out at the old Catholic cemetery. "It will quell rumors and unite the community," he said, taking off his cap, scratching his bald head. "And it sure is a pretty marble orchard for our young ones too."

"What are you talking about, Jack?" Mama asked him when he dropped into the empty porch rocker beside her.

"Well"—the old man shifted in his seat, pulled his lanky frame toward her—"I'm talking 'bout folks thinking bad things here."

Flannery stepped out onto the porch. "What bad things?" she couldn't help but ask, alarm prickling her flesh.

"Killings," Mr. Henry said, shifting his eyes. "Folks are saying Hollis was so distraught about his dear brother, he took his own life out there. That maybe Patsy shot Danny. We don't know—"

Mama clutched her chest.

"Now see here, Mr. Henry," Flannery said. "*I know.* My sister wouldn't stomp a blade of grass, and Danny likely did his own self in just like Hollis said he did."

"She wouldn't," Mama echoed.

Mr. Henry held up a hand. "Folks is speculating; that's all, Jean. Running their flaps. So I thought burying the kids together would bring us all together. Keep us together. Keep folks from gossiping."

"Gossiping?" The word wormed itself into Mama's brow. "Jack, Saint Luke's closed decades ago when it burned down." Mama bunched up her forehead tighter.

"Not the church's cemetery though, Jean. And it has plenty of space," Mr. Henry said. "Fine headstones. We'll do a grand one for Hollis, Danny, and your girl, too. My Hollis never let a day pass that he didn't look for those two or worry for their whereabouts. He devoted his days to finding them, raising money for the school prom they'd missed, honoring them. Good son, good brother. We give them a proper burial in Saint Luke's, we'll give them poor souls a good Catholic anchor, the one and true, for eternal rest."

Glass Ferry still had its share of churches: two Methodists, and one Pentecostal in the hollows, a Disciples of Christ, the Colored Christian Church, and a Baptist place of worship for the 826 folks living there.

The Butler family belonged to the Truth Disciples of Christ, or at least Mama and the girls did, even though Honey Bee'd never had the fancy to show up but a handful of times and then only because he'd been henpecked by Mama's friends to attend their kin's baptismals and weddings. Sometime during the service, he'd steal out, and Mama and the girls would find him waiting in the lot to tote them home, his tie loosened from its knot, his pressed collar flipped up, tickling his chin, the dark jacket slung over his shoulder.

Mama'd ask him why he couldn't stay put long enough for the sermon. Honey Bee would grin a little embarrassed and tell her she should've joined him for the fine sermon out here. Then he'd point to the sky, the countryside, the grasses and trees, birds and other critters.

Flannery placed a hand on Mama's shoulder and told Mr. Henry, "We're burying Patsy with Honey Bee and my brothers. With *our* kin on Butler Hill."

"Honey Bee," Mama said, as if suddenly remembering. "It would kill Daddy's good soul knowing his baby girl was buried in the Catholic cemetery like that. I have to bury her beside my Honey Bee and my precious boys, Jack."

"Jean—"

"My family."

"Suit yourself." Jack Henry stood, stuffed his hands into his pockets, and left.

# CHAPTER 29

Mama called on her preacher, Isaac Nefas, to conduct the funeral service. On a dismal day, Flannery and Mama buried Patsy's remains in Butler Hill Cemetery, overlooking the river.

They'd hushed up Mr. Henry's suggestion and had the small coffin of bones placed in the ground next to Honey Bee, Patsy's brothers, and her grandparents, surrounded by their ancestors, a couple of outlaws, and a few slave graves.

Flannery and Mama and a handful of folks, mostly from Mama's canasta club, along with old man Henry, Junior and his wife and kids, and a few others, huddled on the hill under umbrellas as Pastor Nefas rang the dead bell four times, calling for prayer for Patsy's soul and scattering away any lurking evil spirits.

When the service was over, Mr. Henry sidled up to Mama, tipped his brown felt hat, and put his hand on Patsy's casket. "Jean, it ain't right how you separated those two," he said, and pianoed the little coffin with his fingers, tapping out his grievance. "I knew Danny was smitten with her. Hell, he might've even married her. And I would've paid for Patsy's burial in the Catholic cemetery." He shook the dampness off his hand. "Put her beside my good boys."

Mama's eyes widened. "Now see here, Jack. She belongs here. And Butlers don't accept charity."

"You are a foolish woman, Jean Butler." His old voice was weak, watery.

"I will surely not be beholden to you again, only to have you come back collecting later like you did on my dear Honey Bee. You'll not get another red cent of Butler money," Mama said.

Mr. Henry flinched at the mention of collecting granny fees. "Taxes had to be collected according to the law. Honey Bee knew this. And I know Hollis had been going light on your homestead taxes for some time."

"Butlers earned that, what with all you took when we were barely scraping by," Mama said. "We hardly made it out of the Depression."

"We all pay our dues, Jean."

"Lord, Jack." Mama's voice dropped to a scalding whisper. "You know Honey Bee and I have paid ours dearly."

"Now, Jean, we're not talking about—"

Flannery placed her hand protectively on Mama's shoulder. Mama patted it. "Paid with blood," she spat, seeming to draw a fire from her daughter's grip.

"Ssh, Mama, don't upset yourself." Confused, Flannery looked at Mr. Henry and her mama locked in a secret moment.

"It's bad doings what you've done here, Jean," he said. "It's still not too late to have her transported over to the Catholic cemetery for tomorrow's service—"

"I will not!"

Mr. Henry looked over to the huddle of old-timers waiting to lower Patsy's coffin into the ground. "Just saying it ain't right to separate those two after all this time," he whispered.

"What ain't right, sir, is your boy took my girl. Took my girl right over that cliff," Mama huffed.

"We know Patsy went off on her own accord."

"She wouldn't have driven herself into the river like that. Your boy did that." Mama cut an accusing hand out from under her umbrella into the mist.

Mr. Henry hissed low, "She seduced my boy, sure as a Kentucky summer is long and hot. *She* caused that accident."

Mama gasped. "Is that what you think, Jack Henry? Is that what you're telling folks now?"

"Just calling it like I know it, Jean."

"Well, we're done then. *Good 'n' done.*" Mama's eyes filled. "Leave. You can leave right now, Jack Henry, and let us mourn her without your filthy, false accusations."

"I'm hurting too, Jean." Mr. Henry rubbed a tight fist over his damp eye, tucked his teeth under a grimace. "Lost both my boys." He stabbed an eye to Flannery.

Mama reached for Flannery's cold hand.

"Go," Mama whispered.

When everyone departed, four men quietly came forward and lowered Patsy's small coffin into the hole.

Flannery and Mama gripped each other and looked away, Mama's muffled sobs soaking Flannery's shoulder. They stayed that way until the sound of shovels and falling earth struck hot in Flannery's ears and a tightening wrenched her throat and the sadness rumbled—until she could no longer trust her weakened legs to carry Mama home.

The next day the state trooper came back to the Butler house.

Claymore Green stepped out of his police cruiser and pulled his tall frame up to the porch.

"Mrs. Butler. Mrs. Hamilton," Trooper Green greeted. "I hope I'm not disturbing you." He had a clipboard with papers.

Flannery didn't say a word and clasped her trembling hands behind her back.

Mama held out her hand. "Come on up and have a seat, Trooper."

Flannery moved the newspaper off the rocking chair and remembered. Remembered where she knew the trooper from. She'd seen him in the *Glass Ferry Gazette's* newspaper a few years ago, read about him right here on Mama's porch. The trooper had gotten into a bit of trouble about tickets he'd turned in at the end of his shift.

Yes, that was it. A sort of depression had taken hold of the young lawman, the paper reported. Law officials found out no one had showed up for court, or paid fees on the tickets Trooper Green handed out for almost a year after his mother died.

His mama's car had been struck while crossing a train track. Unable to bear any more misery, cause anyone more suffering or sadness, they said that during the young trooper's shift he began visiting the cemetery where his mama was buried.

A year passed before a court clerk discovered the indiscretion after one of Trooper Green's tickets landed on his desk. The clerk had been surprised to see it was written to his grandmother, who'd died ten years ago, and every single citation from the trooper had been issued to dead folks, the names plucked from their gravestones.

Nothing came of it, Flannery recalled, just some light-duty desk work for a short spell, meetings with the police chaplain, until the incident was good and hushed.

Flannery snatched a glimpse of the trooper. She supposed everyone had a bit of blue book in them, or at the very least, was just a blink away from getting themselves on that list.

Now, Trooper's shoulders seemed to relax, and there was warmth on his strong face when he looked at her mama, a softening inside him.

"Ma'am, I'm glad to see you're feeling better." Trooper Green gave her a smile. "You're sure looking fit today."

"Thank you, Trooper Green. I do feel better now that we got Patsy back and had her a proper burial. Do have a seat," Mama patted the chair, perking.

"God rest her," he murmured, and sat down. "Ma'am, my captain wanted me to wrap up this case. Before I close it, I'd like to make sure I have everything right. Mind?"

"Of course not. Will you have a glass of tea?" Mama asked.

"No, ma'am. Thanks. I need to ask a few more things about your daughter. Sorry for prying, but it's important. Did Patsy have a temper?"

"Heavens no," Mama piped. "Patsy was more like me, where Flannery"—she smiled kindly at her daughter—"is a lot like her daddy."

Flannery felt her face warm, but stayed put and rested her back against the porch beam.

"I know it's been a long time, but did Patsy have any reason to want to harm Danny? Did he do anything to make her upset that you might recall?" Trooper pressed.

"Lord a'mercy!" Mama startled. "I raised my girls as good Christians, sweet girls. My Patsy wouldn't do harm to anyone. I know that as well as my name." She fluffed her frumpled duster, tugged at the collar. "Better than anyone."

Flannery wanted to scream, to shout out that it had been Hollis Henry. *It was all Hollis Henry.* Instead she crossed her arms and said, "That's just old gossip, Trooper. Instead of accusing my sister, you need to find the person who pulled a gun on them, maybe. Maybe somebody forced them off the road like that after shooting at them and hitting Danny."

"Sorry, ma'am," Trooper said, turning to Flannery. "I don't mean to disrespect. We're just trying to find out as much as we can." He tapped the clipboard with his pen. "Now, about the guns you have in the house—"

"I told you, Trooper." Flannery walked up behind her mama. "There's just my daddy's old shotgun in the closet and the outlaw's pistol." She rested her hands on Mama's shoulders.

Mama opened her mouth to say something.

"Nothing but those. Right, Mama?" Flannery lightly squeezed Mama's shoulders and patted. Confused, Mama nodded and folded her hands in her lap.

"Mind showing me that shotgun?" the trooper asked. "I'd like to be sure that I record it on paper."

"Sure, Trooper. We'll be right back, Mama." Flannery walked over to the screen door and held it open. Inside the foyer, Flannery opened the closet for him. "In there." She stepped aside, looking once over her shoulder to the parlor at Honey Bee's old secretary.

The trooper reached inside, lifted the shotgun, and inspected, then leaned it back against the wall, poking his eye to the top, bottom, and sides of the tiny coat closet. "Thanks, Mrs. Hamilton." He wrote something down on his clipboard.

Relieved, Flannery shut the door. And then, to cast suspicion away from her, from Patsy, everything, she wrung her hands, thinking how she could cinch it all.

"Anything else, Mrs. Hamilton?" The trooper looked at her busy hands.

"You know, Trooper"—she herded him closer to the door— "back then those Henry boys were always trouble."

Trooper straightened. "How so?"

"Seems everyone knew, talked about those two brothers snuggling too close to the batwing." Flannery patted her backside pocket where guys kept their bourbon flasks.

The trooper lifted a brow.

"Well"—Flannery licked her lips—"those boys were always drinking, and I suspect it wasn't any different prom night, maybe a bit extra to celebrate."

"Hollis said no one was drinking."

"Patsy wasn't drinking. Never drank a drop. But Hollis now, that's another story."

The trooper scratched his chin with the clipboard.

"Especially Hollis. *Lit.* Now that I think back, Trooper, I'm pretty sure I'd smelled the whiskey on him . . . lots of other times, too. But on that night, I'm sure I did." She wrinkled her brow in thought. "Yes, I did, though I'm sure I didn't want to get Patsy in trouble with Mama."

Trooper frowned. Flannery waited for him to write it all down, but he didn't.

"My classmates said Hollis never went anywhere without his ol' batwing," Flannery said. "Did ya'll find his flask in the wreck?"

Trooper Green looked lost in thought. Like he was thinking hard, maybe wishing someone else would do it for him.

Holding his gaze, she could almost see his thoughts there. The young trooper wouldn't disgrace a fellow lawman. Above all, he would protect Hollis's memory and the brotherhood they shared. As thick as kin. "All lawmen are related, and those relations are thicker than blood," Honey Bee had once remarked to Uncle Mary while discussing the business side of whiskey.

"Just in case something comes up, I better file this with the other open cases. If you can think of anything, no matter how small—" Trooper said.

"I'll call."

Trooper turned to leave. Flannery touched his arm and said quietly, "I know you got to take it all down, but please don't tell Mama. She's been through so much. It would break her heart."

A small relief seemed to wash over his face, and Trooper Green quickly gave an understanding nod.

Flannery followed him back out to the porch.

Mama jumped up from the rocker and asked, "Trooper, are you finished here?"

"Yes, ma'am. I've finished for now." Trooper shot Flannery a concerned look and laid a gentle hand on Mama's arm. "You take care."

When he left, Mama said, "Does he think Patsy would shoot someone? Why would he have that notion?"

"Don't worry, Mama. The gun they're looking for was smaller. We only had the shotgun and the James gun when Patsy went missing. Remember?"

"Yeah, Honey Bee's old hunting gun," Mama said as if relieved. "I don't know what he did with his old snub nose he was so fond of."

"Don't you fret none about that. Not a bit about anything. I'll worry for both of us." Mama folded herself back into the rocker. Flannery rubbed Mama's back, a chill scuttling a choke collar around her neck.

# CHAPTER 30

It wasn't a week after the funeral when Flannery met up with the trooper again.

She awakened one morning to find Mama gone. Flannery called the state police post and reached Trooper Green. Frantic, she asked him to check down at the river. "I'm throwing on some clothes and will be there as soon as I can," Flannery told him.

Flannery made it to the boat dock just as Trooper Green was peeling off his shirt and shoes. Mama, once again, stood up to her shoulders in the muddy water.

Trooper charged into the river with Flannery not far behind him.

Mama screamed at him and waded out deeper. Her head slipped under and bobbed back up just as the trooper tried to clutch her into his arms.

Even though he was taller and had a good footing, Trooper had a hard time latching on to Mama, and she pulled him under twice. By the time he and Flannery got her back to shore, the trooper was both furious and spent. After checking her out for injuries, he made her sit in the backseat of his cruiser and called for an ambulance on his police radio. "That was very foolish, Mrs. Butler. Not only foolish, but downright dangerous. Next time, I'll have to lock you up."

Mama's eyes filled, and she begged, "Please, oh, please, Trooper, get me back my baby's pearls. *Pleeease* . . . I miss my baby girl so much. It's all I have left of her." Her cold, wet hands shook as she reached out for him. "I need to hold the pearls and remember how beautiful she was in them. Remember her in her pretty yellow dress. The lovely pearls that put a sparkle in her eye. You should've seen her, Trooper."

"Ma'am, I understand, but—"

"She had a sweet smile when I clasped them around her neck that night. I can't, won't, have only *that* keepsake . . . a dirty, nasty ribbon to hold to her memory," Mama said weakly.

"Mama, *please*," Flannery said, not wanting anyone to know she'd brought home the small piece of evidence from the wreck. "Trooper Claymore, just let me take her home. I won't let her out of my sight."

The trooper lightened at the sight of Mama's tears and draped his dry shirt over her shoulders. He patted her arms. "Come on now, Mrs. Butler. Let's get you to the hospital and make sure you're okay." He turned to Flannery. "Can't do that again, ma'am. She's becoming a danger to herself. I have to get her checked out, or it'll all be on me."

Mama recovered from her swim within hours, but the doctors couldn't fix her broken heart. During her stay, doctors ended up trying something new for her nerves, this new pill, and another, some more new in a syringe another day, and then back to that better new, and again a *sure* new pill five days later, until they were convinced Jean Butler's nerves were rested and the old woman was strong enough to be dumped someplace else.

The doctors tried to figure out what to do with Mama and spent a good deal of that time just talking.

In town running errands, Flannery overheard folks talking too. Talking a lot. Talking sideways, anyways, and no-ways, trying to make sense of it all. Many gossiped it was ol' Joetta that had done the sheriff in, same as she must've done to his younger brother. Others swore and argued the ghost drew the teens to Ebenezer Road on prom night and sent them off to their cold, watery grave. That Hollis had even done himself in. And more than a few argued ol' Joetta was punishing Jean Butler, tormenting her for allowing her daughter to run off from Glass

Ferry and die like that. Patsy Butler was surely the murderer, a few prattled.

Lots of scared talk that folks puffed themselves up with to make them feel bigger and less frightened.

Flannery visited Mama at the hospital in the mornings and returned at night to tuck her in. She wanted to bring her flowers, but she couldn't make herself look at them, pick them up. Twice she walked into the small florist shop inside the hospital, and twice the scents ran her out and left her shaky and gagging.

The third time Flannery managed to pick up a bundle of cheerful sunflowers, Mama's favorite. She plucked them up from a glass shelf, carried them low where she wouldn't see them, keeping her grip sealed on the lip of the vase, holding it as close to her knee as she could without dropping it. But when Flannery reached the cash register, her legs knocked a little. Quickly she placed the flowers on the counter and opened her purse.

"That'll be four dollars and twenty-four cents," the clerk said, centering the Coke-bottle-green vase, pushing it back toward Flannery. "Now aren't these perfect for the gloomy skies we've been having." She smiled.

Something closed in Flannery's throat, and it became hard to breathe, hard to think through the pounding in her chest, the blood rushing up to her ears.

The lady caught Flannery's arm. "Honey," she said, "do you need to sit down?"

Flannery tried to blink and pull herself out of the toppling panic, but the anxious feeling grabbed ahold and wouldn't let go.

She jerked loose of the woman's grip and rushed out of the shop, fleeing down a long corridor.

A minute later Flannery found herself outside, in back of the hospital, bent over, taking in large gulps of air. Soon, she felt her legs getting back their grit, and she latched on to the corner of the building to straighten herself.

"Damn you, Mark," she said hoarsely, and smacked the concrete wall. She was missing more than what he and that old delivery doc took long ago, knew she would always feel her ex's choke leash on her neck, his bite on her skin.

Flannery pulled herself up and went back into the building. A doctor met her in the hall and said he would keep Mama a few more days, but advised Flannery to take Mama away from Glass Ferry. "Take her to a home for the idiots, if you can't care for her. The asylum," he suggested. "Her mind is failing. They can restrain her, best deal with her kind there."

"A home for idiots? Restrain her?" Flannery repeated his words.

"Yes," he said, in a mood to rush. "They are equipped to care for these creatures."

"Creatures? But—"

"Mrs. Hamilton, we're a hospital. We care for the ill. Not the *addled*. Now please, I have patients waiting."

That night when Flannery came to tuck Mama in, she found her tied to the bed with leather straps. Mama's arms were pulled up high and wide, ugly, stretched to the rails, and her legs were spread and fastened to the metal sides, her gown hitched up to her waist.

Mama pulled a helpless gaze to Flannery. Her lips quivered, but nothing came out.

"Mama! Who did this to you?" Flannery rushed to her side and went to work on the straps, loosening the knots and pressing the nurse call button in between her frantic efforts to get Mama free.

A nurse came in. "Mrs. Hamilton, what do you think you're doing?" The heavyset woman pushed Flannery's hand away from the last strap.

Flannery shoved the nurse's arm back.

"Mrs. Hamilton, you need to stop. You can't do that. The doctor gave orders for restraint." The nurse pulled up a strap.

"And I'm giving orders to release her." Flannery bumped the nurse aside.

"She tried to escape. We had no choice, Mrs. Hamilton. This afternoon we found her in the nursery ward. She was delusional, and argued with a nurse, accusing her of harming the babies—"

"I don't believe you." Flannery released the last strap, threw it on the floor, and pulled down Mama's gown to cover her nakedness. Quickly Flannery snatched the covers and stretched the thin blanket over her mama's shivering body.

"Mrs. Hamilton, I must insist—"

"Get out. Out. Dammit." Flannery cursed the nurse and rubbed Mama's ankles.

"*Flannery,*" Mama moaned.

"Shh, shh, Mama." Flannery gently patted Mama's reddening arm, rubbed the indents the strap had left behind.

A doctor came in behind her. "Mrs. Hamilton, you can't—"

"*You* can't! You can't tie her up like that. Like a dog. I'm taking her home," Flannery said.

"She needs her medicine tonight. And Doctor Owen won't be back till the morning," the doctor said. "He'll have to sign her out."

"I want her released now," Flannery said, dismissing him. She pressed her hand over Mama's.

"Help me," Mama whispered.

Flannery cringed. Mama's plea, her frail voice brought back Patsy's last plea for help. "Now," Flannery ordered the doctor, and then again louder over her shoulder, "right now." Flannery turned and showed him the fury in her eyes.

"Doctor Owen is the only one who can do that, little lady," the doctor clipped as he walked out the door. The nurse shuffled after him as if she wanted to talk to him without Flannery hearing.

Mama tried to rise, but slumped back whimpering. Flannery pulled her chair up to the iron bed and took Mama's cold, shaky hand. "Just rest, Mama."

They both remained silent for a good spell.

Finally Flannery said, "You'll be okay."

"I just wanted to hold the newborns," Mama said weakly. "The nurse said she couldn't be bothered to rock them."

"It's okay." Flannery tried to smile.

"That one nurse was the worst." Mama sniffled. "Said I wasn't even worth the air in the resuscitator can. Pinched my arms down with her knee while the large one put those tight straps on me." Mama rubbed her smarting arms.

"I'm sorry, Mama. You're safe now." Flannery leaned over and hugged, squeezed her gently.

"I was scared."

"I'm here now." Flannery shifted. "Mama, listen, the doctors want you to leave home. I want you to come back to the city with me."

Mama's tired eyes grew big. "Live in Louisville? Leave home?"

"It'll be nice. There's a cute studio down the street from me. A neighbor mentioned it'll be available at the end of the summer. And there's a big fabric store around the block. You can sew up a storm, make us some pretty dresses. Wouldn't that be nice?" Flannery forced a smile and pulled Mama's hand to her mouth and kissed it lightly. "Sew as much as you want and—"

"Leave Glass Ferry? Leave Patsy and Honey Bee and the babies?"

"We'll come back and visit the graves. I promise. The doc thinks it would be good for you to get away. We can sell the old house now. It's too much for you, Mama." Flannery rocked Mama's hand in hers. "Too much work."

"I—I just wanted the pearls. I didn't mean to cause—"

Flannery saw embarrassment in Mama's eyes.

"I know." She hated that Mama needed that old broken strand, those precious pearls, the broken lifeline, precious moments that were lost to both of them.

"I heard the nurses call me crazy. That one mean one called me a ninny and said it would serve me right to go to the old cuckoo asylum."

Flannery rubbed Mama's hand. "You're not going anywhere but with me."

Mama grew quiet for a few minutes, then said, "Where will I put all my stuff? And Patsy's and Honey Bee's? I can't leave my baby boys' cradle. All those things from my life, their sweet memories I kept to keep giving me life? I can't lose any more of them, not another single piece. It's all I have left now." Mama balled up the hospital sheet in her other hand, squeezed.

"You have me. And don't you worry none; I'll help you pack everything you need. We'll try to take as much as we can, and we can always store the rest."

"When? When do I have to say good-bye?"

"I don't have to be back to teaching until late August. I have to get my classroom ready for September. We'll leave in August. Okay, Mama?"

A shame and brokenness filled Mama's eyes as a hopelessness settled into her frail shoulders and rocked them both, and she sobbed, bobbing her head in defeat.

"All is lost." Mama covered her trembling lips, smothering a cry. "Just like with your brothers. Just like then . . ."

Flannery couldn't look at her, knew that she could never look at her again if she didn't do something. She pulled her tired bones up from the chair. Kneeling down beside the bed, she laid her head on Mama's belly like she had when she was young and needed comforting.

In a few minutes, Mama stroked her hair. "My baby," she said softly.

*I'll go to the trooper tomorrow. Tell him everything. I must do the right thing for Mama.*

"My angel, my good girl," Mama said in a splintered voice. "You're all I have now. Oh, Lord, I couldn't live without you. Couldn't bear it. Thank you, Heavenly Father, for my sweet Flannery."

Hearing that, Flannery stiffened, knowing she could never tell. Not ever. And filling with brokenness and drowning misery, she allowed herself a moment, just a small one, and pressed her mouth into the folds of Mama's gown and found a measure of relief in her Mama's soft arms. She sobbed quietly for babies, Mama's and her own, and for what she'd done, and what she'd become.

Flannery vowed to do away with the pearls. Maybe it would help some. *Yes.* She'd bury it all, and shed herself of the secrets, the lies, and now the deadly sin of omission that had stained her and would surely send her to Hell.

Flannery stayed at Mama's side till midnight, growling at the nurses with her eyes, keeping them out of Mama's room with her hovering arms.

When the shift changed, a nurse appeared, saying she knew Mama from their early school days before she'd moved away to another county. Quietly, she told Flannery to go home and rest, promising she'd watch over her dear old chum.

The kind nurse convinced her, and, exhausted, Flannery went home to shower and rest.

# CHAPTER 31

Early the next morning in Mama's sewing room, Flannery found an old, empty cookie tin that Mama had set aside for stray buttons. Minutes later Flannery walked toward Ebenezer Road with the tin in one hand and Mama's small gardening shovel in the other. On Ebenezer, she saw the big bull gate that blocked cars from going down the dead-end road.

She stopped and called up the voices: hers, Patsy's, Danny's, and Hollis's. They were always louder here, her conscience haywiring with her racing worries.

Flannery slipped easily around the gate and hurried past the cemetery and over to the elm. She began digging around the tree at a weak spot where she found soft dirt that didn't run into shallow roots.

After she dug a hole big enough, Flannery opened the tin and touched the bullet and Mama's lovely pearls. Patsy had looked so beautiful that evening. And Flannery cringed, remembering her sister standing right here, frantic to find them. "Don't go . . . Help me . . ."

Flannery wept at that, and again begged God to forgive her, dropping her sins and grief into the dark Kentucky soil, soaking it with regrets and more prayers. She thought maybe if she'd given her sister the pearls Patsy would have made it to the prom. Made it to Chubby's even. Flannery should have been proud of her beautiful sister, happy to see her, happy to wait on her in front of Violet, Bess, and the others that night.

What Flannery wouldn't give to change it all. To give Patsy the night she'd dreamed of, instead of the jealousy and harsh words she'd left her with. Give those stolen minutes back to her sister that she had let the devil snatch away.

Flannery covered the hole with the mound of soil, tamping it down with her foot, piling dead leaves on top, hoping to lay to rest her own tormented soul.

# CHAPTER 32

*2002*

When Jean Butler passed away in the summer of 2002, Flannery took her ninety-one-year-old mother back home to Glass Ferry and buried her in the marble orchard on Butler Hill, right beside Flannery's baby brothers, Patsy, and Honey Bee, and under the arms of the two-hundred-year-old chinquapin oak.

Flannery had taken care of her mama up to the very end. Made it her sole duty and daily drive to give Mama the peace she knew she had stolen from her, and to earn herself a half measure of forgiveness, if forgiveness could be earned. Though Mama would never admit to it, she'd thrived in the city. Her mind had cleared, and a long-lost spark returned to her step.

Mama'd made friends at the Knights of Columbus, where she attended bingo twice a week. Found some more folks at her neighborhood church, and formed a canasta club, and also did some seamstress work for the dry cleaners down the block. Less and less she mentioned Glass Ferry. And less and less Flannery thought about what she'd left behind.

After one of Mama's new friends learned about Jean Butler's husband and his distillery business, it wasn't long until some men came calling on her and Flannery.

They were young businessmen, sons of a bourbon king, who were curious about Honey Bee's recipes, his old ways with the whiskey.

Lately, Louisville and the rest of Kentucky had embraced their bourbon roots, seen a global promise in that colorful past, and soon, new artisanal distilleries were popping up everywhere. A boom, there were now more bourbon barrels than people in the Commonwealth.

In the end the men paid Flannery top dollar for the recipes, and like Honey Bee, only with an operation larger in scale, those smart young folks began toting their barrels of River Witch across seas and back, aging amber liquor aboard ships, letting those grandmother oceans spank the very fires into their newfangled whiskey, using Honey Bee's old ways.

Flannery and Mama bought a small cottage on the Ohio River and lived comfortably off the sale. Flannery still taught at the elementary school, had herself a few friends in the faculty, and kept busy tutoring several days a week after school.

Occasionally, a fellow teacher would introduce Flannery to a man for a dinner date, maybe a movie, but it never turned into anything more than Flannery wanted it to—a nice night out and only this.

She and Mama would go home to visit, but just that: a day visit to the graves, then Flannery would drop Mama off to see old friends. Flannery always grabbed a book and read under the elm on Ebenezer until the light began to fade, dirtied, and it looked dingy and done, like someone had washed it too many times.

She couldn't explain to herself why she was drawn back, other than maybe she was like some hardened criminal pulled back to the scene of the crime, who needed to pocket a secret token from his victim, relive it all, like the villains in those old Jerry Bruckheimer TV shows she watched every Thursday evening. Flannery reckoned visiting Ebenezer was her theft, her ugly trophy she held tight and offered up to Patsy.

The day Flannery buried Mama on Butler Hill, a young couple attended the graveside service. They had a familiar feel to them, like she should've known them, but Flannery was sure they'd never met.

After everyone left, the couple approached her. "Miss Butler?"

"Mrs. Butler Hamilton," Flannery corrected absently.

The young woman approached her shyly. "I'm JoLynn Puckett, and this is my husband, Ben." JoLynn pulled her husband to her side, and he shook Flannery's hand and offered a warm smile.

"We're sorry about your mama. We wanted to pay our respects," JoLynn said. "I left flowers on the graves up here for your family. . . ."

"Thank you." Flannery looked around, suddenly noticing the small bouquets on her baby brothers', Honey Bee's, and Patsy's graves. "That's very kind of you." Flannery made to dismiss them so she could have a private moment.

"Ben and I live in your house now," JoLynn said. "It's a beautiful home. We bought it two years ago from the people you sold it to."

Flannery looked at them curiously.

"Well, I . . . Ben and I just wanted to ask, that is, if you're not in any hurry, if you might like to have lunch with us today? I made some tea and sandwiches. A nice luncheon for after the service."

Surprised, Flannery brightened at the invitation. She was not in a hurry to get back to Louisville. She never got in a hurry about much these days, dragging around her sixty-six-year-old bones.

"Nothing too fancy, but we have country ham and biscuits, and a nice salad we made from our garden. There's tea. Oh, and lemon pie," JoLynn pressed. Ben nodded and smiled warmly.

Flannery looked down the hill at the big old house peeking through the trees. She would love to see it. Love to walk into those rooms and pretend Mama, Honey Bee, and Patsy were with her.

The day was sunny, breezy, and not too hot. The young couple seemed kind, and the visit would cheer her.

"Thank you, lunch sounds nice. Just give me a moment to say good-bye to Mama, and I'll be down in a bit."

The Pucketts told her to take her time and left.

Flannery reached to the funeral spray lying atop the casket, then jerked her hand back. She grimaced and forced herself to take a flower and then quickly tossed it into the freshly dug grave that awaited, blowing a soft kiss. "Mama, sleep well with your babies and Honey Bee and Patsy. Our kin. All gone too soon. But all together now."

Flannery stepped over to Honey Bee's grave and placed a kiss to his headstone, then moved over to her brothers' and did the same, dusting off the scattered acorns on their old stones. At Patsy's grave, she rested a hand on the marble. "Sweet dreams, dear sister. Mama is with you now."

Flannery drove down the hill, pulled up to the house, taking it all in, the freshly painted porch, a new tin roof. Stepping out and under the willow, she smiled. Someone had placed a wrought-iron settee with cushions near the tree.

She touched the lacy leaves, brought a soft branch to her nose and inhaled the earthy scent of green, admired how tall it had grown. Lightly she hummed "The Tennessee Waltz" and swayed her arms a little. "*Yes, I lost my little darling the night they were playing the beautiful Tennessee Waltz . . .*" Flannery sang softly. Spun around once, the elixir of home lighting music in her bones.

How many times had she dreamed of Wendell Black taking her to a dance one day, practiced her twirls right here under a moonlit weeper.

She wanted to savor everything good from her childhood, spin again. The clap of a screen door stopped her. If JoLynn Puckett had not been standing on the porch watching, Flannery would've twirled, would've knelt and kissed the earth, kicked off her shoes, stripped her stockings even, and wriggled her toes in the sweet bluegrass to feel the years of her youth once more, feel her family who had once felt it all with her.

*Memories.* Those times when Mama and Honey Bee would place a quilt under the tree for a picnic of cold fried chicken, stuffed eggs, buttered biscuits, and custard cake Mama'd made, sending the girls back to the house for the china, silverware, and linen napkins to make it fancy.

Uncle Mary would stop by and take his seat near the trunk,

whittling on a piece of wood with his knife, carving out a little bird, a dog, spinning tops, or some other whatnots for Patsy, Flannery, and Mama.

Flannery ran her heel lightly over the patch of earth. "The ground is still bald." She chuckled. From her and Patsy's doings. Honey Bee used to also set up a big washtub there in the summer when the girls were little, wearing that grassy seat out.

Laughing, splashing, she and Patsy had cooled off in the bucket behind the willow's green, draping curtain. The twins would wave at Mama and Honey Bee sitting on the porch, drinking their lemonade and sharing smiles.

Tilting her head to the sky, Flannery took a whiff of the sweet summer memories and pulled them into her old soul.

"That old willow there," JoLynn called out as she stepped off the porch, tucking a cell phone into her back pocket, "is sure a pretty one."

"My sister and I planted it with our daddy when we were four. He said he wanted a proper kissing tree for his girls and their children to get hitched under one day. Said every homestead should have one."

JoLynn grinned as she walked up to Flannery. "We sure love it. I spend my reading time here."

"A fine tree. A fine spot for hitching, even." Mark had rushed Flannery to the courthouse for a quick, cold ceremony, not allowing her to call Mama or any of her college friends. The courthouse clerk had pulled out a Bible hidden under a mile-high stack of government paperwork, and handed it to Flannery, saying she could pick out a verse if she liked and he would read it for them. Mark grabbed it from her, thumbing through the pages to the Book of Ephesians, tapping the written verse— "Wives, submit yourself"—his self-righteousness and expectations laid out in Scripture and a nod to Flannery's required faithfulness.

"It's my dream for my son," JoLynn said, smiling.

Relieved that it wouldn't be cut down, Flannery patted the trunk. It would live on. Now a Puckett tree that would be cherished. "A fine weeper and a sure keeper."

"I wish you could meet my son, Ben Junior, but he's off to conservation camp this week. He loves playing under this tree."

"Camp John Currie?"

"You know it?" JoLynn asked, surprised.

"My sister and I attended when we were ten."

And they'd gone, but not too eagerly, Flannery recalled. Especially Patsy. She'd thrown the biggest hissy ever. Mama'd fussed at Honey Bee. "You can't leave Patsy here, you can't," Mama insisted in the car. "It's a barbaric place. She's not strong enough to survive this wilderness—"

Frightened, Flannery and Patsy had wriggled free from the conservation officer's hold and fled back to the automobile. The twins knocked on the rolled-up windows, imploring their parents to take them home.

"No, Honey Bee," Mama said, reaching for his arm. "It's not a safe place for our young ladies. For Pat—"

Honey Bee'd fired back, silencing Mama. "That's exactly why I will. Our Patsy has to learn to protect herself."

Patsy ran down the dirt road after the Butlers' automobile, begging, crying for her mama and daddy to come back, take her home, until a conservation officer chased her down, dragged her into a barrack, sat her down on a bunk bed, ordering her to unpack.

That long, hot week, the girls boated on Kentucky Lake, learned archery, canoeing, fishing, riflery, and other skills to make them strong Kentucky women.

Flannery earned the certificates Camp John Currie awarded, and Patsy proudly received all her badges except for the one in riflery.

That had hurt Patsy the most, because toward the end of the course she had almost won herself the title of top marksman, outshooting every girl and even the officer when he challenged Patsy to target practice with him one morning after a breakfast of lumpy, cold oatmeal. Patsy had nailed the bull's-eye on the wooden board, besting the man and also leaving him red-faced and a little hot around the collar.

On the last day before the awards were doled out, the conservation officer had placed rifles in the girls' hands and lined them
all up to shoot.

After firing a few rounds, Patsy put her gun down. Clutching
her belly, she teared up. The conservation officer hollered for
her to pick up her gun and get back into formation.

Bawling, Patsy grabbed her rifle. In a second, she doubled
back over and dropped the weapon. The gun discharged into
the officer's canteen that was sitting a few feet from his boot.

The man ran over to Patsy and shook her. Shook her again
and again, thundering. Patsy shrieked, claiming she'd been hit
by gunfire, then pointed an accusing finger at Flannery who had
been shooting rounds beside her. Patsy's face was dirt-streaked
and pinched, her hands pressed to her stomach.

"Here, right here," Patsy said hoarsely, and poked her belly,
tears leaking onto the officer's boots. "S-shot."

"Fibber. I never!" Flannery said.

"Did so." Patsy gasped.

The officer narrowed his eyes and slowly lifted Patsy's shirt.
A fat, angry hornet flew out, sending the man stumbling back
and all the other girls running.

For two weeks, Patsy carried around a silver-dollar-sized
bruise, and earned herself Honey Bee's good favor and a bag of
licorice treats he'd bought for her bravery to boot.

"I hope your son earns all his certificates." Flannery smiled
at the young mother.

"Fingers crossed." JoLynn grinned and held up a hand, locking one finger over another. "Come on inside, Mrs. Hamilton.
Ben Senior's gone down to the barn, but he'll join us shortly."

She took Flannery on a tour, showing her the new curtains
they'd hung in the parlor, pointing out the soft floral print, the
many updates, the sassy yellow fabric they'd upholstered the
Butlers' tired settee and drab chairs with, a warm geranium
paint coating the walls.

Flannery nodded approvingly when JoLynn showed her the
stone shower, marble basin, and new commode that had re-

placed her and Patsy's old pink bathroom. Inside the bedrooms upstairs, new carpet hid the old wooden floors she and Patsy used to race pennies across, twirl Uncle Mary's spinning tops upon.

A couple of rooms had been skinned of their thick wallpapers, replaced with periwinkle, poppies and soft yellows, and other cheery colors of paint.

Still, the house looked pretty much the same in most parts, felt like the cheerful home she and her family had shared long ago, before death had taken hold.

In the master bedroom stood Mama and Honey Bee's old walnut set. The seven-foot headboard with its wheat-scrolled border that had been carved out across the top. The washstand still jutted out in the corner with the pretty rose marble top that Honey Bee'd hauled back from a Tennessee quarry for Mama's birthday one year.

The couple had kept the furniture. When Flannery'd sold the home, Mama said she'd leave most of the bulky pieces behind for the buyer. Flannery was glad to see those people had done the same for the new owners. And she was somewhat surprised the young couple liked the heavy, dark furnishings. Most young folks preferred modern pieces.

JoLynn read Flannery's mind. "I'm twenty-eight, but my mama always said I was born a hundred, if a day. There's a shine in old things. I believe antique stuff has a soul and deserves to live on. Believe every scratch and scar has earned its right to exist with the living." JoLynn walked over to the curtains to draw them back.

Flannery looked around and noticed the nicks and bumps in the wood, left from the Butlers' lives. "Where did you move from?" Flannery asked. "I feel like we've met."

"Knoxville, Tennessee. My Ben is the new pastor here at the United Methodist Church. I'm a nurse now across the Palisades at County Hospital. Sorta followed in my great aunt's footprints, folks like to say."

Flannery thought how Honey Bee had wanted her to follow in his footsteps. Wondered how that path might've been. Would she have had all those babies, one of the finest stills, with famous whiskey recipes, and owned vast parcels of land like the Kentucky pioneer, Catherine Carpenter? Flannery regretted she hadn't fought hard enough for the road Honey Bee'd set for her, and for a minute regretted she'd sold those recipes too quick.

"She was a midwife, and I was always pretending to be her with my baby dolls," JoLynn said. "I was born in Lincoln County, Kentucky, and we had relatives scattered all around these parts. Had kin living right down the road there." JoLynn parted the curtains and pointed.

Flannery followed her finger toward Ebenezer Road.

# CHAPTER 33

"Right on Ebenezer," JoLynn said. "My great aunt, Joetta Deer. Maybe you heard of her?"

"Joetta?" Flannery said, surprised.

"Yeah, I was sorta named for her. Mama—she's deceased—just added Lynn to Jo in memory of the aunt she was so fond of."

"Everyone's heard of Joetta. Such a tragedy."

"When I was little, Mama used to bring me here to Glass Ferry, out to visit Ebenezer. I'd help put flowers on the graves. We'd clean up the weeds as much as we could, but it was hard to keep up, hard to come all this way. My parents both worked," JoLynn said. "But we would try to visit a couple times a year and make the trip at least once. Mama said there should always be flowers there for her baby cousins, Uncle Ebenezer, and her sweet Aunt Joetta. *God rest.*"

Flannery said, "I didn't know any Deer kin were still around."

"Most of us settled in Tennessee in the '40s and '50s, and a few stayed put like Joetta," JoLynn said. "But my old heart's always been in Kentucky. Mama would drive by your place here, and I remembered how beautiful it was. Declared I'd have it one day so I could make sure my relatives' graves would always have flowers. Stopped by once when I grew up, and left my contact information with the owners to call if they ever had a notion to sell. One day they did, and I knew I had to have it."

"I hadn't heard the Murphys put it up for sale," Flannery said.

"It was too much for them, getting on in years like that. A lot of upkeep. The very first thing I did was plant a big flower garden out back. I'll make sure and share some with your kin on Butler Hill, too," JoLynn said with a sweet, sad smile, her eyes suddenly watering.

"Thank you. Joetta's grand-niece," Flannery marveled.

"In the flesh." JoLynn pulled a tissue from her pocket and dabbed at her eyes. "Oh. I almost forgot. Speaking of flesh. I believe I have something that belongs to your family. Let's go down to the dining room."

Flannery followed her downstairs.

JoLynn ran a loving hand along the massive cherry sideboard, bent over, pulled open the bottom drawer of the chest, and lifted out a little photograph and a wooden box about the size of a small book. Nervous, she handed the box to Flannery. "When Ben was painting and laying carpet upstairs, he moved some of the furniture and found these. I tried to get them to you."

"It's lovely." Flannery rubbed the smooth wood, touched the tiny pearl inlay on the lid.

"We called the Murphys, but it didn't belong to them. The initials carved on the box are *J B*. I guess it's Butler."

"I've never seen this." Flannery inspected the box. "It could have been Mama's." The hand-carved box had a delicate scroll border and a tiny lockset drilled into it.

"We didn't open it," JoLynn offered a little more nervously. "I didn't want to . . . to intrude, or risk busting the lovely wood. We wanted to mail it to you, but I couldn't find your address."

"It's locked," Flannery said, and shook it. Something solid was inside.

"Sorry, we didn't find a key." She handed Flannery the photograph.

Flannery narrowed her eyes, pushed her spectacles higher on her nose. "This is my mama. But how—"

"I wondered if that was Mrs. Butler sitting on the bed there with Aunt Joetta, holding her newborns. Or another relative of yours."

"Yes, it must be."

"Are those the same babies up in your cemetery? The headstones up there are so old we couldn't read the names very well." JoLynn tapped the back of the photo.

Flannery flipped the photograph over and saw in faded ink, *1931, April 22, Paxton and Preston Butler with Mother and midwife Joetta Deer.*

"Oh my, yes. My mama's handwriting. But I've never seen this photo. My brothers only lived about a week. The summer diarrhea or such claimed them and a lot of infants back then, I believe she told us."

"I'm sorry, Mrs. Hamilton," JoLynn said sadly, and cast her eyes down.

Flannery peered closer. "I never knew Joetta delivered them. My sister and I were born in the hospital, you know."

"Aunt Joetta died in 1931," JoLynn said quietly.

"That explains it. We didn't come along till '36."

"Mama said Aunt Joetta delivered lots of babies around these parts. Guess the apple didn't fall far and all. I'm a delivery nurse too."

Flannery peered closer at the photo, seeing the resemblance between Joetta and JoLynn.

"Your brothers were beautiful boys, ma'am," JoLynn said.

"May I keep it?" Flannery asked.

"Sure. I made a copy, and I have plenty of other pictures of my aunt that my family has passed around."

Flannery studied the old black-and-white picture again, looking at Mama sitting on the bed, tired but smiling with her babies in her arms. "From the date here, Mama was twenty, and it looks like Joetta wasn't much older. Both handsome women."

JoLynn said, "I believe my mama said Joetta was close to thirty in this picture. But she didn't know for sure. Joetta started midwifing when she was barely twenty. My family said she brought over a hundred babies into the world and never lost a'one in delivery."

"Remarkable lady," Flannery said quietly, studying the photo some more.

Flannery never dreamed Mama knew the midwife like that. Though she now remembered that anytime someone said anything about old ghost Joetta, mused about or poked fun of her legend, Mama would shush them, demand they never utter Joetta's name in her house. Usually it was Patsy doing the poking—Patsy who hated Joetta's tale. Though Patsy could never really say why, just tried to make Flannery feel the same.

"Well, you must be starved," JoLynn said. "Let's get you that lunch I promised."

JoLynn and her husband shared a fine meal with Flannery.

Flannery enjoyed the young couple, and they welcomed her warmly and asked her to spend the night, but Flannery declined.

JoLynn was easy to talk to, and Ben reminded Flannery of Honey Bee, the goodness in her daddy, and he'd told her to visit anytime. By the time lunch was over, Flannery insisted they call her by her first name.

JoLynn took down Flannery's address, promising to write, and told her she and Ben would visit her in Louisville one day. They hugged on the porch, and still something more tugged at Flannery's heart, was tucked in JoLynn's solemn eyes, she felt.

Flannery held up the wooden box, gave it another shake.

JoLynn frowned, her gaze set on the box before she caught Flannery studying her. JoLynn looked away.

For a second Flannery doubted the key had indeed been lost. Wondered why the keepsake had been hidden, why Mama would hide the key unless she'd lost it.

Ben came out onto the porch, said good-bye to Flannery, and told his wife he'd be in the barn finishing chores.

JoLynn gently took Flannery's arm and helped her down the porch, giving her guest one more hug.

Flannery thanked her again and put the box onto the backseat of her car. She pondered on what Mama had thought was so important inside that it had to be locked away from her girls.

*2012*

Nearly a decade had passed since she had buried Mama.

Flannery had placed the wooden box JoLynn had given her on the mantel in her home, admiring the rich, reddish tones on the locked keepsake, never bothering with it much, just enjoying the beautiful wood and its carvings, resolving that Mama probably kept old compacts, makeup inside she didn't want her young twins getting into, and had placed the pretty box out of reach of clumsy hands that might break it.

Years passed, and Flannery mostly forgot about it, but JoLynn hadn't forgotten about her.

Flannery returned to Glass Ferry once a year to visit Ebenezer and the Butler cemetery. JoLynn always flagged her down as she was leaving, inviting Flannery in for a chat, tea, or a meal.

The two became close. JoLynn surprised Flannery with monthly letters, unheard of in this day and age when advertisements and scam flyers littered mailboxes.

JoLynn called her once a week too, making sure to keep telephoning if Flannery was out and until she reached her. And twice a month when the young mother and her family came to Louisville to shop, JoLynn made sure to stop in and visit Flannery.

Ben Junior even dubbed her Aunt Flannery, and when the Pucketts' sitter canceled on them for the parents' second honeymoon trip, the boy spent a week in Louisville with Flannery. Ben Junior had trouble with his fractions and Flannery enjoyed helping him learn. She told him to think of fractions as slices of pizza pie. "Ben," she'd say, "five tenths is like five of the ten slices of a pizza, and we all know that when I've eaten five of ten slices, I've eaten half the whole thing." He got that real fast. They'd celebrated at a pizzeria.

And when Ben Junior was married under the weeping willow last spring, Flannery was invited. She couldn't have been prouder if it had been her own son, and felt Honey Bee was looking down, pleased to see one of his dreams come to life.

Flannery had stayed at the Puckett home last Christmas for

the first time, enjoying Ben Senior's fine Christmas Eve service he'd preached over at the United Methodist Church, seeing Ben Junior's pretty new bride, and helping JoLynn prepare a grand Christmas feast.

Flannery had brought a box of Christmas oranges she'd purchased from the farmers' market in Louisville, and the family stuffed their Christmas stockings with them, the aroma of fresh, tart fruit permeating the house, a cheer against the winter storm brewing outside.

Flannery stood back to admire the stockings hanging from the mantel above a cozy fire. JoLynn came in from the kitchen and handed Flannery a small package.

"Open it," JoLynn said.

Flannery hadn't bought gifts, just the oranges, and she hesitated.

"Go ahead," Ben Junior and his bride and Ben Senior cheered, smiling.

JoLynn pushed. "It's not a purchase."

Flannery unwrapped the gift and found a beautiful, hand-quilted Christmas stocking with *Aunt Flannery* embroidered on it that JoLynn had made.

Flannery's old eyes filled as she looked around the home of her family, the ones gone and the ones who were now given to her. She breathed in the festive air and could almost smell the Christmas pine Honey Bee would chop down for the parlor, imagine his rugged face, a twinkle in his eye—hear Patsy's excited giggles and Mama's musical laughter echoing. *Family.* It was all intoxicating, and something she'd thought she would never have again, never feel again.

"My seams are a little crooked, but I hope you like it." JoLynn grinned.

Speechless, Flannery could only bob her head and stare at the precious gift.

Taking the present from Flannery's spindly fingers, JoLynn stuffed an orange gently inside and hung it in between the Pucketts' stockings.

"We can't have anyone waking up Christmas morning without a stocking. You're family too," JoLynn announced with a sniffle. "*Our family.*"

The Pucketts gathered around Flannery, pulling her into their arms.

JoLynn was a young mother who was wise and kind in old ways lost to this frenzied world, her family gentle and hard-working. Flannery loved JoLynn, the sweet family, and the new life and laughter they breathed into the Butler home—her.

In 2014, Flannery was delighted to find out she was going to be a great aunt, that Ben Junior and his wife were having a baby.

Excited, Flannery took her brothers' wooden cradle to Glass Ferry to surprise them with it. The crib had been so dear to her mama, and she couldn't think of anything finer to give her new family—this precious baby coming into her life.

But when she opened the rear car door to show JoLynn, her friend had paled. A second later, JoLynn teared up, and she told Flannery to take it back. It was their first and only disagreement.

"I thought the kids might like it," Flannery said, hurt. "Look at the fine workmanship on the wood. There's a perfect sweep on the carved rockers here." She tapped the base. "It's sturdy enough for my grandnephew or niece, twins even—"

"I'm sorry, Flannery," JoLynn said. "I can't have it for my grandbaby."

"But it's antique, and you like antiques." Flannery raised a hand to the Puckett house packed with old furnishings.

Trembling, JoLynn shook her head and said, "No. Not that."

"But—"

"Take it back!" JoLynn ran to the house.

Bewildered, Flannery stared after her, wondering what had gotten into JoLynn.

On the drive home, Flannery reasoned that JoLynn must want something more modern for the young couple, a piece without history. Maybe JoLynn thought it was bad luck for her son and daughter-in-law to have it.

Back home, Flannery had a neighbor lug her brothers' crib

back into the garage. That evening JoLynn called and apologized for her strange behavior, leaving it at just that, an apology and no other clue as to why the earlier outburst.

A few weeks passed, and JoLynn stopped in Louisville to visit Flannery. JoLynn seemed back to her old self, the crib business forgotten, her chatter happy, her hugs warm.

# CHAPTER 34

*2016*

Flannery pulled her Buick up to Ebenezer Road, the June sun warming her seventy-nine-year-old body as she stepped out of the car on the eve of her and Patsy's birthday. Still spry for her age, she opened the trunk and pulled out the small hand shovel and towel.

The grass seemed a bit higher, wilder, the old tree beyond the rusty bull gate a little more beaten and broke-limbed than on that day, but it still felt like it could've been yesterday. Was one of those memories where it would always be yesterday for Flannery.

Under the elm, Flannery pressed her knees into the towel and shoulders into her small gardening tool, wedged her gnarled hands down deeper between the dirt and cookie tin. Carefully, she worked the soil with her bony fingers, separating the earth until she unplugged the cookie tin.

At last she held it up, heard the rattle of pearls against copper, and lifted her head, letting her prayers wash the sky.

She'd come back every year for the last four decades, checking. Each time digging it up, inspecting the pearls and bullet inside, then burying it all back again. But this year the doctor told Flannery her ticker wasn't strong. Told her to slow down some.

Flannery worried she couldn't wait for another year to pass.

She'd have to touch the pearls one last time and say a final good-bye.

She pushed the shovel aside, and Honey Bee's wristwatch broke loose from its clasp and slipped off her arm, falling onto the tin.

Alarmed, Flannery picked it up. The drop had cracked the old, brittle crystal. Peering closer, she spied the dead second hand. Flannery shook the watch, tapped it a few times, and held it up to her ear. *Broke. Everything breaks eventually, like me too.*

That old watch had been running forever, grabbing the extra life since the '40s without so much as a hiccup, and here it stopped. Stopped as sure as it started when Honey Bee'd given her those extra eight minutes when she was born.

For as long as Flannery could remember, like her, Honey Bee had set the Zenith watch exactly eight minutes fast. He'd said he started doing it on the day she was born, and told her many times, "In eight minutes your life can change, Flannery girl. And when you were minutes behind your sister, ol' Doc knew you were in trouble. Mama's cord caught hold of you and wouldn't let go, damn near killing you and her, till the doc cut you out. That eight-minutes-late arrival changed your life and changed mine. You weren't born eight minutes late; you were born eight minutes on time to steal from the devil. And I aim for you to hold on to that time for when that thief comes a'calling."

He'd reminded her another time too when they were on the river and had passed the spot where the men had come after them. *"Always guard your eight minutes. Lord knows I wish I had them for your brothers. If only I'd gotten to them sooner . . ."* Honey Bee had grown quiet for the rest of the day, stoking something troubling inside him.

She wrapped the watch around her thin wrist, fastened it, and then tapped once. No use. Her eight minutes had finally run out.

Dusting off her dress, she trudged over to her vehicle with the tin. Inside the car, she mulled over what she had to do. Cradling the container, she knocked her knuckles on the lid a few times, thinking, then reached over to the passenger side and pulled out the diary tucked inside her purse, setting it beside her.

Flannery studied the soft-sky-colored journal and glanced at the old button tin in her lap, cutting her eyes back to the diary again. She'd been hauling the old diary around everywhere since she'd discovered it. *Wouldn't dare let that out of my sight.*

After a minute she inspected Honey Bee's watch again. Flannery had the urge to tap it once more, and after giving it three sharp raps, she pinned the crystal to her ear. The silence thickened. A sadness sunk her shoulders, but then she straightened in relief.

Plucking up the diary, Flannery placed it carefully inside the tin atop the pearls and bullet, stared thoughtfully out the window.

She needed to make one last stop. She started the car, pulled off Ebenezer, and drove over to the Butler cemetery.

Inside her family's graveyard, Flannery saw the grass had been mowed, weeds plucked around the tombstones, and, like JoLynn had promised, fresh flowers perched atop the graves in polished urns. Flannery glanced through the trees, down at her childhood home.

Standing amongst the graves, Flannery studied her broken wristwatch and made one last reckoning with God. Finished, she drove down the hill past the Puckett house.

In the rearview, she saw JoLynn step out onto the porch, wave her dish towel, heard the concern rising in her voice. "Flannery, wait. *Flannery,* where—" JoLynn ran onto the gravel road, calling after her.

But Flannery couldn't. Wouldn't dare stop, not this time.

Moments later, Flannery drove through the Palisades, whirred down and around old Kentucky roads bathed in dappled yellows and cloaked in a peacefulness that clung to its crags. The trees were a bit scragglier at the tops than when she and Patsy had driven it, some a lot taller and thicker at their bottoms, though the rock face jutted strong, resolute.

Flannery rolled down her window and inhaled the honeyed breezes of mountain laurel, pine, and yellowwood blossoms.

Soon she saw the sign and pulled into the State Police Post Seven's lot and parked.

Inside the stale building, a young receptionist looked up from her sandwich. With a mouthful of food, she asked, "Can I help you, ma'am? Are you lost?" She took another bite.

"I'm Mrs. Butler Hamilton," Flannery announced to the woman hunched over her desk.

"Haven't I seen you with the Pucketts?" The girl pinched off another glimpse under her flurry of thick false eyelashes. "Do you need to call them?"

"I'd like to speak with Trooper Claymore Green."

"Ma'am, Captain Green is in a meeting," she said flatly, swallowing the bite before setting the sandwich aside, "but if you'll tell me what this is about, I can call another trooper for you." The receptionist placed a hand on the phone, waiting, the bother set plain in her purple painted lips, the steady tap of a long nail with a cartoon painted on it.

"I'll wait for Captain Green." Flannery rubbed the rusted cookie tin in her grip, pressed down her skirts.

The receptionist shook her head, wagging pumpkin-streaked curls. "I told you, he's busy. What's this about?" the receptionist needled, eyeing Flannery's dirt-stained hands, beat-up old wristwatch, and odd package.

"I have some information for him about an old matter. An old family matter and my missing paddle. And a few others who've been missing theirs."

"Ma'am"—the receptionist sighed—"it could be a while. We're very busy here. If you'd like to leave word stating what this is about, maybe I can have him call you later." The receptionist took a big bite of her sandwich and then pulled out a telephone message pad from under a pile of papers.

"I need to see him about one of his old files—an open case. I'd like to close it for him," Flannery clipped, dismissing her.

The girl choked on her food and had to swallow twice before she grabbed the phone.

Flannery shuffled over to the wall where a row of empty folding chairs sat, and took one, rattling the pearls and bullet inside the tin as she hugged it to her lap.

The receptionist made another phone call, whispering, spinning her chair around, turning her back to Flannery.

Flannery pried open the lid on the button tin and pulled out the small blue leather journal again.

Six months ago, a retired teacher from the elementary school dropped by and had admired the curious wooden box sitting on Flannery's mantel. When Flannery told her she didn't have a key, the woman pointed her to an antique dealer who went through all of his old keys, finding the one that opened the locked box that JoLynn had given her.

Flannery hadn't risked breaking open the family keepsake, harming the heirloom, and was thrilled to find the antique key fit—until she saw what the memento held, saw what she couldn't allow others to see, until now.

Inscribed inside, on the wood bottom, it read *To Jean, Love Honey Bee,* and was filled with an old diary that had belonged to Mama.

Footsteps fell across the buffed linoleum, smacking, startling the quiet. The receptionist glanced sideways at Flannery, pursing her lips. Flannery watched until the young girl disappeared into the mouth of a sterile hallway.

Crossing her nylon-lined legs, Flannery guessed the woman had surely gotten her stockings from a plastic egg. Settling back in her seat, she opened the diary to the first page. She had read it before—many times—but it deserved one last reading.

> *1931, April 7*
>
> *It won't be long now. I'm much stronger, and the fever is gone, though midwife Joetta Deer has ordered me to bed rest until my delivery.*
>
> *Oh! My darling husband has cheered me once again. Honey Bee traveled to Lexington and bought this fine journal from a stationery store so that I may fill it with our blessings. Then he carved a*

*beautiful box from the felled cherry on Butler Road*
*for me to safeguard it in.*
*Dear Lord, thank You for Your goodness. Thank*
*You for my good Honey Bee.*

Flannery shut the leather journal and ran a gnarled finger
over the smooth cover, glanced at her busted watch. In a minute
she opened the book again and carefully flipped through the
yellowed linen pages until her eyes came to rest on Jean Butler's final entries. She admired the fanciful oval handwriting her
mother had penned, lightly traced the elegant Spencerian Script
that nowadays could only be found on an antique Coca-Cola
sign tucked inside an abandoned filling station off some forgotten state road.

Her eyes filled a little, and she slipped a finger under her
glasses and wiped away the dampness.

*1931, April 20*
*The stork is coming this week. I just know it.*
*I can feel it somehow, in my bones, in this sweet*
*spring air. Honey Bee painted the nursery and has*
*fussed for days in the barn, finishing the walnut*
*cradle he's making. It is beautiful and big enough to*
*hold triplets, even.*
*Lord, don't I look like I swallowed three*
*pumpkins. Dear Honey Bee pokes good-naturedly*
*that I may have been sampling in the watermelon*
*patch too long.*
*I never told a soul, but the day I learned I was*
*pregnant, I found two yokes in my morning egg.*
*Won't my darling Honey Bee be surprised!*
*Thank you, Gracious Lord.*

*1931, April 22*
*My baby boys were born at nine O five tonight.*
*They are striking lads. Honey Bee is worried about*

*their long hair, and says their strength could be
stolen. He frets that a baby born with a full head
of hair may be weakly because all the might has
been spent on the hair. My own granny used to say
a babe born with long hair is born looking old and
will surely have a short life. But Joetta insists they
are fit and strong. We are blessed!*

*Honey Bee says his sons look just like him.
Joetta thinks so too. She proclaimed them the
handsomest baby boys in the county, surely the
most handsomest babies she has ever delivered, and
the only twins she's ever seen.*

*Before Joetta left, she showed me how to nurse.
She said there's nothing finer than mother's milk to
keep the sickness away from my babes, and claimed
her two- and three-year-old boys were still nursing,
and nary an illness has struck either one.*

*My milk was thick and flowing, and my strong
boys were greedy and quickly rooted and filled
themselves before falling fast asleep.*

*We named our precious sons Paxton and
Preston.*

*Paxton Beauregard Butler and Preston Lee
Butler!*

*Thank you, Dear Lord, for my precious, darling
angels.*

*1931, April 22*

*Joetta's house burned down not two hours ago.
She has lost everything dear to her. There is nothing
left. The Good Lord called her beloved Ebenezer
and their three boys to His home.*

*I'm positive it is my fault, though Honey Bee
begs different. He says he insisted on Joetta's help
and pleaded with her to come for the birthing,
paying her handsomely for her services. But the
fire broke out while she was delivering my babies.*

*How could it not be my doing? I took her from her home, her sweet babies, her gentle husband, to tend to me.*

*Dear Merciful God, please keep Ebenezer and his baby angels in Your heavenly arms and protect them until Joetta can once again hold them.*

*Forgive me, Father, forgive my sins and weakness.*

1931, April 26

*Joetta has been staying with us until her kin can call for her. Yesterday, she made pillows for my darlings' cradle. Together we embroidered a circle of sweet cherubs onto the pillowslips' hem. Joetta helps me with the babies, and my little angels seem to brighten her mood.*

*Honey Bee says she's helping too much. He worries about her spending every second with them. Lately, Joetta doesn't want me or Honey Bee holding them much, and is bothered when I must nurse them. She insists too much coddling will make them weak, and too much nursing will make them needy.*

*Today, in the dark morning hours I caught her in the nursery offering her breast to Paxton. We argued, and I accused her of trying to steal my sons.*

*Joetta fled, crying. I tried to go after her and apologize, but she disappeared onto Ebenezer Road.*

*Forgive me, Heavenly Father, for my anger and jealousy.*

1931, April 29

*My heart is broken. My precious sons, Paxton and Preston, are dead. Gone! Murdered in their sleep. My husband is surely lost to me as well.*

*Honey Bee caught Joetta in the nursery clutching the pillow. But it was too late to save my sweet angels from that madwoman's hands.*

*Joetta has vanished. And I fear for my beloved husband.*

*I watched him take a rope from the barn, and now he has gone looking for her. Honey Bee has surely locked arms with the Devil himself!*

*O' Merciful Father, forgive him. Save me. Save us all.*

*1936, June 15*

*After a most frightful delivery, my beautiful babies were born yesterday. Patsy Jean came first at 11:36, and eight minutes later, the doctor cut out her bald-headed twin, Flannery Bee.*

*Doctor Stinnett said I will heal quickly and that our precious girls are fit as a fiddle. But my darling husband was beside himself, and argued with him about Patsy's well-being. Then Honey Bee left abruptly.*

*A short spell later Honey Bee returned with a razor, and shaved off Patsy's thick crop of long hair, every single strand. Doctor Stinnett called for the law and had my dear husband removed from the hospital.*

*Thank you, Heavenly Father, for our sweet, darling girls. O' Merciful God, look upon Patsy with Your watchful eye and shield her from evil. Protect us always, protect us all.*

The pages darkened. Flannery rose slowly into Captain Green's broad shadow.

"Mrs. Hamilton," he said, a surprise in his smile, "it's good to see you again."

From behind, an outside door opened, and footsteps drew

near. A hand landed on Flannery's shoulder. She turned and met kind eyes.

At forty-two, JoLynn looked a little older than her years, burdened with the old ways and knowing eyes.

Captain Green looked questioningly at the women.

Quietly, JoLynn slipped her hand into Flannery's and squeezed once. Twice. Then again, an approval in the woman's supportive grip.

Finding strength, Flannery pressed back and handed Captain Green the diary and the tin with the pearls and the bullet—the Butler family's first lick by the Devil himself, and her family's first heartaches and the later ones—all the sins of her and JoLynn's families.

# ACKNOWLEDGMENTS

My deepest gratitude to Beau "Honey Bee" Brasington for your dear friendship and because *there's a paddle for every ass.*

Many thanks to Deborah and Gwen for generous first reads and gracious help. I'm so glad Nashville happened and am doubly grateful for your friendship and wisdom.

A special thank you to Sgt. Jerry Huckleberry of the Louisville Metro Police Department Dive Team for your valuable knowledge.

Big thank yous and my greatest appreciation go to my fantastic editor, John, and to Vida, and Paula, Debbie, and the fabulous hardworking team at Kensington.

To Kris Mills-Noble, Creator Director, Kensington, I love this cover, and the beautiful work you give to my novels. Thank you.

Lauren, because I promised, and you are loved.
*Lauren's Poem*
A beauty named Lauren Jernigan
promotes books to the moon and then back again
She Tweets and Posts
She Hollers and Boasts
until her books outshine the best of 'em
Additional *Lauren's Poem* contributors
(because it took four authors):
Karen Abbott, Joshilyn Jackson, Sara Gruen

To my dear agents, Stacy and Susan, you guys are everything; thank you is never enough.

George Berger, a special thank you to you, my dearest writer friend and author. I remain your number-one fan always.

For Joe, my first reader, my first everything, thank you. I love you like salt loves meat. To my beautiful children, Jeremiah and Sierra, I love you more.

Thank you, dearest reader, for bringing me into your home.

# THE SISTERS OF GLASS FERRY

## Kim Michele Richardson

## ABOUT THIS GUIDE

The suggested questions are included
to enhance your group's reading of
Kim Michele Richardson's
*The Sisters of Glass Ferry*.

# DISCUSSION QUESTIONS

1. Do you believe that the spirits of dead people who died horrifically and left unfinished lives stay with the living to try to make things right?

2. How does the geography of where one grows up—the weather, the plants, the lakes and the rivers and the sky—affect character, or does it?

3. Discuss Honey Bee's superstitions. Do you have any related notions, wives' tales, or beliefs that were passed down to you from your family?

4. Production of Kentucky bourbon has boomed, reached its highest peak, and, worldwide, people are trading their other spirits for the native bourbon. Nutrition journals and clinical studies claim bourbon boosts healthy hearts, improves brain function, fights cancer, regulates diabetes, and more. Currently, there are 6.6 million barrels of bourbon in Kentucky, or 1.5 barrels for every person living in the state. How do you feel about the benefits and burdens of alcohol consumption? What's the place of that industry in the larger economy? In health care?

5. How have midwifery and baby deliveries changed over the years? Has it come full circle?

6. If you are not a twin or a triplet, did you know twins (etcetera) growing up? Discuss multiple births decades ago compared to now.

7. How has police forensics changed since the '50s? Since the '70s? What specialty law enforcement units such as the Hostage Negotiation Team, S.W.A.T. team, horse

patrol, dive team, etcetera have been created to aid in police investigations and bring swift recoveries?

8. With all the deadly car accidents and other mayhem surrounding high school proms, how can we make that uniquely American celebration safer? Should the event be modified, eliminated?

9. Up until the 1990s, police had their hands tied when dealing with domestic violence. A policeman in Kentucky and other states had to witness the misdemeanor assault, a battering against a woman or child before they could arrest the perpetrator on the scene. How have laws to protect women and children changed in your state? What new laws could be implemented to strengthen the fight against domestic violence?

10. Discuss the treatment of the mentally ill today versus decades ago.

# Connect with

# U(s)

Visit us online at
**KensingtonBooks.com**
to read more from your favorite authors, see books
by series, view reading group guides, and more.

**Join us on social media**

for sneak peeks, chances to win books and prize packs,
and to share your thoughts with other readers.

facebook.com/kensingtonpublishing
twitter.com/kensingtonbooks

## *Tell us what you think!*

To share your thoughts, submit a review,
or sign up for our eNewsletters, please visit:
**KensingtonBooks.com/TellUs.**